A RARE BEAUTY

A RARE BEAUTY

Sally Stewart

This first world edition published in Great Britain 2002 by
SEVERN HOUSE PUBLISHERS LTD of
9–15 High Street, Sutton, Surrey SM1 1DF.
This first world edition published in the USA 2002 by
SEVERN HOUSE PUBLISHERS INC of
595 Madison Avenue, New York, N.Y. 10022.

British Library Cataloguing in Publication Data

Stewart, Sally
    A rare beauty
    1.   Love stories
    I.   Title
    823.9'14 [F]

    ISBN 0-7278-5851-3

Except where actual historical events and characters are being
described for the storyline of this novel, all situations in this
publication are fictitious and any resemblance to living persons
is purely coincidental.

Typeset by Palimpsest Book Production Ltd.,
Polmont, Stirlingshire, Scotland.
Printed and bound in Great Britain by
MPG Books Ltd., Bodmin, Cornwall.

One

Francesca dawdled along Mount Street, aware that she was deliberately trying not to think about the interview ahead of her. A shop window offering a circular bath decorated with taps disguised as gold dolphins held no interest, but the next window did. Looking at her wistfully through the glass was an old and simply carved wooden donkey, but the long-dead medieval craftsman had fashioned it with love and a simple conviction that Christ had ridden into Jerusalem on just such an animal; there was comfort for a sore heart in merely looking at the donkey.

She lingered too long in front of the window and finally had to run the remaining hundred yards to the Edwardian grandeur of the Connaught Hotel. It was a far cry from a modest flat in Earls Court Square, but no doubt suited the man she'd come to meet – the Condé Luis Fernando Esteban y Montilla. The very name sounded extravagantly foreign, and she was ready to guess that el Señor Condé had no difficulty in living up to it. Democracy might have taken root at last in Spain, but its aristocrats weren't known even now for easily rubbing shoulders with the hoi polloi.

Inside the hotel she was conducted to the lift by a small uniformed page who smiled with such pity that she could see him identifying her – not someone who was likely to be paying a *social* call on the Count: she'd probably come about a job. Well, in a way he was right. The room she was shown into was so bright with spring sunshine that she was blinded for a moment into thinking it empty; then a man stepped out of the shadow, immediately correcting her expectation of meeting an elderly grandee who deserved the courtesy of a visit rather than a telephone call. The man she was confronting was perhaps ten years older than herself, dark-haired, lithe, and impregnably self-assured. Deep-set eyes studied her with insolent thoroughness, registering her awareness of being deeply at a disadvantage; but it didn't dispose him to be merciful. Count Esteban seemed to have no time or inclination for the courtesies that ordinary people felt it necessary to offer each other.

'I'm afraid the page has brought you to the wrong room. I was expecting someone else.'

Of course he was; she knew who he'd been expecting: a fair-haired, entrancing girl whose beauty not even an agency photograph could ever diminish.

'There's no mistake; I'm Francesca Brown . . . but you were waiting for my sister, Felicity.'

She saw him glance down at the photograph in his hand as if to find some faint resemblance that might confirm what she'd said.

'We're not alike,' she said quietly, thinking it preferable to point that out before he did so himself.

'Your sister is unwell . . . unable to be here?' he asked instead.

'She left for New York yesterday morning.'

A frown pulled his dark eyebrows together. 'I don't understand. Your sister confirmed that she would keep *this* appointment.'

Francesca gave a small, tired shrug; it might have suggested to him that she was doing what had had to be done before, but Count Esteban was too concerned with problems of his own to notice.

'I'm sure she intended to be here when the appointment was made, but her plans changed . . . very suddenly.' It was the truth – at least, as much of the truth as she could bear to reveal – but Esteban, staring at her inimically across the width of the sunlit room, waited for more explanation and she had to concede to herself that he was entitled to it.

2

'A letter was waiting for me last night in which Felicity asked me to telephone you with her apologies. A telephone call seemed too inadequate, and I decided to bring her apologies in person. If I'd known earlier, I should have tried to contact you in Spain; but no doubt you've come to interview other people here as well.'

A smile touched the man's mouth for an instant, but it did nothing in Fran's view to humanise him or lessen her feeling that she'd have done better not to come at all. 'There *are* no others to interview, Miss Brown! Your sister was the final choice made for me by an old family friend who lives in London. This morning's meeting was meant merely to confirm the details of the arrangement.'

He spoke with a quietness that was more deadly than a shout of rage, and she was painfully aware of his anger. Felicity, ever careless of exact truth as well as of people's feelings, had simply asked her to cancel an interview she didn't intend to keep. The Count had more to despise her for than that.

'I'm sorry . . . very sorry,' Fran muttered unhappily. 'The only excuse I can offer for my sister is that it suddenly seemed vital to her to . . . to put everything else aside and go to America.'

'The vital incentive was a love affair, I suppose,' said the Count brutally. 'Commitment to the job I'd offered her couldn't be allowed to stand in the way of *that*. I suppose I should thank God I'm discovering now, rather than later, the peculiar code that governs her conduct.'

Fran's pale face flushed with colour. The comment might be harsh, but it was justified, and there was nothing more she could offer in her sister's defence.

'I'm sorry,' she said again. 'I only came to apologise for Felicity; having done that, I'll leave you to get on with your search for someone to take my sister's place.'

Luis Esteban was tired, angry and disappointed, but he was belatedly aware that the girl in front of him need have done no more than leave a message at the reception desk downstairs. Francesca Brown had gone to more trouble than that, but perhaps she was in the habit of clearing up the havoc left behind by a different sort of girl altogether. His old friend, not usually impressionable, had been enchanted by Felicity Brown. This girl wouldn't stand out in a crowd, but the inevitable comparison with her beautiful sister must be something else she'd had to grow used to.

'You should have done what you were asked,' he said suddenly. 'Telephoned instead of coming here.'

'Yes, I should,' she agreed after a moment's silence. As usual, she hadn't measured up to Felicity and he was intent on making that clear; but the unkindness of it at least had the useful effect of making her angry. She offered him a cool nod by way of goodbye and walked towards the door, but then stood waiting for him to open it for her. It took a moment for the challenge to be accepted, but he finally did so and she left the room with the feeling of a small but important victory scored.

The flat, when she got back to it, was full of reminders of her sister's brief stay: tapes played but not returned to the rack they were kept in, books and magazines leafed through and thrown aside, clothes discarded and left behind made up the cheerful chaos in which Felicity liked to live, calling her too vividly to mind. Against that assault memory could no longer blot out what had happened: Richard Weston, the man she'd been expecting to marry herself, had fallen headlong for Felicity instead. The notes they'd both left behind had been tenderly, genuinely, full of regrets, but they *knew* darling Fran would understand – because she always did understand everything.

To cope with the ruin they'd made of her life, Fran had forced herself to think about the other victim of the plot: the Spanish aristocrat expecting to meet Felicity. It had seemed a necessary act of reparation for her sister's outrageous behaviour, to keep the appointment herself; but she couldn't think why now. Looking back over the interview, Fran accepted that the Count had been right:

she'd have done better not to go to the Connaught at
all.

Two evenings later her doorbell rang at the time of day
her neighbour on the floor above often chose to call; but
Fran wasn't ready to explain even to Anita the extent to
which her future plans had suddenly been wiped out. She
went reluctantly to the front door, but the visitor standing
there was not her friend; instead, the landing light shone
on the lacquer-smooth black hair and harsh, dark face of
Count Esteban.

'Miss Brown . . . do you remember me . . . Luis Esteban?
You called to see me at the Connaught.'

'I hadn't forgotten,' she confessed unsmilingly.

'May I talk to you, please?'

She was tempted to refuse, but to close the door in his
face seemed more churlish than she could manage. In the
end she held it open and led him to a small sitting room that
seemed at once altogether *too* small for the physical size
and personality of the man who followed her in. Determined
not to be intimidated by him, she took refuge in courteous
formality.

'I can offer you sherry – perhaps not the brand you're
accustomed to, but certainly Spanish at least.'

Esteban bowed. 'Thank you . . . dry and chilled, if
possible.'

His voice so clearly doubted the chances of her bringing
him anything but the lukewarm, sweet concoction beloved
of her countrywomen that it was a pleasure to put in front
of him a delicately engraved glass frosted with the ice-cold
Manzanilla she'd poured into it.

'No tapas to eat with it, I'm afraid,' she said politely,
'but perhaps it doesn't matter in London; here, you don't
have to wait until ten o'clock before you dine.'

His eyes surveyed her across the width of the small room.
'You seem very familiar with Spanish habits, Miss Brown;
you must have visited my country.'

5

'Yes, I've been to Spain,' she agreed, 'but that isn't what you came to find out, I imagine.'

He stared at the straw-coloured liquid in his glass for so long a moment that she wondered if he was suddenly regretting having come at all. 'No,' he said finally, 'I'm here to ask if *you* would like the job your sister decided not to take.'

In the silence that surrounded them she heard the slam of a taxi door in the street, and Anita's voice calling goodnight to someone outside . . . It was a perfectly normal evening, except for this stranger, who seemed to fill her small room with the potential for danger of a marauding leopard.

'Without knowing precisely what the job is, I'm certain that I should *not* wish to take it,' she said at last. Even to her own ears it sounded blunt to the point of rudeness, but perhaps that didn't matter when courtesy seemed not to be the Count's long suit either.

'The job *is* one you're qualified to do. The medical agency that offered me your sister's name assured me this afternoon that you're equally well trained and experienced as a physiotherapist but also free to take on a new patient.'

'Yes, but not any patient of yours, if that is what you are offering.'

She expected an outburst of some kind, but his thoughtful stare seemed more puzzled than angry. 'Why refuse so quickly? You don't know *me* well enough to reject the offer simply because I make it. Does some kind of pride stand in the way of accepting a job that was to have been your sister's?'

'I certainly prefer to find my own,' Fran agreed calmly. 'What appeals to Felicity doesn't automatically appeal to me, and I lack her thirst for adventure – or so she tells me. Why don't you hand your problem back to the agency?'

'I did,' he answered, 'with the result that I've interviewed six candidates since I saw you last. Three of them were pleasant, middle-aged women looking for a docile patient; my niece is *not* docile. Two more were from quite the wrong milieu, and I didn't consider them. The sixth might have just done, but she lost interest when she discovered where she would be required to stay. Galicia is in the north-west of the country – as far removed from the conventional picture of sun-drenched, castanet-rattling Spain as it is possible to get. My home at Cantanzos is beautiful in its own fashion, but as green and windswept as England.'

'What about *my* milieu, señor?' Fran enquired gently. 'Perhaps that would be quite wrong as well!'

Esteban's eyes met hers in a frowning stare. 'Your background is the same as your sister's – therefore *not* unsuitable because naturally I checked.' He put the question aside with a gesture of impatience. 'Why not consider the important thing: what your job would be?' Her little shrug reluctantly agreed and he went on in careful, flawless English. 'My niece Juanita is sixteen. Four months ago she was injured in a car crash that killed her parents – my sister Mercedes, and her Italian husband; they were driving back across France to Milan.'

The brief story was told in a voice so devoid of emotion that he might, Fran thought, have been referring to a day when the weather had been unexpectedly unpleasant. Perhaps this was the Spanish way of dealing with grief, but it seemed too stoical by far for an injured adolescent who had had to survive the dreadfulness of seeing her parents killed in front of her. About to suggest that the undocile Juanita might need love as much as medical attention, Fran was warned by the Count's expression to remain coolly professional instead.

'How was your niece injured?' she asked.

'Both her legs were broken. I am assured by the surgeon who treated her that the bones have mended now. There is no physical reason why Juanita should not walk normally again, but she refuses even to try, or to consider any other suggestion that is put to her. For the moment she is staying in the south with my mother, who is too frail herself to endure Juanita's behaviour for much longer. That is why

I am desperate to find someone who might both help and control her.'

'Why look here? Why not find a physiotherapist at home?'

'Because my niece would treat her like a servant and, hating all things Spanish at the moment, take no notice of anything she said. Juanita can speak English, though she will pretend otherwise – she prefers her father's language: Italian. My sister and brother-in-law spoiled her; without them she's become impossible.' His set expression seemed for a moment to flicker into something more wryly human. 'Your face gives you away, I'm afraid. You'd like to point out that I'm a callous brute! Well, acquit me at least of misleading you. The job I'm offering you is not a sinecure, but the woman I spoke to at the agency insisted that you enjoy devoting yourself to suffering humanity. I can't help thinking that the people who have to try to live with Juanita also come into that category, but if *our* plight fails to move you, there is my niece herself – undoubtedly in need of help.'

Fran took a long time to answer, while he seemed content, now, to wait in silence for her to make up her mind. She could stare at him for a moment because his own glance was on a watercolour hanging above the fireplace. He'd made his offer coolly enough, deliberately excluding the slightest bid for sympathy, but he'd made it fairly as well, not concealing its difficulties. If his London friend had been equally honest, it was astounding that Felicity had ever considered the job at all. Fran admitted to herself something else as well: caught off guard for a moment, his face looked strained and tired. Count Esteban *wasn't* indifferent to his niece's condition, only frustrated by his own inability to improve it. Then, as if aware of being watched, he suddenly stared again at Fran.

'Will you come to Cantanzos, or not?'

The decision had been taken, she found, almost without conscious thought. 'Yes, I'll come, and do my best to help. If Juanita's problems are only physical, I'd feel confident of getting her to walk again; if she doesn't *want* to get well, then she'll need more help than I am qualified to give her.'

For a moment, while he continued to stare at her, she had the feeling that he regretted having offered her the job; his sombre expression almost said so. She was right about his sudden indecision, but wrong about his reasons for it. For once he was blaming himself for having made a mistake. Although Francesca Brown wasn't the disarming beauty that her sister clearly was, she had qualities of her own: courage – something that appealed to a Spaniard – was there, and also a quietly effective dignity; but she was no match for a girl who would enjoy trying to destroy her.

'Miss Brown,' he said hurriedly, 'on reflection I believe I should withdraw my offer. Your visit will not do after all.'

It should have been hurtful, but she could see no contempt or unkindness in his face; astonishing though it seemed, he was merely looking concerned.

'Don't withdraw the offer, please,' she heard herself insist. 'I should like at least to try with Juanita. Apart from that, I've reasons of my own for wanting a change of scene, and I'm well used to rainy weather!'

She wouldn't, he thought, explain what the reasons were, nor did he want to be told; but he was sufficiently acquainted with grief himself to recognise it in the girl in front of him.

'Very well . . . come for as long as it takes to get my niece walking again, or at least for as long as you can put up with her tantrums,' he finally agreed. 'I'll ask the agency people to book your flight and send me the details so that you can be met at Santiago.'

He stood up, apparently ready to end the interview, but Fran's diffident question halted him. 'Must your niece go on living in Spain now? It sounds as if the poor girl might be less unhappy in her old home in Italy.'

'She might, if it were remotely feasible for her to live there, but for as long as she remains my ward, she'll have to put up with Cantanzos. It shouldn't be too much of a hardship.'

Fran stared at him, reluctant to believe that there wasn't some small seam of gentleness running through the granite out of which he seemed to have been carved. 'Don't you ever make allowances? Are people always required to match *your* expectations, even when they're hurt and lost and lonely – and your niece must be all of those things?'

'Your heart is touched, I see, by the vision of an orphan at the mercy of an unfeeling guardian! Keep your sympathy, señorita; Juanita will not thank you for it, or even co-operate with you, because you arrive with a burning desire to help her.'

He saw a flame of anger turn Fran's hazel eyes to green. It brought her pale face to life, dispelling his first impression of her, but he put the small discovery aside. She would still be unnoticeable at Cantanzos.

'My servants speak very little English, I'm afraid; perhaps you can manage some Spanish?' he suggested.

'Enough, I expect,' Fran agreed calmly.

'From which I deduce that you speak it like a native! It's unusual, if I may say so, in an Englishwoman.'

'Perhaps, but someone . . . an old friend . . . encouraged me to learn. He's a brilliant historian, and recently published a book about the Spanish Civil War; it was impossible not to share his interest in the subject.'

The sudden bitter mockery in Esteban's face warned her that she'd spoken without thought. 'Good of you to be "interested", Miss Brown, in a three-year slaughter that tore Spain in two and still embitters all our memories!'

'I understand something of what the war did to Spain,' she answered quietly. 'I should have said that I am interested in what has happened to your country since then.'

'Then we must hope you can stay long enough to find out! Cantanzos is not Madrid, though; it's on a peninsula jutting out almost as far west as Cape Finisterre. Your finger won't exactly be on the pulse of national affairs.'

'But *you're* very content with it nevertheless,' she pointed out.

'It's my home.' And that, she could see, removed any doubt in the matter.

He moved towards the door and this time she made no attempt to stop him. 'Arrange to come as soon as you can, please,' he said briefly, and then let himself out of the door.

She was left with a sudden sharp sense of the room's emptiness without him; el Condé, unpleasant though he was, made an impression. But, alone again, it was time to consider what she was now committed to: probably the most unpremeditated and rash adventure of her life to date. The more she looked at it, the worse in prospect it became, and the only grain of comfort she could find was that she might last long enough at Cantanzos to be safely out of London when Felicity returned with an enslaved and ecstatic Richard, chained to her chariot wheels.

Two

The Iberia Airways flight swathed gently through layers of cloud and nosed its way down to the runway at Labacolla. Rain was falling steadily and, though having been warned that Galicia was often wet, Fran couldn't help feeling depressed by it. She retrieved her luggage from the carousel and stood waiting to be claimed herself. Luis Esteban had said she would be met, and it didn't occur to her to doubt that, if he said a thing, it happened. Even so, the crowd around her had thinned and disappeared by the time a small, stocky man came towards her.

'Señorita Brown? I am from Cantanzos, Pepé is my name.' The carefully spoken words seemed to be the extent of his English and they weren't augmented by even the vestige of a smile. He merely gestured in the direction of the exit, hung himself about with her suitcases and marched off, apparently unconcerned to see whether she was following him or not. Like master, like man, she decided: both of them anxious not to be accused of any friendliness or warmth.

There was a tantalising glimpse, as they drove away, of Santiago's cathedral towers fretting a cloud-hung sky, and she promised herself that she would come back to the city in whatever free time she had. The great church built to honour James, the apostle, housed one of the most precious shrines in Christendom; for a thousand years pilgrims had made their way to it in search of peace in this world and salvation in the next. She would join the procession when she could, in a much-needed pilgrimage of her own.

With the car now heading south towards Vigo and the

Portuguese frontier, Fran commented to Pepé in his own language on the English dreariness of the weather. He agreed, after some thought, that it was indeed *muy lluvioso*, then lapsed into silence. Presently she tried again. Cantanzos was quite near the frontier, was it not? He nodded reluctantly. Portugal, not far away on the southern side of the River Mino, was not of interest to him, and she was to understand why. He was a Spanish *hombre*, a Galician – what did the rest of the world matter to him?

She admitted defeat and stared at the landscape instead. Its gentle green hills veiled in rain might have been those of Somerset except that there were still two-wheeled carts being pulled by yoked pairs of oxen, under the watchful eye of the countrywomen who walked beside them. The fields about them had the unmistakable look of land still tended by hand, still prized as something loved and irreplaceable. Then at last Pepé turned off the main road and their route now ran alongside a little river that gradually widened into an estuary. On one side of it a fishing port climbed the hills in a picturesque huddle of whitewashed walls and faded pantile roofs. On the northern bank of the river a long promontory poked its way into the sea, and Fran remembered what the Count had said: his home was on a peninsula. He hadn't mentioned that it obviously lay in the path of every depression and gale driving in from the Atlantic, but such exposure helped to explain his own personality and the dourness of his servant; Cantanzos was not a place for weaklings, they both seemed to say.

At least the approach to it prompted Pepé, as they turned off the coast road, to wave at the ancient stone archway they were about to drive through. Fran assumed that he was anxious for her not to miss the tableau engraved on it: a leopard about to capture a unicorn. It was uncomfortable to recall a moment when she'd associated with her employer the very same dangerous grace and cruelty of the animal carved on the stone. The idea was absurd, of course; Luis Esteban was a man like any other, simply made more arrogant than most by wealth and privilege, and hardened by the streak of cruelty that often underlay the surface smoothness of the Spanish male. But it didn't sound as if Juanita was at all inclined to play the part of the gentle unicorn; she could safely ignore a bloodthirsty coat of arms and concentrate instead on the grounds Pepé was now driving them through.

Unfamiliar shrubs huddled for protection from the sea winds under clumps of massive pines, but a drift of wild flowers hinted at softer days. Beyond the trees the castellated top of an immense wall seemed to encircle the entire peninsula, and its message was clear: the Count's home was his castle, and visitors came by invitation or not at all. With another twist in the drive she saw that Cantanzos was indeed a castle. The next archway led to a stone-flagged courtyard, and at one corner of it a grey tower heaved itself into the sky, keeping watch over a sea that seemed bent on washing the castle away.

'Cantanzos,' Pepé bestirred himself to announce unnecessarily. *'La casa del Condé.'*

Fran stared at the huge building in front of her. Nothing, she told herself, looked its best in drenching rain. On a fine day – and surely even Galicia must sometimes have them – it would look less like a prison than it did now; but she was painfully sure that, in sunshine or in rain, she would never feel at ease in this forbidding relic of the past. Its grey stone walls spoke too clearly of old repressions and cruelties. She wanted, almost more than she could bear, to be back in dear, familiar London. The events of recent weeks had been shattering, but they didn't excuse the madness that had led her to accept the Count's offer.

'*Señorita?*' Pepé's sharp query made her realise that she'd halted too long in front of a hugely impressive doorway. She *had* chosen to come; now she must see the rest of this strange interlude through, and begin by following Pepé's broad back into a cavernous hall that would have swallowed her entire flat in one easy gulp. The chairs and chests that broke up the vast empty spaces seemed the sort of furniture that giants might comfortably have used, and Fran had a glimpse of a banner-hung roof and a stone chimney breast engraved with the same cheerful coat of arms she'd seen outside; then a middle-aged woman dressed in black came through a shadowed doorway.

'Miss Brown . . . I am the housekeeper, Señora Fernandez. Allow *me* to receive you, because the Count does not return until this evening with the Señorita Juanita.'

The speech, delivered in Spanish, made no allowance for the fact that it might not be understood, and the woman's voice and face contained no warmth or hint of welcome. She didn't even smile at Pepé in the course of giving him a volley of instructions. Then she turned back to Fran again.

'Come . . . I show you your room, Miss Brown. Then you may care to rest . . . the Count dines always at ten.'

It sounded as far away as the last trump for someone who had lunched sketchily on an aeroplane at noon, but the faint relish that Fran detected in the housekeeper's voice ruled out any sign of dismay. If the Señora had said dinner would be served at midnight, or not at all, it would still have been necessary to smile at her with cheerful unconcern. She followed her guide up a wide stone staircase, softened only by a central strip of dark-blue carpet and presided over at each turn of the stairs by a figure in full armour. By now ready to believe that the Count kept some of his ancestors inside them, she knew that, when the opportunity presented itself, she would have to lift their vizors to make sure that they were empty.

The housekeeper ignored the broad corridor on the first floor, turned at the top of another flight of stairs, and announced that here were the rooms of the Señorita Juanita. Here also her English attendant would sleep. The woman's attitude seemed to indicate that neither of them was worthy of the grander rooms on the floor below, and Fran was glad of a stiffening twinge of anger. The Count wasn't above allowing his servants to be infected by his own opinion of Juanita.

A moment later she was positively thankful to have been spared the first floor. Her chamber – it was a ridiculous word but the only one that came suitably to mind – could have slept six people in comfort; the dull afternoon light squeezing through its small windows lost heart and gave up before reaching the distant shadowy corners of the room. The windows overlooked the pine trees and castle wall; but she could see nothing beyond but grey sea and even greyer sky. The chill gloominess of the huge room combined so perfectly with the hostile face of the housekeeper that Fran was almost inclined to smile; she knew she wasn't in the middle of a Mrs Radcliffe melodrama, but Cantanzos was doing its best to make her feel so.

'The Señorita likes her room? She will find herself comfortable here?'

The question should have sounded polite but wasn't well intentioned, and Fran knew she was expected to be cowed by such unaccustomed magnificence. Well, she was damned if she was going to concede an inch to the woman who stood watching her; it was the moment to reveal that she could hold her own in Spanish and even indulge in a little gentle irony.

'I am sure I shall be comfortable. It is kind of you to make me so welcome, señora.'

She successfully outstared the housekeeper, then felt ashamed of herself for a petty victory.

'Your bathroom is across the corridor, shared with Miss Juanita. This evening one of the maids will come to guide you to the salon.' Fran nodded and Señora Fernandez swept out of the room, closing behind her an oak door grown black with age. The sound of it settling heavily back into place brought back the unpleasant sensation of having allowed herself to be immured in a prison. Shades of *The Mysteries of Udolpho* again! Suppose she could never get the door open and only the stony-faced Señora Fernandez knew she'd been left there at all? She even ran to the door and felt panic spread inside her until she realised that she was struggling

16

to turn the wrought-iron latch the wrong way. Hunger and unhappiness were making her light-headed. It was a relief to hike across the room to the windows instead and brave the cool, damp air that flowed against her skin when she opened them. The prospect outside looked uniformly grey, much the same dismal colour as her own future. Defences suddenly down at last, she could no longer see the tumbling sea for the tears that trickled down her cheeks. It was time to admit that she was lost, hurt and desperately lonely. Her mind wanted to stray to agonising images of Felicity in New York with Richard, but that way heartbreak lay. She would somehow think instead of a damaged girl years younger than herself who needed help in putting her own broken life together.

Fran was stowing underclothes in the drawers of an immense chest when a knock on the door was followed by the appearance of a maid carrying a tray. She brought not only tea but a dish of *churros*, the small sugary doughnuts beloved of Spaniards – a peace-offering from the housekeeper? More probably, Señora Fernandez had included the *churros* as a test, and the expression on the maid's face as good as said so as she pointed to the dish.

'For the Señorita . . . we know the English eat at strange times and cannot wait until the dinner hour.'

Fran handed back the dish with a smile, because the duel with bloody-minded Cantanzos was beginning to amuse her. The doughnuts had to be resisted, even if she fainted with hunger at Esteban's feet before she got to the dinner table.

'Thank the Señora for me. The tea will be most welcome, but these are not required. What is your name?'

'I am Marilar, the sister of Pepé.'

It came as no surprise. She shared a faint family resemblance with her brother, as well as his miserly way with words and total refusal to smile. Fran thanked her all the same for bringing the tray and didn't understand the puzzlement that had now crept into the maid's face. The English were arrogant, and their women talked loudly in a barbarous tongue they expected everybody else to understand. This Marilar knew because Pepé had told her so . . . she would have to ask him why this *Inglesa* didn't behave as she was supposed to do.

When she'd gone, Fran spooned sugar into her tea to make up for the food she'd turned away, drank it with gratitude, and then climbed on to her high bed. If the afternoon had been fine she would have walked outside, but to go out in drenching rain would do nothing but convince the household that the English deserved the label of madness so often attached to them. She propped pillows behind her back, intending to read about Santiago's cathedral, but sleepless nights and hectic days got the better of her. By the time her patient was helped along the corridor, she was sound asleep and only woke in time to get ready for dinner because doors slammed on the floor below, hinting at the arrival of guests who *did* merit the grandeur of the first floor.

Downstairs in the great hall Luis Esteban was flicking through a pile of mail when his guests walked in: Pascal Vargas and his sister, Inez. They were not only friends of long standing but distant cousins as well, and Doña Inez especially had become a frequent visitor to Cantanzos since the death of a husband much older than herself. Greetings out of the way, she selected an antique chair that seemed to frame her beauty adequately and then smiled at her host.

'Caro . . . what a climate! It is lovely to see you but how much I wish I could persuade you to leave this sodden place more often and come to visit us instead. Your mother agrees with me, you know.'

He smiled at her but shook his head. 'Inez, darling, I live here because I am Galician, born and bred! It's where I belong. Seville suits my mother very well, but I'm like a fish out of water down there.'

She smiled briefly at the suitable choice of phrase. Luis

18

had been careful to speak lightly, but the words had contained a message that she knew she'd been meant to take seriously.

'Is Juanita here?' she asked next.

'Yes, I brought her back an hour ago . . . in exactly the same frame of mind as when I left her with my mother.'

Inez held out long, thin hands in a gesture of despair. 'My dear, she needs help – psychiatric help – even if you don't like to admit the fact.'

'There's one more thing to try first,' he said quietly. 'I suspect that it may only prove to be another false hope, but if it *is* a mistake, it's been made now. I've brought Juanita an English physiotherapist from London. She must be given the chance to see what she can do.'

Inez gave a little moue of disapproval. 'I've been in Andalucía too long, obviously. I didn't know you were even thinking of such a thing.' A faint suggestion was left hanging in the air that a mistake wouldn't have been made if she'd been consulted first, but she managed to sound regretful when she spoke again.

'My poor Luis, I'm afraid it won't work at all. Juanita will hate your Englishwoman. You must cancel the arrangement and let me find someone suitable.'

He gave a little shrug. 'The suggestion comes too late, *querida*. Miss Brown arrived this afternoon. I hope you don't object to meeting her at dinner!'

Inez was silent for a moment; the truth was that she did object, but she knew better than to say so. No one could be more effortlessly grand than Luis himself, but there were times when he swung quite ridiculously the other way. 'Let us meet her by all means,' she agreed, 'and hope that Miss Brown doesn't find Cantanzos more than she can manage – Juanita is quite enough to contend with!'

'What's the nurse-person like, Luis?' Inez's brother asked, suddenly entering the conversation. 'I'll guess at a resemblance to the English nanny we had as children: frumpish and *very* firm; I grew fond of her in the end, but

19

I can't say the same for my sister, who was, of course, thoroughly rebellious and ungovernable!'

Not minding this description of herself, Inez smiled at the Count. 'Is that apt for Miss Brown – frumpish and firm?'

Luis refused the challenge. 'You'll have to make up your own minds about her. I saw her very briefly and she made no strong impression beyond seeming competent at her job.'

'Nondescript,' Inez decided with a faint, satisfied smile. 'I doubt if she will do at all, and I think it's your own impression too.'

'Perhaps,' he admitted slowly, 'but largely because in her present frame of mind Juanita will refuse to accept anyone that I could have found to help.'

Inez nodded agreement. 'Then in that case Miss Brown will soon return to England and we can start again.'

Luis thought for a moment of the face of the girl he had seen in London. He certainly couldn't recall it feature by feature, but memory retained an image that didn't quite match Inez's easy assumption of a mistake soon written off. It was more likely that Francesca Brown's philosophy required the strong to rescue the weak, and he knew with strange certainty that, her appearance notwithstanding, she was to be numbered among the strong.

'Shall we wait and see?' he suggested finally. 'Meanwhile, Inez, here is Señora Fernandez to show you to your room. Pascal, you're in the tower with me, as usual.'

It was still the Cantanzos rule to stick to traditional Spanish habits – men and women sleeping in separate areas of the house. Inez had once laughingly accused her host of accepting the worn-out legacy of centuries of Moorish occupation, but it had made no difference to the way their bedrooms were arranged. More irritatingly still for a woman who'd been widowed for over a year, Luis insisted on observing a period of mourning that she found antiquated and absurd. She had no doubt that he wanted to marry her and, in his own good time, would make the proposal she was waiting for; but she was not a patient woman, and the waiting was hard. There would be problems ahead, of course, not the least of them her intention of removing him from Cantanzos for at least a part of every year; but the first step was to become his wife. He wouldn't be able to hold out much longer; she was expert at measuring her effect on men and Luis Esteban, self-disciplined though he was, needed her very badly. She smiled brilliantly at him now, and then nodded to the waiting housekeeper; it was time to be conducted upstairs.

Three

O n the floor above the one Inez de Castro was being led to, Fran surveyed the wardrobe she'd brought with her. It looked inadequate, to say the least, for dinner with the Count and his guests; she'd reckoned on silent meals with the housekeeper. But there was another small problem as well: Galicia was not southern Spain, and she could easily imagine the sort of glacial atmosphere in which Luis Esteban was accustomed to dine. Damn elegance; she would put her money on warmth, and no doubt find herself relegated to the servants' hall tomorrow evening.

It was something to smile at while she hurriedly changed her clothes, but the truth was that she was trying not to think of other things: had Juanita already been helped to bed, or was she also going to be downstairs, waiting to make it clear that the sooner her English attendant went home the better? Fran wanted very much to meet her for the first time alone, not entangled in the hostility that seemed to exist between the Count and his niece. She was ready and waiting when Marilar tapped at the door, but her smile still got no response and they walked down the wide staircase in silence.

A fire of logs burning in the huge hearth of the hall produced flickering shadows and a slightly more welcoming air, but Marilar plodded heavy-footed towards double doors that opened into a room Fran subsequently learned to call the salon. The maid disappeared and she was left to walk into it unannounced, to find that she was being stared at by a group of people standing in front of another fire-lit hearth. Their message seemed clear: unlike herself, they belonged on this alien, windswept promontory. The sheer unfriendliness of it gave her the stiffening of anger that she needed. There was colour in her face by the time Luis Esteban left the couple standing by the fire and came towards her – the leopard himself, hiding teeth and claws for the moment.

'Good evening, Miss Brown . . . I'm sorry that I was not here when you arrived, but no doubt Señora Fernandez made you welcome.'

'She showed me to my room,' Fran agreed coolly.

His dark eyebrow lifted in a mannerism she remembered; she hadn't answered him humbly, as he expected, and in general people did do what he expected of them. Fran registered the fact and feared that she would continue to disappoint him in future; but he managed a faint smile and indicated his other guests.

'Let me present you . . . Miss Francesca Brown – the Marquesa de Castro, and her brother, Don Pascal Vargas.'

The Marquesa's hand touched hers in so minimal a greeting that Fran wondered whether she'd been meant to curtsey instead. Don Pascal was kind enough to bow, as if he didn't mind meeting her; but Fran's attention now was on the person she hadn't yet been introduced to – the girl she had come to help. Juanita Fiocca sat apart from the others, crutches propped against the side of her chair. In an odd moment of silence Fran was aware of several things: Esteban's niece had the black hair and olive skin of her Spanish mother, but otherwise nothing seemed to link her to the other people in the room. She was entirely, defiantly, alone and intended to go on being so; more surprisingly, she was very overweight and downright plain.

'My niece, Juanita Fiocca,' Esteban said quietly. 'As you see, not as active as we would like.'

Fran put out her hand, then withdrew it again because Juanita merely gave an indifferent nod before resuming her inspection of a log smouldering on the hearth. The legs stretched stiffly in front of her looked too frail to support her heavy body, mutely confessing to wasted muscles that

23

hadn't been used for months. Fran's heart was suddenly wrenched with pity for a girl who had rejected recovery because she rejected what life had done to her. No sinecure, the Count had said; he might have said that the job he'd offered was impossible. Juanita's eyes looked at nothing but the inward vision of her own ravaged life, and anyone who tried to persuade her away from it became immediately an enemy.

'Good evening, Juanita,' Fran said in Spanish. 'I'm very glad to be here.'

It earned her another insolent stare. 'How nice,' Juanita commented briefly.

Fran saw Esteban frown, and hastily plunged into a conversation with Don Pascal. 'Are you and your sister natives of Galicia, señor, inured to the sort of weather we imagine only belongs to England?'

It was the Marquesa who answered. 'No Spanish *woman* is resigned to rain, Miss Brown, or to the unspeakable mackintoshes and rubber boots that you English seem prepared to wear.' Fran resisted a strong desire to rush to the defence of all things English and decided that someone else could find the next topic of conversation. It was Don Pascal, busy refilling glasses for his host, who broke the silence.

'Some Manzanilla for you, Miss Brown? I'm afraid you'll have to accustom yourself to *our* way of serving fino . . . I believe you treat it differently in England.'

Fran permitted herself a glance at the impassive face of Luis Esteban before smiling at his guest, grateful for a comment that had at least been made pleasantly. He looked, in fact, a pleasant man altogether, despite the resemblance to his sister. In him their family features had been blunted into something more ordinary than the Marquesa's stunning beauty. *Her* face had the flawless precision of some precious cameo, and Fran acknowledged it to herself with regret – a little less perfection would have made it easier to like her. Perhaps Juanita thought so too, unable not to be aware of the contrast she must present to the other woman. On the other hand, maybe the Marquesa *had* tried to take the girl in hand and failed; it was too soon to pass judgement on these alien, complicated people she found herself among.

Fran sipped her dry, delicious sherry, hoping that she needn't drink much of it before she was finally given some food, but her watch said half past ten before a white-gloved servant appeared in the doorway to announce that dinner was served. Esteban went across to his niece.

'Time to move, my dear. Shall I help you?'

Fran saw her nod sullenly and allow herself to be pulled to her feet; then, with the crutches in place, she shuffled slowly towards the door the servant had opened into the adjoining dining room. The rest of them followed at Juanita's pace and settled themselves round the massive oak table. The heavy furniture seemed appropriate to a room hung with crimson curtains and ornately framed portraits of the Count's ancestors. It contrived to be airless and cold at the same time, and Fran felt thankful for the warmth of her own cashmere sweater, which must surely be more comforting than the Marquesa's beautifully frilled silk shirt. They were served with food that was delicious but over-elaborate for someone unaccustomed to eating so late at night. Fran enjoyed the hot, spicy soup and good Spanish bread, but helped herself sparingly from a dish of scallops served rather strangely, she thought, with bacon and oranges in a thick, rich sauce.

'You don't like our Galician cooking?' Esteban asked after a glance at her plate.

'I'm accustoming myself,' she said with a faint smile.

Inez flashed an amused glance at her host. 'My dear Luis, I doubt if poor Miss Brown likes anything here at all – it must be so very different from anything she is used to.'

'High tea at six in my London slum,' Fran agreed solemnly. 'Count Esteban has seen where I live, and has a very good idea of what I'm used to.'

'Count Esteban thought your home was charming,' he said unexpectedly, 'and he would prefer that you called him Don Luis in future.'

Her startled glance met his across the table; a dark, grave stare denied the possibility that he was amused, but she was at least certain that her employer was quite as complicated as anyone else she was likely to meet. What was more, she suspected him of liking to disconcert other people; but Inez reclaimed his attention and Fran looked instead at Juanita, now making no attempt to talk to anyone and simply cramming food into her mouth in a way that explained the heaviness of her face and body.

They were nearing the end of the long meal when a remark Pascal had intended for Fran was overheard by the rest of them.

'The holiday season is at hand, Miss Brown, but I'm afraid you will see very few English people up here – they seem to prefer the sun and the south.'

Inez promptly threw up her hands in protest. 'Please, caro, don't remind us of the horrors in store. You ought to know by now what Luis feels about the foreign tourists who invade Spain every summer.' She turned to stare at Fran. 'It must be an embarrassment to you – the way your compatriots behave on the Costa del Sol.'

The words were sympathetic, but her dark eyes were bright with malice; the woman was a Spaniard, Fran reminded herself, bred up to giving no quarter.

'A minority of ill-mannered hooligans put us to shame, of course,' she agreed quietly, 'but the English aren't the only foreigners who "invade" Spain. If you really don't want them, why encourage them to come? I assume that the hideous hotels that disfigure a once beautiful coastline have mostly been built by your own entrepreneurs?'

Pascal smiled at her. 'Well said, Miss Brown! If we want the revenue the tourist industry brings – and we undoubtedly do – we must put up with its disadvantages.'

Luis Esteban frowned at him, but addressed himself to Fran. 'We certainly have only ourselves to thank, but remember that, when the tourist industry began, this was still a desperately poor country. We opened our doors expecting that our guests would conduct themselves in the Spanish way, with restraint and dignity. Have you seen how they behave after a week of steady drinking?'

'No, but we read about them, and I can't defend their conduct,' she was forced to admit. 'All the same, I refuse to believe that they are more than a minority of young people; your authorities and ours must find some way of teaching them better manners.'

Juanita suddenly lost interest in food and launched herself into the conversation. 'The English are the *worst*; everybody knows that,' she said viciously. 'We don't want them here . . . we don't want *any* of them here.'

There was silence round the table. From the expression on Esteban's face Fran supposed that the Marquesa's subtle baiting was permitted, but not this clumsy frontal attack. She hadn't decided how to deal with it, and nor apparently had he, before Juanita struggled to her feet, groping for her crutches. 'I hate this place,' she shouted. 'I *won't* stay here.'

It was Pascal who got up to open the door for her; her guardian remained at the table, silent and set-faced.

'The stairs,' Fran murmured, half-rising from her own chair. 'How will she manage them?'

'Leave her alone,' Esteban said harshly. 'She *does* manage on her own, and prefers to.'

Fran stayed on her feet, confronting him across the table. 'I don't think I was brought here to "leave her alone". Doesn't it occur to you that what she *can't* manage is her own unhappiness? She's sixteen – scarcely more than a child – and her only solace at the moment is in stuffing herself with food and hating the people put in charge of her. Isn't it time you decided how to deal with *that*?'

Her eyes challenged him, seeing his anger, which was as fierce as her own, but not the near-despair that he also felt about his niece's condition. It was the Marquesa who answered first.

'You met Juanita for the first time two hours ago,' she

said coldly. 'Allow us to know her a little better than you do. You seem ready to believe that she's been given no encouragement to recover, but that isn't true. She *wants* to suffer. In doing so she can reduce the life of everybody around her to ruins; it's her revenge for what life has done to her. Tell us, by all means, how we should deal with that!'

'If what you say is true, she is a sick child,' Fran answered despairingly. 'I'm not competent to heal her mind.'

'How should you be?' Inez agreed. She hesitated fractionally, then went on after a glance at her host. 'It was quite unfair to have encouraged you to come here – I believe Don Luis already realises that; indeed he has as good as said so.'

It made several things clear, Fran realised. This beautiful, ruthless woman shared Esteban's life to the extent of receiving all his confidences. She was even sure enough of herself to reveal on his behalf opinions he hadn't expressed himself; but it was to him that Fran put her next question.

'*Would* you prefer me to leave?'

'I should prefer you to remain, if you can bear to,' he said deliberately. 'My impression was that you wouldn't give up so easily, but perhaps I was wrong about that.'

His eyes were offering the challenge now, and she must pick up the gauntlet he'd flung down. Pride demanded it, as well as her longing to help Juanita if she could; but there was also a less worthy ambition that she had to recognise: she wanted very much indeed to deny the Marquesa the pleasure of being proved right.

'Our arrangement stands,' she agreed at last. Then, nerves strung tight by the tension in the room, she took refuge in a last-ditch attempt at humour. 'If everything else fails, perhaps sheer dislike of the English will persuade your niece to fling her crutches at me!'

'Then at least she'll have to manage without them,' the Count pointed out, without the flicker of a smile. 'That will be something gained, will it not, Miss Brown?'

She nodded, aware of the oddness of their situation. Both

of them had somehow been trapped into accepting it by the Marquesa's intervention; without that, Luis Esteban would probably have advised her to go home and she'd have agreed that it was the only sensible thing to do. Now, God alone knew what would happen next, but her only immediate certainty was that she must get out of the cold but overcharged room. The day had been long and full of strain, and she felt mortally tired. The morning would have to be time enough for her next confrontation with Juanita, and *that*, after all, was what mattered; she wasn't there to cope with Luis Esteban or a woman who, inexplicably, seemed to want very much to see the back of her.

She said a brief goodnight and managed to smile at Pascal Vargas when he held the door open for her. There was no sign of Juanita in the hall or on the staircase so, probably on her hands and knees, she'd got herself back to her bedroom. Fran shut the door of her own room, then had to lean against it, fighting the wave of loneliness and despair that washed over her. It was insanely wrong for her to be in this hostile, alien place; she belonged with more gentle people. Clothes left where she stepped out of them, she fell into bed and, with tear-stains drying on her cheeks, slept at last to the sound of the sea washing against the rocks beneath the castle's encircling wall.

Four

S he awoke to the rasp of Spanish voices outside her windows, but the other sounds she had grown used to were missing: the sea was quiet now, and wind and rain no longer drove against the glass. It was time to climb down from her high bed, buckle on her armour and start to come to terms with Cantanzos and its inmates. A glance out of the windows produced the first surprise: it was unexpectedly beautiful. An opalescent mist was dissolving as the sun rose and, even as she watched, sea and sky were gently suffused with colour. She bathed and dressed quickly in jeans and sweater, and ran down the staircase. At six o'clock the great entrance Pepé had led her through the previous afternoon might still be locked and barred, but there must be other ways in and out of the castle. Bars of sunlight already striped the hall floor, and Marilar, sour-faced as ever, was there, polishing the stone flags with a mop three feet wide.

'*Buenos dias*, Marilar.' Fran spoke cheerfully, but the maid merely stared with disapproval at a girl who got up before she was supposed to.

'Breakfast will be brought to your room, señorita, but not until eight o'clock.'

'Then I have time for a walk, if you'll show me which door to use.'

She was led in silence along a corridor that skirted a warren of small rooms – no doubt the domestic heart of the place – and escaped at last into the outside world, wondering what it was about Galicia that made its inhabitants so determinedly morose. This morning the rain-washed, pine-scented air smelled delicious and there were surely far worse places in which to live. From her windows she had seen that the top of the encircling wall carried a path wide enough to walk along; she would begin with that, if she could find the steps that led up to it.

They were in front of her almost at once, but after climbing up she stood watching the last, silver shreds of vapour melt into a hyacinth-coloured sea. The ebbing tide splashed gently against the rocks piled up against the seaward side of the wall, and the sound awoke a childhood memory of the sea washing the shingle of a Cornish beach. She was suddenly homesick for England, still aware of the pain of all she had lost: the wise and loving man who had been her father, and the charming scholar she'd believed she was going to marry. It was thanks to her father that she'd been able to grow up *not* hating her beautiful, feckless sister. Felicity, coming back to London from abroad, had been taken in and made welcome, and in Fran's flat she'd inevitably been introduced to her sister's fiancé. From that had begun the train of events that led to this sunlit morning at Cantanzos.

'One of our more gentle days, Miss Brown,' said a voice suddenly.

She turned to find Luis Esteban climbing the steps behind her. Like herself, he was dressed informally this morning and looked slightly less unapproachable as a result.

'You're out so early that I'm afraid you didn't sleep. Were you plucking up the courage to tell me that you want to go home after all? I couldn't blame you after my niece's behaviour last night.'

She didn't know whether, regretting his choice, he was making it easy for her to go, or merely feeling sorry for the failure she was facing. He watched her while she thought about it, her body slender and upright against the immense backdrop of sea and sky. The breeze lifted her soft brown hair – as different as could be from a Spanish woman's hair. It wasn't surprising, of course; she was different altogether.

But he was conscious once again that, if they'd both made a mistake – he in bringing her and she in coming – he hadn't been wrong about her stubborn refusal to admit defeat.

'I thought we agreed last night that I should stay,' she said after a long pause.

'Yes, but you were looking at the sea just now as if you were a mermaid longing to swim away in it. Don't you like my home any more than you relish your job here?'

His voice warned her that the question wasn't one for answering lightly. She turned to stare at the grey walls of Cantanzos rising out of the green hillside. A flag on top of the tower moved gently in the breeze – she could see its leopard, bright against a crimson background. When she looked at Esteban again he'd half-turned away from her and there was time to study the man himself as well. The sunlight showed up the frosting of silver that touched his hair and the thread of an old scar pale on the brownness of his face. She could see the lines of strain and sadness engraved there as well, and understood something she hadn't registered before: his sister's death was a grief he still struggled with.

'It doesn't matter whether I like Cantanzos or not,' she finally said in answer to his question. 'It's your niece who concerns me. Does her specialist know that she's still dependent on crutches?'

'He knows and, of course, disapproves. The crutches should be forgotten, thrown away; but Juanita persists in clinging to them, presumably to remind us that she will accept nothing we can offer her in place of what she's lost.'

'Perhaps she clings out of fear,' Fran suggested quietly. 'She's afraid of falling, of course, but also afraid of what else life might do to her if she gives it half a chance.'

Expecting him to argue or just walk away, she wasn't prepared for what came next.

'You disapprove of me very strongly, don't you?' he asked abruptly. 'All your English instincts are outraged by the streak of cruelty in us that you like to think is only appeased by killing bulls for entertainment or, in my case, ill-treating an unhappy orphan. Well, you are wrong; but this *is* Spain, Francesca Brown, not England!'

She almost smiled, so unnecessary did the warning seem to be. 'Oh, I realise where I am, but Doña Inez was right last night to remind me that I don't know enough to approve or disapprove of any of you yet. I shall learn in time about Juanita, if she will let me stay long enough: the rest of you I'm fortunately not required to learn about at all.'

A faint grin touched Esteban's mouth, surprising her by its genuine amusement. 'Put in my place, and with such gentle firmness! All the same, I should never have asked you to come here, because Juanita will hurt you if she can, and I have the feeling that you've been hurt already.'

It was even more unexpected than his smile, and as perceptive as it was painful; but she couldn't confess that he was right. Instead she steadied herself with a breath of pine-scented air and did her best to sound cheerful. 'Don't ask me to turn tail. National pride is at stake even if you do regret having brought me here.'

He had one final surprise in store. 'For the first time in my life I'm no longer sure *what* I think. Is that any comfort to you?'

Fran shook her head. 'No comfort at all, I'm afraid. You're required to be *el gran Condé* – undisputed lord of Cantanzos, supremely certain of yourself at all times, and more than a match for the rest of us!'

She smiled as she said it, suddenly aware that, if it was possible to find something to laugh at, she would be able to cope with life at the castle after all. His expression was unreadable now and she could only be certain that the *gran Condé* wasn't accustomed to providing amusement. It was scarcely to be wondered at, of course: he must have been aware of his importance in the local scheme of things almost from the moment he was born.

'I came out to explore,' she remembered with relief.

'Perhaps I should make a start before Cantanzos is veiled in rain again.'

'Quitting the field of battle, Miss Brown?'

'Regrouping my forces, Don Luis!'

It gave her the last word as she walked away, but the unfortunate truth was that her forces didn't amount to very much – against him, or against the sick, unhappy adolescent who didn't want her there.

By the time she went back indoors with a handful of wild flowers to brighten her room, the sun was already losing heart against an onslaught of cloud sailing in from the Atlantic; before the morning was out, Galicia would no doubt be true to itself and the rain would be slashing down again. Still, she'd seen Cantanzos in sunlight, and even caught a glimpse of its owner smiling briefly.

When her breakfast arrived, it was brought by a young maid she hadn't seen before, who not only offered the information that she was called Constancia but gave it cheerfully. Fran thanked her for the orange juice, coffee and heaped dish of rolls, solemnly agreeing that they might be sufficient to sustain her until lunchtime. The little maid thought this so richly funny that Fran found herself laughing too, and the sudden moment of light relief planted an idea in her mind.

'Constancia, does the Señorita breakfast now, as well?'

'In half an hour I bring her tray.'

Fran hesitated for no more than a moment or two. 'Will you bring her tray to *me* this morning, please, and let me take it to her?'

Constancia looked puzzled, but agreed. 'If the Señorita wishes.' Like the rest of the staff, she knew why the English woman had been brought to Cantanzos; unlike most of them, she sincerely pitied her.

Half an hour later Fran knocked at Juanita's door and heard a sulky voice call '*Adelante*' in reply. A tape player on the bedside table blared out the insistent beat of pop music, while Juanita sat up in bed, flicking through the pages of a magazine. Boredom was replaced by sudden rage as she saw who had come in.

'Did my dear uncle say you'd got to do the servants' work for them? I thought you were here for *my* benefit, not theirs.'

Fran told herself that she was very sorry for Juanita, that the malice that brimmed over so easily was better out than in . . . All the same, if they were ever to get on terms with one another, the ground rules had to be laid at once or not at all.

'We're all servants of a kind,' she said levelly, 'even your uncle, who has to serve Cantanzos. It isn't my job to bring your breakfast, but I asked Constancia to let me do it. I wanted to come and see you.'

'Well, you've had that pleasure; now you can go away again.'

'So I can,' Fran agreed cheerfully. 'It would be much more of a pleasure to walk out, but unfortunately I'm being paid to put up with you!'

Juanita blinked, repeating the words in her mind until she was sure she hadn't misunderstood them. This English-woman had meant to be insulting – she probably imagined that her tin-pot little island still counted for something in the world. Juanita congratulated herself that it wouldn't take long to make matters clear.

'Don't you call yourself some sort of nurse? I thought they were supposed to do their work for love, not for the rate of pay.'

'True,' Fran agreed calmly, 'but even nurses must eat.'

'Eat yourself sick at my uncle's expense, if you like, while you've got the chance. You won't be here long – Inez will see to that.'

'I don't think it rests with her. My instructions are that you're stuck with me until I've got you walking again.'

Juanita's hand moved suddenly to the tape machine, and the noise became a roar that made conversation impossible. She lay back against her pillows, looking pleased, and picked up the magazine again. It was the moment of truth, recognised by both of them.

Fran put down the tray on a chest of drawers, shifted the crutches out of reach, then switched off the tape machine; on second thoughts she carried it over to the wide window sill. War had been declared now and half-measures would only earn the girl's contempt.

'Would you like your breakfast? The rolls are delicious.'

Juanita glared at her, unable to deal with the conflicting tangle of feelings in which she knew herself to be trapped: rage, helplessness, hurt, and most certainly hunger. Just at the moment hunger had the upper hand; the rolls would be delicious, especially heaped with the fresh butter and sweet apricot jam that went with them. She needed them and, short of crawling across the floor to her breakfast tray, had no way of getting them. It was tempting to shout for the food to be brought to her, but she knew it would be a mistake; this wicked Inglesa who stood watching her was capable of removing the tray altogether. Instead, she held out her hands in a gesture that looked half-plea, half-command. Fran relented to the extent of putting the tray on the bed, then walked across the room to stare out of the window.

Ten minutes later Juanita said grandly, 'You may take the tray now. I've finished.'

She had done just that, Fran discovered. The basket of rolls was empty, the jam and butter dishes scraped clean, although there had been food enough for two or three people. For a moment, looking at the tray, she felt oppressed by her own helplessness . . . where was she to start helping a girl so determined to go to ruin in her own way?

'I was hungry,' Juanita said suddenly.

'You were angry,' Fran corrected her. 'A moment ago you were mostly angry with me, but you eat too much all the time because you're angry with life.'

It seemed touch-and-go whether the girl would scream at her to get out of the room. If that happened, she could see no way of getting back into it again and might as well start packing her suitcases to leave altogether; but Juanita was as unpredictable as her uncle. Instead of shouting or screaming, she beat her hands in sudden desperation against the counterpane.

'I *hate* Cantanzos, and my uncle . . . I *hate* Spain! I want to go home to Italy . . .' Her voice broke on the words, because she *had* no home, and the parents who had loved her were dead. She turned her face away, fighting the tears that until now had been frozen in her cold heart.

Fran wanted to weep herself for the injuries that life allowed people to suffer years before they were able to deal with them. Juanita had been a victim twice over – of her parents' self-indulgence, and of the tragedy that had deprived her of them so abruptly. Now, her only defence was to reject help from anyone else.

'You'll be able to choose where you live, eventually, but first you must start walking properly again.'

'I'll walk when I want to,' Juanita shouted. 'Not with *your* help, though. Esteban brought you here. I hate him; he said my father caused the accident – I *heard* him say it.'

The anguish in her voice was hard to argue with, but Fran knew she had to try. 'It was something you certainly weren't meant to overhear, born of the dreadfulness of the moment,' she suggested. 'Don't hold it against your uncle for ever, and try to remember that *he*'d just lost someone he loved.' She hesitated, afraid of rushing her fences, then took a flying leap at them. 'Will you let me examine your legs?'

There was a moment when she thought the girl might agree; but Juanita's face set in its expression of sullen resentment again and Fran knew that her first battle had been lost.

'Don't bother to refuse; I shall ask again, but now I'll leave you in peace.' She replaced the crutches and tape machine by the bed, then picked up the breakfast tray and walked out of the room.

Left alone, Juanita tried to feel pleased with herself – she'd routed the Inglesa, as she knew she would; soon

Esteban would have to send the woman home. Then, clearly, she heard the echo of her father's voice, talking about the English – stubborn people, he'd reckoned, who never seemed to know when they were beaten. He'd smiled as he said it, remembering his own boyhood and times shared with English soldiers during the war. She knew very well what he'd have said now: she was wrong to hate Francesca Brown and a fool not to accept her help. The tears she'd tried to hide a moment ago brimmed over again, and this time she could do nothing to stop them.

Downstairs, because there seemed nothing else to do, Fran walked out into the courtyard, and instantly froze in her tracks as two enormous dogs hurled themselves towards her; but the sight of their flattened ears and waving tails gave them away: these two were as soppy and sweet as the Great Dane she'd loved as a child. She was trying to persuade them that she could only manage one set of front paws on her shoulders at a time when Don Pascal came hurrying from the coach house that now garaged the castle cars.

'*Buenos dias, señorita* . . . I'm sorry . . . these silly animals only look alarming. I'd have held on to them if I'd known you were here, but I can see that you aren't in the least afraid of them.'

He could also see that Francesca Brown, smiling at the dogs, and with the sun on her hair, wasn't the unremarkable girl they'd been introduced to the night before. He remembered his sister's estimate of her, delivered the moment she'd left the room. It had seemed a reasonable assessment then, but he was inclined to think that for once Inez might have to admit that she'd made a mistake.

'Tell me the names of these beauties,' Fran suggested, wondering why she was being stared at for so long.

'Well, the one trying to nibble your ear is George, and the more bashful one is Henry.' His grin widened at the expression on Fran's face. 'I'm afraid you don't believe me, but there's a simple explanation: Don Luis's mother has an English companion, Miss Entwhistle, whose brother breeds these creatures in England. Mr Entwhistle, a keen royalist, works his way through the kings and queens of England whenever a dog's name is needed. Having got up to date with the monarchy, he starts at the beginning again!'

'Simple, when you know,' Fran agreed smilingly.

Pascal was still examining her. 'You look happier this morning,' he said with pleasure. 'I hope that means you're going to stay at Cantanzos.'

'I'm not a guest, señor, to choose whether I go or stay. In this morning's confrontation with Juanita I'm afraid I lost; if I can't do better than that, there'll be no point in staying.'

The Spaniard shook his head. 'Don't despair, and don't give in to her; Juanita despises people who allow themselves to be trampled on. She's too intelligent not to appreciate you in the end.'

Fran felt grateful for the show of confidence; Pascal Vargas was kinder than his sister, and a different man entirely from Luis Esteban.

'Are you and Doña Inez here for a long stay?' Fran thought she might safely ask without seeming impertinent.

Don Pascal shook his head. 'It's not just a visit for me; it's a job. I'm here to learn to help look after Cantanzos. My cousin isn't just the chief landowner in these parts; the Estebans have always been involved in industries right across the north – like steel and shipping. He works too hard and, until now, I've worked too little. I hope that's about to change!'

Fran smiled at the honest comment but hadn't replied when the Marquesa emerged from yet another doorway and came towards them. Unlike most women first seen at night, she was just as flawless by day; it was all Fran had time to notice before Doña Inez spoke sharply to her brother.

'Caro, Luis has been looking for you for the past half-hour. You are here to start work, remember; others can surely exercise the dogs.'

As if aware of the discourtesy of ignoring Fran altogether,

Pascal turned to her with a charmingly rueful smile. 'Are elder sisters as autocratic as this in England, señorita?'

'More often than not, I believe,' she agreed solemnly.

He gave her a little parting bow, and walked away with the dogs escorting him, one on each side. Left with the Marquesa, a vision this morning in white trousers and an emerald-green silk tunic, Fran decided not to wait to be told that she was there for Juanita's benefit, not Don Pascal's. But she was still trying to think of a suitable exit line when the woman in front of her suggested with a graceful wave of the hand that they should take a walk together. It was as unexpected as a royal command and offered, Fran thought, just about as little possibility of refusing. There wasn't much hope that she'd enjoy anything Inez de Castro had to say, but she nodded and fell into step, trying not to feel like a lamb being led to the slaughter.

Five

S he was taken through another archway into a secluded
walled garden that seemed to have little connection with
what she'd seen so far; here, protected from the worst of
the Atlantic weather, the first roses were already in bud,
reminding her that even northern Spain was a good deal
further south than London. She gestured to the beautifully
tended flower beds and spoke the thought in her mind.

'It isn't like the rest of Cantanzos; did some castle lady
once insist on a rose garden?'

'Don Luis's mother,' the Marquesa answered. 'She no
longer lives here, preferring Seville, but it's kept as she
planned it. I expect it pleases you – we know about your
national obsession with flower gardens!'

Fran smilingly agreed and, because the Spanish woman
had sounded not unkindly amused, confessed to something else as well. 'You were right last night to point
out that all this rather feudal splendour is not what I'm
used to. Cantanzos requires adjusting to in all sorts of
ways!'

'Its feudal ways offend you, perhaps? You find it unac-
ceptable in this day and age for one man to own so much,
have such control over the lives of so many people?'

Fran remembered her conversation with the Count, in
which he'd seemed unexpectedly human enough not to
be isolated by rank from everyone else. 'I could say that
it seems unfair,' she answered at last, 'but the tattered flags
hanging in the great hall say something too – of battles
fought against the Moors, the French, perhaps even against

41

fellow Spaniards in the Civil War. The Estebans seem to have earned the right to own a bit of Spain!'

'I think so too,' the Marquesa agreed, then smiled brilliantly. 'I could wish that the "bit", as you call it, wasn't so often veiled in sea-mist or rain, but these are natural elements to a Galician like the Count. I shall have to accustom myself to them!'

The message wasn't direct, but Fran registered it without difficulty. Not sure whether she was meant to offer congratulations or not, she said instead, 'Don Pascal spoke of being here not simply on a visit. Will *he* have some adjusting to do as well?'

'Rather a lot, I'm afraid. For the first time in his life he must learn to be busy! My very dear brother is kindness itself, charming to everyone he meets, especially to women, but he's easily distracted from the idea of working, and *that* is what he is here for.'

Message number two, Fran acknowledged to herself; the reasons for the Marquesa's invitation were becoming very clear. Presumably she was already certain of her own future at Cantanzos, but she and the Count would have their work cut out if they intended to turn Pascal Vargas into a dedicated toiler in the vineyard with never a moment to 'stop and stare' or make another human being feel important. She hoped they'd fail; she liked him as he was.

Now turning back in the direction of the castle, Doña Inez fired her final shot. 'I should be talking to you about Juanita, of course. I hope last night's behaviour convinced you that what she really needs is a professional psychiatrist. The longer you stay, the worse the delay will make her, in my opinion.'

Fran told herself to accept that it was an opinion honestly held and therefore rightly put into words. 'I'm not sure that the Count agrees with you,' she suggested cautiously. 'He hasn't asked me to leave.'

'Because, having brought you here, he feels some embarrassment in doing so; but if you agree with me that Juanita needs proper treatment, you won't wait to be asked. If you cherish any faint hope that she'll accept *your* help, I can assure you that the hope is doomed.'

There was a good chance, Fran knew, that the damned woman was right, but it was against every instinct she possessed to say so. Perhaps seeing something of the struggle in her face, Doña Inez went on in a gentler tone of voice.

'Miss Brown, believe me when I say that I want Juanita cured quite as much as you do – for her own sake, of course, but also for the sake of her uncle, whose painful responsibility she is.'

There was a little pause before Fran answered. 'I'll promise you this much: if I can make no headway at all, I'll go without being asked; but if I can see a chance of helping Juanita, I shall stay.'

A hint of triumph shone for a moment in the other woman's smile. 'Then the matter is as good as settled, I'm afraid. Now forgive me if I leave you to continue your stroll alone.'

She walked away with the self-conscious grace of someone who knew that she was worth looking at. Fran registered the fact with wry amusement, comparing it with the more English attitude of hoping not to be noticed at all. She'd noticed the difference before – even Spanish women who weren't beauties had the conviction that they'd be watched because they were females; it must do wonders for their self-esteem. She put the thought aside, knowing that she was simply wasting time out there. Her battle lay inside the castle, and at the moment it was Juanita who occupied the high ground to fight on, not herself.

She climbed the staircase and emerged into the corridor leading to her own room. Expecting to see the opposite door firmly shut, she was astonished not only to see it wide open, but to see Juanita herself, still propped up in bed, apparently waiting for her.

'You've been ages downstairs . . . I thought your job was

43

to look after *me*.' Delivered in Miss Fiocca's surliest voice, it wasn't a very promising start; but Fran told herself that any start was better than none.

'Don Pascal was introducing me to the two friendliest inmates of the castle I've met so far: George and Henry!'

'I don't like them,' Juanita said predictably. 'Apart from the fact that they belong to my dear uncle, they try to knock me over, the stupid animals.' She stared with resentment at a girl whose smile seemed far too cheerful for the position she was in. 'You're in sodden, downtrodden Galicia now. Don't expect *people* to be friendly here; they've got more sense than the dogs.'

Fran shook her head. 'Yesterday I might have agreed with you: this morning at least began with the sun shining. Cantanzos suddenly looked so beautiful that I thought it might grow on me in time.'

Juanita's scowl became a disagreeable smile. 'You'll also be disappointed if you expect to grow on anybody here. The Count will keep Pascal too busy to even throw a glance in your direction, and Inez will see to it that his attention doesn't stray from her. No pickings here for you, my dear Miss Brown.' The worldly drawl was so good an imitation of Inez herself that it prevented Fran from being angry.

'Thank you for making matters clear. I was wondering which of them to try to charm first!' Then she brushed the idea aside. 'Come off it, Juanita – you've been reading too many lurid romances. You know very well why I'm here. I'm not a bold adventuress on the make, simply a sober, hardworking physiotherapist with a job of work to do.'

'You aren't the one who was supposed to come,' Juanita remembered suddenly with glee. 'You're only a makeshift. Luis came back furious and told my grandmother that another girl had let him down.'

'The girl happened to be my sister – less sober than me, and much more beautiful.'

'Pity . . . she might have given Inez something to worry about!' Juanita considered the promising idea for a moment, then went on with such venom in her voice that it couldn't be dismissed as simply another attempt at self-dramatisation. 'I hate *her* most of all – she's trying to persuade Luis to send me away. I want to get out of Cantanzos – *Dios mio*, how I do. But not to some place where mad people go . . .' Her voice trembled and stopped abruptly, and Fran glimpsed the terror that she was staring at. The situation was becoming understandable now; no wonder a hurt and muddled adolescent faced the world with her fists raised, and crammed food into her mouth for comfort.

'Juanita, will you listen to me – by which I mean open your mind as well as your ears to what I'm going to say?'

The indifferent shrug that she got in reply provoked her into using a tone of voice the girl in front of her hadn't heard before. '*Answer* me, please.'

Startled by the sharpness, Juanita turned to face her. 'All right – there's no need to shout at me. Stuck here, what can I do but listen?'

'That's the point,' Fran said more gently. 'You're only stuck here because you've allowed yourself to be. I can't undo what's happened and give you back all you've lost. Nor can your uncle, although I'm sure he wishes that he could. As far as I know, there's no physical reason why I can't get you walking again, but if you were given notes and X-rays when you left hospital, I need to see them.'

Juanita's usual expression of mulish obstinacy was back on her face again, but Fran had glimpsed the fear that held her locked into immobility. Somehow she had to be released from it, but dealing with her was a perilous matter. It would be the easiest thing in the world to drive her into total withdrawal, but in her present frame of mind only antagonism seemed to spur her into making any effort at all. Fran sent up a silent prayer that she was doing the right thing, then spoke again.

'I know you don't want *me* here – don't, in fact, want anyone at all. But why not consider that for the moment I'm the best chance you've got of escaping from Cantanzos in

45

the long run? If you can take charge of your own life, you'll be able eventually to leave a place you seem to hate. If you don't start walking again, you'll be here for good.'

There was so long a silence that she'd almost accepted failure when Juanita's grudging voice said what she needed to hear.

'There are some doctor's reports and things – pictures – in the drawer over there. I meant to hide them from you.' She watched Fran walk across the room to fetch them before adding an angry rider: 'You're a worse bully than that cow Inez, and you don't even *look* as if you are.'

Fran turned briefly to smile at her. 'I know – it's quiet ones like me that you've got to watch!'

That evening, getting ready for dinner, she found it hard to believe that it wasn't much more than twenty-four hours since she'd arrived at Cantanzos. Her London life had receded so far in time and space that it seemed to belong to someone she could scarcely remember. Locked in her struggle with Juanita, she was almost unaware of what she'd lost herself. The pain of it was only put aside – she knew that clearly enough. It would be waiting for her again, whenever the moment came to leave Cantanzos; but she could spare it no part of herself now, if she wasn't to fail with Juanita in the end.

Walking into the salon before dinner that evening, she noticed what she'd been too tense to register the night before: the room might have been found in any country house in England, with its comfortable chesterfields and armchairs covered in flowering chintz. Persian rugs made pools of colour on the polished floor, and delicate, gilt-framed watercolours hung on the walls. The heaviness that had seemed so overpowering in the dining room and hall were missing here; it was a charming room in which to feel comfortable and at home. But it wasn't empty as she'd thought: Luis Esteban stepped out of the embrasure of one of the long windows and stood watching her.

'You're prompt because you are hungry, I expect,' he said calmly. 'I'm afraid English stomachs never accustom themselves to our peculiar hours of eating.'

The leopard sounded almost amiable, tempting her to relax in his company – probably only for the pleasure of turning on her as soon as he grew tired of the game. She smiled cheerfully, remembering that she'd decided how to deal with him. 'I have it on good authority that it is we who are strange – Marilar made the matter clear as soon as I arrived.' For a moment she was tempted to tell him about the *churros* that had had to be refused, but he was still too much of an unknown quantity, a man whose sense of the ridiculous she'd had too little chance of testing.

'Miss Brown . . . it is time to make something else clear. What I said earlier was true – I should *not* have brought you here. The error was mine, and if you fail with Juanita – as I think you will – the failure will be mine as well. Doña Inez tells me that you're determined to go on trying. I should like to tell you that there would be no disgrace in accepting defeat – probably only sound common sense.'

He moved across the room to the huge stone fireplace, to deal with a log that had shifted on the hearth, and she watched the firelight play over his dark face. He looked tired and . . . sad was the word that came to mind, as it had done once before. She acquitted him of harshness now; he simply didn't know what to do with a girl who remained his responsibility even though she rejected him. The Marquesa had been right to point out that his own life was suffering. Fran gave him credit for not referring to it himself, but he must be longing to be free of a niece who seemed determined to hate the woman he intended to marry.

He turned round to find himself being watched, and the faint lift of his eyebrow seemed to say that he wasn't accustomed to being observed any more than he was used to being laughed at. An autocratic man, *el Condé*; she must try to remember the fact and not treat him as she had treated Richard Weston.

'I shall accept defeat if I have to,' she said quietly. 'My first attempt with Juanita this morning wasn't a great success, but at least she changed her mind afterwards about letting me see her hospital records. Now I can at least be certain that it's only fear that keeps her from walking.'

Esteban's frown didn't fade. 'Her legs are only part of the problem; even walking again, isn't she going to be the same hostile, greedy, impossible adolescent she is now?'

It was the Marquesa's view he was repeating; Fran thought they were the very words the woman would have used. 'Perhaps, but we have to start with her somewhere,' she insisted, 'and it doesn't help if the rest of you do nothing but wring your hands and say that she's impossible.'

She flung the words at him, too concerned to care that his employees probably didn't make a habit of open criticism. He hadn't decided how to reply when the door behind them opened and Inez walked in. Dressed this evening in black, except for a scarlet silk shawl whose long fringe swept the floor, she was self-assured beauty personified – the cruellest possible contrast to the dumpy girl who swung herself into the room behind Pascal.

They went in to dinner, and the long, elaborate meal was a repetition of the one the previous evening except that there was no outburst this time from Juanita. She simply withdrew from the conversation and ate with the concentration of a starving refugee who didn't know where her next meal was coming from. Fran saw the expression on Esteban's set face when he glanced at her, and thought she could guess what was in his mind. Inez was right: the situation was next to impossible, and as soon as the stubborn creature he'd been fool enough to import had been persuaded to go home, his niece must be put in the hands of doctors capable of dealing with her.

For a moment his despair almost persuaded Fran that she was allowing wishful thinking to get the better of her. Juanita pushing chunks of bread into her mouth, crutches propped against her chair, was a sight to depress any guardian; but

48

while Inez held forth confidently about the political state of Spain, the girl suddenly looked up from her plate, met Fran's eyes across the table and . . . gave an infinitesimal wink! A discouraged keeper's heart lifted on a small but definite wave of hope. The cause wasn't yet lost if humour as well as intelligence lurked behind Juanita's heavy features. She was mostly hostile, and undoubtedly greedy, but perhaps not impossible after all.

Fran smiled back at her, and wondered if Esteban was listening as intently as he seemed to be to the Marquesa's authoritative attack on half the members of the country's present government. Pascal joined in the argument for the pleasure, Fran suspected, of contradicting his sister; but Juanita did nothing but yawn, and eventually got up from the table in her usual graceless fashion. Another gruelling day at Cantanzos was over.

Six

Her next early-morning walk along the castle ramparts was enough to persuade Fran that it was something she would miss when she was back in London. Already she was becoming accustomed to this wind-blown, sea-surrounded world, and she could easily understand the spell it cast over anyone who belonged there. Lucky Inez de Castro, even if she didn't think so, to have such a home in view. Then, as if the thought of the Spanish woman had conjured up her brother as well, Don Pascal suddenly materialised at the next flight of steps leading up to the wall.

'Good morning, Francesca,' he said, apparently forgetting that they hadn't reached Christian-name terms. 'I hoped that if I brought George and Henry along as a bribe, you'd allow me to share your walk!'

She liked him and enjoyed his company, but she could have done without the friendliness he seemed determined to offer. 'Francesca' indeed – God knew what the Marquesa would make of that! The blame would somehow be hers for encouraging an impressionable man to lift his nose from the grindstone. She might have made some excuse to abandon her walk but had to smile instead, because the dogs, having heard their names, stood on hind legs to lick her face with loving gratitude.

'Picture of two well-trained English animals being given their morning exercise,' she murmured. 'It's hard to believe that such ungovernable creatures belong to *el gran Condé*!'

It was Pascal's turn to grin. 'Luis pretends that it was Entwhistle who ruined them as puppies, but it doesn't stop him loving them. Why do you call him by that ridiculous name?'

'Not ridiculous at all; it's how I think of him – autocratic and powerful; someone who doesn't have to stop and consider how other peoples' lives are led.'

Pascal's cheerful face grew unexpectedly thoughtful. 'I'm afraid you don't like him. I suppose the outward appearance is what you say, Francesca – which, by the way, is a name I like very much said as the English say it. But Luis is *not* a tyrant – just a man who inherited huge responsibilities when he was still quite young.'

'But didn't mind doing so, I can't help thinking! There are people who feel that huge responsibilities, and the privileges that go with them, rightly belong to them. Count Esteban seems to me to be one of them.'

'Shall I tell you about him? His father was a Spanish aristocrat of the old school, so stiff and formal that he used to put the fear of God into me when I was a child – for all that we're cousins distantly removed. Luis never talks about him, nor about a childhood that must have been cruelly unhappy.'

Fran looked sceptical. 'A strict father doesn't necessarily mean an unhappy child.'

'No, but a mother who hates her home surely does,' Pascal said unanswerably. 'The Condesa was different, you see; she came from the south, as Inez and I do. She loved dancing and gaiety and the sunlight of Andalucía. When she found that she couldn't ever persuade her husband to leave Cantanzos, it became a sort of prison to her.'

'What happened in the end?'

'Luis's sister, Mercedes, escaped by marrying Gino Fiocca, but by then Marganita Esteban had simply run away. Luis adored his mother, but although he hated her to be unhappy, he could never quite convince himself that she'd had the right to abandon them. Poor Luis.'

'Poor Condesa,' Fran amended quietly. 'Still, I have to

agree with you; his childhood can't have been happy. Yours was, I should think. Am I right?'

'Yes, although we were shamefully poor! My sister's solution was, of course, to choose a wealthy man.' Pascal hesitated for a moment, then went on. 'Inez will marry next time for love, but even that won't be easy. She's a creature of the south, but she'll have to accustom herself to living here because Luis loves Cantanzos quite as much as his father did.'

Fran walked in silence, thinking that life was never simple after all, even for people who seemed born to good fortune. With a glance at her thoughtful face the man beside her went on speaking.

'You don't talk about yourself, I notice. Were you a happy child? I suspect so, because even when you were thrust into a room and watched in the rather insolent way we Spaniards have, you still seemed serene and sure of yourself.'

Fran smiled at the memory of her first introduction into the salon. 'The truth is that you all made me very angry – that helped! My own childhood was a mixed blessing, I suppose. My dear and gentle father loved his daughters equally. My mother doted on my younger sister, who inherited her own beauty. Felicity was to achieve what she had missed herself by becoming the wife of a country doctor – a brilliant, successful life.'

Pascal repeated the question Fran had asked. 'What happened in the end?'

'Father died five years ago; my mother still lives in Cornwall. Felicity followed me into the same training, but she's been more adventurous about her career than I have. It was she who was to have accepted Don Luis's job, but she went to New York unexpectedly instead and I came in her place.' The explanation came out calmly enough, but it took an effort to keep her voice steady, and she disguised it by throwing a piece of driftwood for the dogs to chase. They brought it back between them and dropped it hopefully at her feet, but she shook her head. 'Time to go back, gentlemen. Breakfast will be arriving, and I plan to eat mine with Juanita.'

Pascal looked surprised. 'Is that true? We imagined that she'd have nothing to do with you. In fact, Luis is expecting you to say any day that you're ready to go home; my sister is expecting it, too.'

'I know, but they can't always have what they expect – it's very bad for them!' She said it primly, trying not to smile at his shout of laughter.

'You don't look like her in the least but you *sound* just like our old nanny! We all had these formidable ladies when we were children, you know – it's why we speak such correct and elegant English, of course.'

She was still smiling at the thought when she left him to go indoors, but her face was thoughtful as she walked up to Juanita's room. Inez had been right about her brother: he was certainly kind, but it was Fran's strong conviction that Pascal was missing the charm of southern life. He was doing his best to accept a harsher regime but it didn't come naturally to him. God had put women on the earth for men to be attentive to, and he saw nothing to quarrel with in that.

Delayed by their conversation, she found Juanita already breakfasting with her usual determination to clear the tray of food. Fran had so far postponed that particular battle, being of the opinion that she couldn't fight on all fronts at once; the crutches were the first prop that Juanita had to be detached from.

'You're late. I expect you just happened to meet Pascal again,' was the comment that greeted her as she walked in. 'If the dear Marquesa notices these little strolls, you'll be in trouble, Miss Brown.'

'Pascal will be in trouble. I have a problem of my own.'
'Which is?'

'To convince your uncle that I'm not skiving at his expense. For as long as you insist on appearing downstairs with those damned crutches, he has the right to think I'm just enjoying a free holiday. Even Don Pascal knows that

I'm expected to say at any moment that I've no excuse to stay here.'

Juanita gave a little shrug intended to convey that she didn't care what any of them expected; but she nodded when Constancia asked from the doorway for permission to bring in the *señorita inglesa*'s breakfast.

'When you've finished eating, I want to show you something,' Fran said quietly.

Juanita pushed the tray aside. 'Show me now.'

Fran went to the drawer where the medical records were kept and came back with the X-ray pictures. It was a risk, to confront a disturbed girl with the evidence of a moment in her life that had been terrible, but she could see no way of making progress without it.

'These are photographs of your legs before and after the hospital treatment; look at them, please. These two long shadows are the main bones in your legs – the fibula and the tibia. In the first set of pictures the damage is obvious – here, and here. Now look at the next set: the bones have completely knitted together and, having done so at your age, they're as good as new again.'

Juanita suddenly flung back the bedclothes with a gesture that scattered the X-rays all over the bed. 'These are my good-as-new legs – look at them! If I tried to walk, I'd just fall over, and then they'd break again.'

A sob caught in her throat, and she lay back against the pillows with her eyes tightly shut and her hands clenched into fists. Instead of answering, Fran put her own hands on the wasted legs and began to massage them – gently at first, then rubbing, *willing* strength back into muscles that hadn't been used for months. At last she stopped, pushed the damp hair out of her eyes, and squatted on the end of the bed.

'Your muscles will get a little stronger each day with massage, but what they *must* be given is something to do. It's what they're there for. I want you to start right now, and you must trust me enough to know that I shan't let you fall.'

She saw Juanita's pudgy cheeks turn white, and it was hard to insist in the face of such fear, but she held out her hands. 'You said I was a bully,' she pointed out, trying to smile.

In the silence of the room the issue hung in the balance between them, Fran well aware that if Juanita couldn't find the courage by herself, it would be impossible to force her. Slowly, the girl swung her thin, slack legs over the side of the bed, reached out automatically for her crutches, then threw them down again. She was pulled gently to her feet, but stood there rooted to the spot, unable to move.

'Still holding you, I'm going to take a step backwards,' Fran said. 'That means *you*'ll have to come too; take one step towards me, please.'

Somehow, Juanita slid one foot forward, with an expression of such anguished concentration on her face that it was like watching a small child learning to walk for the first time.

'Now another one – don't watch your feet; I promise you they're still there! Keep *going*, Juanita.'

With a mixture of firmness and cajolery, she was led across the room and back again. Then, when her legs could feel the safety of the bed behind them, Fran released her hands, leaving Juanita standing there unsupported for a moment.

'You're a good, brave girl . . . you *did* it, and I'm very proud of you,' she said triumphantly.

'*Dios mio*, so I did . . . Francesca, I *walked*, didn't I?' She sat down abruptly on the bed, trembling and pale, and ducked her head against her knees. After a moment or two Fran pushed her back against the pillows.

'Your medical adviser recommends a rest now. We'll try again later when you feel strong enough.'

She was at the door before Juanita spoke. 'Am I allowed to call you Francesca?'

'Make it Fran – it's less of a mouthful, and what my friends call me,' said her adviser, smiling as she went away.

They repeated the walk twice more that day, with Juanita gaining a little more confidence each time, but she went into dinner on her crutches as usual and seemed her normal morose self at the table. She said nothing about her first attempts at walking, and Fran felt obliged not to mention them either; it made the bleakness in Esteban's face excusable, she thought, as he watched his niece gobbling food as usual.

The exercises were repeated the following day, but still Juanita scarcely opened her mouth at a midday meal shared only with the Marquesa while the Count and Pascal were visiting a shipyard on the coast. Doña Inez kept the conversation going by releasing the information that she would be leaving Cantanzos the next morning – she was expected to visit friends in the south. Juanita then decided to point out that the Marquesa would be there in time for the great Seville Feria, and turned to Fran with a rare glint of mischief in her face.

'I expect you've heard about it even in England: beautiful horses, overdressed women and very vain men, prancing about and admiring each other – not my uncle's scene at all!'

Trying to pour oil on troubled waters, Fran spoke to both of them. 'Even in England we *have* heard what a wonderful sight it is; but I think I'd still more have liked to be in Seville earlier to see the processions during Easter week.'

The tactful intervention did no good because it was Doña Inez's turn to point out crisply that Juanita couldn't be expected to know whether Seville at any time was her uncle's scene or not.

The uneasy meal over, Fran headed thankfully for her own room, praying that the Count would soon be home to keep his warring women in order – she was tired of both of them.

When she went downstairs that evening, she was disappointed to find Juanita in the salon still with crutches by her side as usual. Then, as Señora Fernandez came to announce dinner and Esteban walked across the room towards his niece, she suddenly heaved herself to her feet. With a touching mixture of determination and nervousness written on her face, she began to move slowly in the direction of the dining room, without a glance at the crutches left abandoned by her chair.

Pascal spoke first – in fact, shouted at his cousin: 'Look, Luis; do you see? Oh, well done, *querida*. Well done indeed.' He kissed her cheek as he helped her into a chair, and for once her face wasn't sullen at all but bright with happiness. When the rest of them were seated, and wine had been poured, it was Esteban who got up again, glass in hand, to smile at his niece. It was the tribute of a man to a woman, not a child. Watching them, Fran realised that Juanita recognised it as such, and that he'd intended that she should. It also occurred to her that the Marquesa's departure the following morning was the spur Juanita had needed; but if Doña Inez had been required to see her triumph, it was she who managed to spoil it as well. She looked across the table at Fran, with a smile on her beautifully painted mouth.

'How clever of you, señorita, but how sly! We were allowed no hint at all that your methods were achieving such success!'

Watching the light die out of Juanita's face, Fran could see no way of limiting the damage – surely done deliberately – but she tried.

'The achievement was Juanita's,' she said quietly. 'None of the credit is mine.'

It was no good; Juanita sat silent through the rest of the meal, eating everything that was put in front of her. Esteban made an effort to draw her back into the conversation, but she didn't even bother to reply, and finally he gave up and returned his attention to Inez again.

The Marquesa left in her own car the following morning, taking with her not only her own special brand of perfumed grace and elegance but also the blue skies and sunlight that had briefly shone on Galicia. Cantanzos was itself again: rainswept, wind-blown and forbidding.

Fran set out on a very damp walk just as the Count stood in the courtyard watching his lady-love drive away. His face was unrevealing, as usual, but she had the strange certainty now that it wasn't because he had no warmth to offer. Perhaps by temperament, and certainly by training, he was a man who would see it as a personal disgrace ever to lose control of himself, but she had no doubt that strong feelings were there. It would be Inez de Castro's difficult but rewarding task to persuade him to abandon his hairshirt of duty and discipline occasionally. She had weapons enough to persuade any man to eat out of her hand, but Fran couldn't help doubting whether she had enough warmth of heart to share.

She put the doubt aside as one that didn't concern her, but when she rounded a sharp bend in the castle wall, collided with the very man she'd decided not to think about. His arms held her firmly for a moment, and his voice sounded amused.

'A fire somewhere, señorita, or was the devil chasing you?'

She disentangled herself, feeling suddenly strangely breathless. 'A theory of my own,' she said as calmly as she could, 'that the faster I walk through the rain, the less wet I get! You'll say it's not scientifically correct, I expect, but it sounds logical to me.'

'I might,' he agreed with a faint smile, thinking as he looked at her that he might have confessed to some errors of his own. His first estimate in London had been that she was a rather plain imitation of her sister. The truth was that she was no imitation at all – instead, someone uniquely herself, more subtle in her appeal than the sort of women who clamoured for a man's attention. Pascal had had the perception to realise it sooner than he had himself.

'You tried to give my niece all the credit last night,'

he said abruptly, 'but she certainly wouldn't be walking unaided except for you.'

Fran saw no point in denying it; she was more intent on getting something else clear. 'Are you thinking that she can be left now, to continue by herself?

The frown she'd seen so often reappeared. 'What I'm thinking is that she remains the unhappy, unbalanced adolescent she's been since she came here. The only difference, big as that is, is that she's not completely dependent on those damned crutches; but if you're about to suggest catching the next flight back to England, I'm afraid I must refuse to let you go.'

It was *el gran Condé*, at his most autocratic again. She was tempted to suggest that a pleasantly worded request wouldn't come amiss, but saw by the flicker of amusement in his face that there was no need: the message had been received already.

'The muscles of Juanita's legs will strengthen quite quickly now,' she said instead. 'The rest of what needs to be done for her requires different help. I might persuade her to stop overeating, but she desperately misses her parents' affection and her home in Italy.'

'About that *I* can do nothing either,' Esteban said curtly. 'Since I can't bring my sister and brother-in-law back to life, she has to stay here until she's old enough to live on her own. I can't help it if she dislikes my home – dislikes me too, I suspect, for being alive when her parents are dead.'

'She didn't tell me not to say this, so I will. She overheard a remark you made – that her father caused the accident.' The words dropped into a well of silence, and she wondered if she would ever cease to regret the impulse that had made her say them. Luis Esteban's face looked carved out of stone.

'She wasn't *meant* to overhear,' he finally muttered. 'It was the truth, as it happens; Gino was tired and shouldn't have been driving, but I would never have wanted her to know it.' His eyes were fixed on Fran now. 'Do you believe that?'

'Yes, I believe it,' she said, 'and perhaps one day you can make *her* believe it too. It would also help if she could think you were a little fond of her; she's much in need of love.'

In the new silence that followed she heard only the mournful cry of a solitary gull beating against the wind, and the wash of the waves against the rocks at the foot of the wall. Raindrops spattered her face like tears and she thought that sea, rain and this unknowable man would be the memories of Cantanzos that she would take away with her when she was finally allowed to leave.

'She does matter to me,' he answered roughly. 'Can't you understand? She's all that's left to me of Mercedes.'

'She is herself as well as your sister's child,' Fran insisted. 'She needs loving for that. We all do. It isn't enough to be a reminder of someone else.'

He stared at her rain-wet face, remembering his impression that she concealed some private sadness. What she'd just said confirmed it: that sort of conviction only came from experience painfully bought.

'To expect to be loved for ourselves alone – doesn't that strike you as a somewhat arrogant claim?' he asked unexpectedly.

Fran shook her head. 'I think it's the only claim we have any right to make.'

He looked at her for a moment, no longer surprised that Juanita had accepted her. The nondescript Francesca Brown – Inez's ill-chosen word for her – was quickly changing things at Cantanzos. His niece was becoming human, Pascal smiled at everyone, and even the servants were beginning to look cheerful. He found himself wondering whether any of them had detected some minute change in himself. It was a stupid thought, of course – quite ridiculous in fact. He brushed it aside and spoke very firmly.

'I have to follow Doña Inez down to Seville tomorrow.'

'For the Feria Juanita thought you didn't enjoy?' Fran suggested innocently.

'Juanita is right for once: I dislike the Fair; but it's time for my mother's annual visit to Cantanzos and she likes to be brought here.' He hesitated a moment and then spoke more diffidently. 'Do you mind being left to cope alone?'

She shook her head, smiling at his idea of them being alone in a houseful of servants. 'We shall manage very well, especially if Don Pascal isn't going with you. He is such a kind man.'

'And you value kindness highly, do you not?'

'Of course – who doesn't?'

He didn't answer at once, then nodded and walked away, leaving her in the gently falling rain. She wasn't aware of it, wondering instead what Cantanzos would feel like when the Leopard himself wasn't there.

Seven

Juanita reverted to the sullen disapproval Fran had hoped was over when she heard that the Count had gone south to fetch his mother.

'What's the matter?' Fran asked. 'Don't you like your grandmother either?'

'No more than she likes me. You could say that we put up with one another.' Dressed only in bra and pants for the morning massage session now in progress, Juanita suddenly sat up and stared at herself in the mirrored door of her clothes closet. 'I look like an elephant. Why don't you tell me so? My grandmother makes it clear enough that no female descendant of hers should look the way I do.'

It took Fran a moment or two to choose the right words. 'Not an elephant but, if it conveys anything to you, you ought to be an English size 12, not the 16 that you probably are.'

'And now,' Juanita suggested with a mocking smile, 'you're about to suggest a regime that will leave me exhausted and suicidal, but wafer-thin in no time at all.'

'I'm about to suggest something harder but much more useful,' Fran answered. 'A slow, gradual reduction in the amount you eat at every meal. You'll lose weight slowly, but at least it will stay lost.'

Juanita's glance met hers in the mirror, resentful, but now with a saving glint of humour. 'I should have guessed that it would be what *you*'d recommend – the hardest thing of all.'

She made an effort at dinner that evening, nevertheless, and helped herself sparingly, even from the dishes she most enjoyed; but she'd relapsed into moroseness again, the joy of showing them that she could walk already forgotten in the pain of this new struggle.

'She needs something to lift her spirits – a treat,' Fran said sadly when Juanita had trailed out of the room on her way upstairs. 'Perhaps, if he were here, Don Luis could think of something.'

The man watching her across the table gave a rueful smile. 'I'm still here; why am I not allowed to think of something – for you as well as Juanita? You haven't been out of the castle grounds since the moment you arrived here, much less paid a visit to Santiago de Compostela. The three of us could drive there on Saturday, spend the night at the parador, and come back on Sunday afternoon. Would that be treat enough?'

Her smile shone suddenly, entrancing him with its sweetness. 'I can't think of anything I'd like more. All I got was a glimpse of the cathedral spires as Pepé drove me away from the airport, and I've been longing to go back. I should think Juanita would love it, too.'

Told of the plan the following morning, the girl, however, seemed more inclined to refuse to go. 'Where's the fun in rubbing shoulders with a herd of tourists? In any case, Pascal's supposed to be working here, not dancing attendance on you. Dear Uncle won't be pleased at all.'

'I doubt if Don Pascal has to account for every hour of his weekend time,' Fran pointed out with unusual crispness. 'The idea is chiefly to give *you* a change of scene. Why not accept the offer with grace instead of trying to ruin it?'

There was a hush in the room that she told herself she wouldn't be the one to break, although Juanita might intend to be equally obstinate, in which case they'd finish up where they'd started: locked in hostile silence.

'You don't have to bite my head off,' the girl finally muttered. 'I may not feel ready to hobble round that great barn of a place. I suppose that doesn't occur to you?'

'It does occur to me, but you can just sit and marvel at a building that has drawn pilgrims from all over Europe for the past thousand years. Think of them streaming over the

63

passes into Spain – lords and knights and priests and beggars, careless of hardship or danger, drawn there only by a burning conviction that salvation could be found at the shrine of St James. If that doesn't fire your imagination and your faith, I despair of you.'

Juanita only shrugged and returned in silence to her exercises, leaving displeasure hanging in the air. Fran went on doggedly with her work, regretting that the outing had ever been thought of, but depressed as well by the fragility of her friendship with Juanita. What it amounted to didn't seem to be enough to be worth staying for, and when Esteban returned to Cantanzos she would tell him that he and his mother must cope with the rest of what ailed his niece.

The day dragged slowly by; the siesta hours came and went, and afterwards Fran walked out into the rose garden. The air was still warm, and early-evening sunlight softened the grimness of the castle's grey stone walls. If Cantanzos wasn't always beautiful, it was undeniably impressive, and its setting was lovely beyond words. She'd leave it with an unsettling mixture of relief and regret, unable ever to quite forget the people she'd met there. Even glum Marilar, from whom she'd recently wrested an unexpected smile, would be worth remembering.

The lengthening shadows reminded her that it was time to go indoors; but just as she was about to move, Juanita came through the archway into the garden. She still walked tentatively, not convinced of being healed, but at least she moved about. It was something achieved, Fran thought; the past weeks hadn't been entirely wasted.

Instead of a greeting, Juanita held out a sheet of paper, and Fran looked down at a charcoal drawing of a pilgrim, complete with medieval gown, staff and cockleshell-trimmed hat; but the pilgrim was herself, realised in a dozen vivid lines.

'It's very clever – brilliant, in fact,' she said, forgetting that friendly relations might still have been suspended. 'Where did you learn to draw like that?'

'Only art lessons at school, but I've always been able

to do it.' Juanita's mouth trembled a little. 'My parents knew – they were going to arrange for me to train to be a dress-designer; Milan, where we lived, is exactly the right place for that.' She suddenly stopped talking and Fran saw the haunting desolation in her face. The accident had taken away her future as well as her parents and she could see nothing left worth living for. That was the burden of grief she struggled with, and to comfort it they'd offered the 'treat' they might have given to a fretful child.

'I'm sorry,' Fran said gently. 'We'll forget the trip to Santiago; but I hope you'll let me keep the drawing.'

'It was *meant* for you,' the answer came back with a snap, 'and of course we're going to see your pilgrim place; you might not get the chance again.'

She still sounded cross, but it was an olive branch of sorts, and Fran smiled at her, resisting the sudden, strong desire to give her a hug. There was no telling whether she'd accept affection offered instinctively or thrust it aside; she was twice as unpredictable as the average teenager, and ten times more vulnerable.

'Does your uncle know about the dress-design plan?' Fran risked asking.

'Of course not; he scarcely ever came to see us in Milan, and I always knew what he thought when he did come: I was a spoiled, insufferable brat who needed a proper Spanish upbringing!'

'Perhaps so, but why won't you believe that he *is* anxious about you now? I'm quite sure he'd be only too pleased to be told that you really know what you want to do. You're a bit too young yet to go back to Italy and make a start, but you needn't waste the next year or two. Study all the useful magazines you can get hold of; learn French if you don't know it already – it *is* the language of fashion – and, above all, keep drawing, *chiquita*. You've got a talent that you must use.'

Juanita stared at her for a moment, registering clearly for the first time the Inglesa's elusive beauty that she'd wanted to pretend wasn't there. Francesca Brown had been hard to sketch; she'd be even harder to paint, because everything about her was subtle and understated. A man might not notice her at all alongside Inez de Castro, but the man would be a fool, Juanita decided now.

'I know what *your* talent is,' she said suddenly. 'You're very good at putting people together again. Is it because you've had a peaceful life – no storms, no Spanish dramas?'

'A small English one,' Fran admitted after a moment. 'I came here in place of my sister – you already know that – but it was a double exchange. She went off to New York with the man I thought I was going to marry.'

Juanita stared at her in genuine astonishment. 'Why did you let it happen?' she wanted to know.

Fran couldn't help smiling at the question, but gave an answering shrug. 'It happened because Felicity came to stay with me and I could scarcely lock her in a cupboard each time my fiancé called! You'd have to meet her to understand – she's very beautiful, but that's only a small part of it; she can't help charming people. No hurt is ever intended; she'd like us *all* to be happy.'

'I'd hate her,' Juanita said fiercely. 'I doubt if you do, though.'

Fran looked back into the past for a moment, then shook her head. 'I haven't been able to hate her since I was ten years old and she took something I thought was mine. My father made me understand then that only deliberate selfishness or cruelty is hateful; Felicity is full of love herself.'

There was a long pause before Juanita spoke again. 'What will happen next? Will she marry the man you wanted?'

'I don't know; they aren't a very well-matched couple. Richard is a gentle academic, very clever and rather serious – not a bit like the men who've attracted Felicity in the past. Perhaps that's what appeals to her – the fact that he *is* so different.'

'What about you?' Juanita enquired next. 'You could have

Pascal for the asking, but even if you wanted a replacement for this man of yours, it would mean staying on here, and putting up with Inez into the bargain.' She suddenly put out her hand in a shy, unexpected gesture. 'You must have been feeling sad when you arrived here. I'm sorry I didn't behave better, Francesca.'

'You're making up for it very nicely now,' she was told with a warm smile. 'Now, I think it's time we went indoors, don't you? Any hour now, God willing, Señora Fernandez will be announcing dinner!'

Chuckling at the English thought, Juanita tucked a friendly arm in Fran's and they walked back to the castle together.

They set off for Santiago the following morning, with Pascal warning them not to expect fine weather.

'It's well known to be just about the wettest place in northern Spain,' he explained as they left Cantanzos behind, 'which explains why its people had the good sense to build themselves a city of arcaded streets; there was no other way of keeping more or less dry!'

When they arrived in the Plaza del Obradoiro, however, the vast square was lined on every side by beautiful, ancient buildings, that glowed like gold in the sunlight they'd been told not to expect. Filling one side was the cathedral itself, its entire facade a wild fantasy of stone balls and lanterns, and curlicues and crosses, with St James himself presiding serenely in the middle of it; but the miraculous result of so much elaboration was simply lightness and grace.

It was already two o'clock – the hour when almost every Spanish institution was shut for luncheon and the siesta that inevitably followed – and Pascal led them first to the lovely Renaissance building called the Hostal de los Reyes Catolicos – once a pilgrims' lodging house, and now one of the most splendid hotels in Europe.

Inside, Fran stared at its galleried grandeur, trying to equate such luxury with the simplicity it must once have had.

'Too ornate for your taste?' he suggested after a glance at her face.

'Too different from Cantanzos,' she found herself answering. 'I can't begin to compare it with anything else! Still, I shall relish staying here and pretending that it's what I'm used to!'

Later in the afternoon they joined the throng of visitors climbing the double staircase that led to the Porticó de la Gloria – the masterpiece of a medieval craftsman simply called 'Matteo' in the cathedral archives. They followed the ritual prescribed by long tradition and bent to touch heads and hands against the hollows in the stone where Matteo's genius could rub off on them. Then they went into the cavernous darkness of the great church.

The interior took Fran by surprise. Its forest of austere stone pillars might have belonged to Durham at home; only the soft ringing of the sanctus bell and the candlelight glowing on the silver figure of St James above the high altar reminded her that she was in Spain; but, anxious not to tire Juanita, they soon went out to sit at a pavement café and watch the crowds sauntering by, until it was time to return to the hotel for dinner.

The next morning, leaving Juanita in bed, Fran rose early to attend the first Mass of the day. She was almost at the door of the hotel when Pascal caught her up.

'I knew you'd want to go back,' he said, smiling at her. 'May I come with you, or would you rather go alone?'

The diffident question was typical, she thought, of a man who was not only kind but full of the unusual Spanish trait of humility as well. 'Come by all means,' she answered. 'Your priests might think you've more right there than a Protestant like me.'

He took her hand to guide her down the steps of the hotel, and then forgot to let go of it. The gesture reminded her so painfully of walks in the past with Richard Weston that she left her hand in Pascal's warm clasp, unable to trust her voice.

They said nothing while the mass lasted, but afterwards he took firm charge again.

'We deserve some good strong coffee – back at the Hostal, or shall we find it somewhere else?'

'At the hotel, please – Juanita might soon be expecting to share her breakfast with us.' Then, as they crossed the sunlit square, Fran smiled at her companion. 'Thank you for bringing us. I shall never forget Santiago.'

'Thank you, Pascal, would sound nicer,' he suggested gently. 'Isn't it time you got over the hurdle of using my name? I call you Francesca.'

She shook her head, disturbed by the sudden gravity in his face. Juanita's opinion didn't have to be taken seriously, of course. Pascal Vargas merely liked women and paid them the compliment of showing it – his attentions were no more serious than that. But for the moment she was the only woman available, and she was different from his Spanish friends; Fran feared that he *might* be inclined to imagine that he was falling in love with her.

'The hired help has to be careful,' she pointed out, trying to make a joke of it. 'Spain might have changed dramatically in the last thirty years, but I doubt if *everyone* has thrown the old formalities overboard.'

'You mean Luis Esteban, I expect,' Pascal said calmly, 'my distant cousin, good friend, and now my employer. But he's not my keeper, Francesca, and whatever formalities he clings to aren't my concern.'

She decided not to labour the point that the Count, being her employer as well, might easily take a different view. Instead, she allowed a waiter to assist her into a chair and left the conversation to lose itself in the small commotion of ordering breakfast. When it had been set out in front of them, Pascal asked a different question.

'I know you found the cathedral beautiful, but can you believe that it has any meaning now? Don't the tourists who come in their thousands every year see it as just a museum piece they're told they ought to marvel at?'

'I can't answer for them,' she replied slowly, 'but I refuse to accept that a place impregnated with such passionate and persistent pilgrimage doesn't somehow affect even the most casual of today's droppers-in. Too many people have been there before them, looking for something, contributing something . . .'

He was about to ask what she'd been looking for herself, but they were interrupted by Juanita coming to join them at the table.

'I suppose you've both been to Mass,' she said accusingly. 'I detect the smell of virtue!'

'Only on me,' Pascal pointed out. 'I suspect that Francesca makes a habit of going to church!' He smiled at her as he said it and, watching him, Juanita thought she'd been right: her Inglesa *had* snared a man who normally enjoyed falling in love and then falling out again. It was harder to guess what Francesca felt about him. In England there was still the lover who'd been fool enough to abandon her. Juanita doubted if Fran could forget him any more easily than she could hate her sister, and Pascal might have a long wait ahead of him. The only certain thing was that the Marquesa wouldn't approve of Fran as a sister-in-law at all. Juanita couldn't help thinking that life was becoming unexpectedly interesting.

It was late evening when they got back to Cantanzos. Juanita was nodding in the back of the car, but Fran, wide awake beside Pascal, registered with a strange sense of homecoming the moment when the light of a rising moon showed her the stone leopard above the entrance archway – not a friendly beast, but he was familiar now, and she could see how clearly he belonged on this wild, wind-blown promontory.

Through the next archway, leading to the courtyard, they found something they didn't expect: Pepé was there, unloading luggage from his master's car. Juanita woke up in time to notice what was going on and was the first to comment on it.

'*Dios mio* – it's Grandmama already, and we weren't here to welcome her; she'll be very put out.'

Fran gave no thought at all to a woman she didn't know. She was reminding herself instead that what she'd said to Juanita was true: Pascal Vargas wasn't the Count's slave; he could spend the weekend as he wished. Even so, she felt sure that Luis Esteban would disapprove of their outing, if only on the grounds that, in his own absence, the rest of them were expected to stay exactly where he'd left them.

The hall was empty when they went in, but the house-keeper appeared to announce that the Condesa had arrived safely with *el señor Condé*. She added the unenthusiastic afterthought that the Condesa's English companion was with her, as usual, then sailed majestically away, no doubt to harry the other servants. It was Señora Fernandez's fault, Fran thought, that they were all, with the exception of Constancia, so reluctant to smile. The castle would be a happier place if Luis Esteban could find himself a different housekeeper.

Juanita lightened the atmosphere with a cheerful wink. 'We're in trouble, it seems! See you in the salon, *amiga*, but don't be late – Grandmama likes to be the last to make an entrance!'

'Who *is* your grandmother's companion – still the lady whose brother bred Henry and George?' Fran asked as they parted company.

'The very same: Maud Entwhistle. La Fernandez hates her because she reckons the Inglesa, as she calls her, ought to rank as a servant with the others, instead of eating in the dining room. I like Maud myself – she's even a match for Inez. It's a pity our dear Marquesa isn't here as well!'

Feeling that it wasn't a pity at all but something to be deeply thankful for, Fran retreated into her own room. Given a choice, she'd have avoided dinner altogether and stayed where she was, but it seemed necessary to take her share of the displeasure the three of them had obviously earned by playing truant at Santiago.

Eight

In her anxiety not to be late, she went downstairs too early and found the salon still empty. Its long windows had been opened because the night was fine and warm, and she stepped out on to the terrace while she waited for the others to arrive. The air smelled sweet, but it was tinged unmistakably, she discovered, by the scent of cigarette smoke. Then she saw the tall figure of Luis Esteban leaning against the balustrade.

'*Buenas noches, señorita.*' He didn't making a habit of speaking to her in his own language and she supposed that the change now was deliberate. The coldly formal greeting was so clearly intended to indicate disapproval that she spoke with exaggerated cheerfulness in return; if it irritated him still more, she didn't mind. 'We weren't expecting you back from Seville so soon.'

'I realise that.'

She soldiered on, ready to explain but not apologise for their outing. 'I expect you're wondering why we went jaunting off to Santiago; it was to give Juanita a little change of scene.'

'Her life here is so unpleasant that she needed to escape?'

Fran took a deep breath, promising herself that she wouldn't shout. 'Her life altogether for the past few months has been full of grief and pain. That doesn't reflect on Cantanzos, but it did her good to be away from it for a few hours.' She steadied her voice and went on before he could answer. 'It was my idea, and Don Pascal was kind enough to arrange the trip. The pleasure it gave Juanita will be entirely spoiled if you now blame her for not being here when her grandmother arrived.'

'I'm not aware of wanting to blame anyone,' he said, speaking English now as she had done. 'But you might care to remember that she's my responsibility. Courtesy suggests that I should at least know where she is.'

Fran had to concede a point she couldn't argue with. 'I ought to have thought of that; I'm sorry,' she admitted. It was true, of course, that the housekeeper had known where they were going; but the stiff-necked grandee in front of her wouldn't expect to have to seek information from his servants.

With her apology made, at least the little confrontation seemed to be over. He buried the rest of his cigarette in the damp earth of the urn beside him and nodded towards the open window. 'Shall we go in? My mother will be down soon, and you have a compatriot to meet as well.' Then an afterthought seemed to occur to him. 'What was your opinion of Santiago, by the way – too ornate, too extravagant for a Protestant's austere taste?'

She halted to turn and look at him. 'If that's what you expect me to say, I'm going to disappoint you. It was beautiful beyond words.' Then, without waiting for him to reply, she walked back into the salon.

Pascal and Juanita were there now, talking to a newcomer who had to be Maud Entwhistle; from straight, bobbed hair to long, thin feet encased in sensible shoes, she was the archetypal Englishwoman of a certain age and kind. Others like her had been scattered round the world for generations, administering discipline, kindness, and a sound knowledge of the English tongue. Fran smiled at her, feeling suddenly thankful to have an ally; Spanish dramas wouldn't stand a chance in the face of Miss Entwhistle's cool stare. But they'd barely been introduced to each other when Pepé threw open the door with a flourish and the Condesa Esteban y Montilla walked into the room.

She was, Fran estimated quickly, in her mid-sixties now,

but she retained the slender figure and upright carriage of a young woman. Her face was haggardly beautiful – the result, perhaps, of a too-strict attention to what she ate – but it was exquisitely cared for and made up, and the black dress she wore made its own simple statement of perfection.

Fran watched her embrace Pascal and her granddaughter, and tried to piece together what she knew about Marganita Esteban: a gaiety-loving charmer who'd abandoned husband and children for a more congenial life, a mother whose daughter had been cruelly killed, and a grandmother of whom even defiant Juanita stood somewhat in awe. She was all these things, and probably more. Deep in thought, Fran suddenly found that it was her turn to be inspected. The Condesa's dark eyes were examining her face and clothes with unnerving thoroughness.

'Señorita Brown, of course . . . I've heard a great deal about you,' she said finally with a brilliant smile.

Fran held out her hand, trying to guess the source of the information – was Don Luis responsible for the odd inflection in his mother's voice, or had Inez de Castro provided *her* version of events at Cantanzos? Wondering how to reply, she was grateful when Juanita filled the little pause.

'I hope you were told that it was Francesca who got me walking again. She's my friend, and I don't want her to go back to England.'

If this was said for her uncle's benefit, he was pouring sherry and apparently taking no interest in the conversation. The Condesa answered instead, sounding sweetly reasonable despite the belligerent note in her granddaughter's voice.

'*Querida*, the señorita is probably anxious to return to her own life in London. I expect she sees her work here as finished now.'

Juanita rose to it like a fish to a baited hook. 'I told you we're *friends* – I want her to come and share my home in Italy with me.'

Torn, now, between astonishment at this new idea and

anxiety as to where the conversation would leap next, Fran struggled to find something soothing to say, but the Countess was ready first.

'Child, your home is here now; this is where you must learn to settle down.'

Fran waited with held breath for Juanita to make the obvious, annihilating reply: that she would follow her grandmother's example in not being able to put up with Cantanzos – but Luis saw the danger too and quickly stepped in.

'Italy, of course, later on, *chiquita*, if that is what you choose; but bear with Cantanzos a little longer, please!' And it was said so pleasantly that even Juanita was disarmed by it.

'Well yes, but I've got work to do that I want Francesca to help me with. She agrees I'm right to want to become a dress-designer; I'll *have* to go back to Milan for that eventually.'

The Countess said nothing, but her glance travelled over Juanita's plump cheeks and still-ungainly body; and then at least she was inspired to temper what she might have said with a little mercy. 'It's an overcrowded profession, my dear, even for hopefuls with real talent; I'm afraid you'll be bitterly disappointed if you set your heart on it.'

'Juanita *has* talent, Condesa,' Fran suddenly put in. 'She can draw brilliantly already. She needs training, of course, but she understands that.'

It was touch-and-go, Fran thought, whether Marganita Esteban threw mercy to the winds and pointed out that a dress-designer looking as her granddaughter did would make any couture clientele shake with laughter; but just at that moment Señora Fernandez appeared to announce that dinner was served, and Luis steered his mother firmly towards the dining room.

At table, she seemed ready to abandon the subject of her granddaughter's future. Pascal thoughtfully led the conversation towards Seville, and Fran knew that from then on they could all relax. The Condesa, encouraged by the two men, was a wonderful raconteuse; the rest of them need only smile and listen.

By morning it was difficult to believe that sunlight had blessed their visit to Santiago. The world was smothered in the Galician version of a Scotch mist – the *orbayu,* Constancia said it was, when Fran met her in the hall.

'*Mucho humedad, señorita,*' the little maid pointed out, wondering why anyone should chose to go walking in it. Still, they all knew that it did nothing but rain in England and probably poor Miss Brown was used to water.

Constancia had been right about the wetness. Fran's eyelashes and hair were pearled with moisture before she'd gone half a dozen yards, and the atmosphere was so densely water-laden that it almost needed swimming through. The pine trees were still for once, and even the sea sounds were muffled by the blanket of mist. The morning had a soft, silvery beauty of its own, but Fran thought she could have done with more light. She'd come out to do some hard thinking, but now she must concentrate instead on just keeping to the path.

One sound did penetrate soon enough: the heavy panting indicating that George and Henry, though not to be seen, were very close behind her. They appeared first as vague phantom shapes, then hurled themselves at her in a flurry of solid tan and white as they recognised a dear friend. Behind them, instead of Pascal as usual, materialised the tall, thin figure of Miss Entwhistle.

'Morning,' said Maud. 'Pascal told me I'd probably bump into you. He wanted to come as well, but I said the dogs might pay more attention to commands if I walked them alone.'

Fran disentangled herself from George's loving embrace and smiled broadly. 'A faint hope, I think. They don't seem to know what commands are!' She was aware of being inspected with interest but didn't mind the friendly scrutiny. Maud's own thought was that this smiling girl was not what she'd expected. According to Pascal, Francesca Brown was as kind as she was beautiful; Luis had conceded only that she was an excellent nurse who had done his niece much good. Inez de Castro had smiled and said that she was 'very English', a comment that Maud hadn't made the mistake of taking for a compliment.

Bending down to talk to Henry, always more bashful than George, Fran waited for the conversation to be resumed.

'Delightful creatures but quite ruined, of course,' Maud said, presumably of the dogs, as they finally walked on together; then, with no perceptible change of voice, she asked a question: 'Are you going to make a long stay here?'

Fearing that length of stay might be thought to go hand in hand with ruination, Fran answered firmly: 'My agreement with Don Luis was to get Juanita walking again. She can manage very well now, and carry on by herself with the exercises I've taught her.'

'But you haven't answered my question,' Maud pointed out. 'Because you don't know what to do?'

'She needs a friend,' Fran said simply. 'She misses her parents dreadfully and so far, at least, refuses to believe that Spain and Cantanzos can offer her anything to replace what she's lost. I think that even Don Luis knows the truth now: she's easily upset still, but she isn't the insoluble problem he thought her. She just hasn't been convinced yet that the accident didn't mean the end of happiness.'

'She was loved too much, if that doesn't sound a stupid thing to say,' Miss Entwhistle observed. 'Gino Fiocca had given up hope of a child by the time Mercedes became pregnant. It's no surprise that Juanita grew up hopelessly overindulged, but it makes it harder for her now, poor child. It's also an unfortunate thing for the future that she seems to dislike Inez de Castro so much.'

'Perhaps it's even more unfortunate that she also seems to dislike her uncle, since he's now her guardian,' Fran pointed out. She waited for Maud to rush to the defence of someone

77

she'd known, man and boy, for almost the whole of his life, but her reply when it came wasn't quite what Fran expected.

'Luis wants to do his best for Juanita, but he doesn't know how to set about it. Aside from the fact that she's a special problem in herself, he's got difficulties of his own.' The measured voice stopped for a moment, then went on again. 'Talking out of turn, perhaps, but you won't make errors of judgement if you understand about the past.'

'Pascal told me a little about life at Cantanzos, and the Condesa leaving home,' Fran confessed. 'It didn't occur to me then that Don Luis ought to find it easy to sympathise with Juanita . . . the circumstances were different, of course, but he had a loss of his own to cope with as a child.'

'*Nothing* that concerns the human heart comes easily to Luis. He was taught not to trust emotion, and it's become a habit to hide what he's feeling. He feels less vulnerable that way, less likely to get hurt.' Maud reflected for a moment and then went on: 'Inez is rather clever at understanding him. She'll make him a good wife if only she can put up with living in Galicia for most of the time. The Condesa wants her as a daughter-in-law because she knows that Inez will at least persuade him to leave it occasionally.'

'Then we must hope she'll also take the trouble to understand her niece by marriage,' Fran said quietly. 'Juanita is intelligent and strong-willed, but she can't do without help yet. She'll insist on going back to Italy eventually, because she regards it as her home; but for as long as she has to stay here she needs encouragement, not ridicule for being ungainly and still too overweight.'

Maud didn't comment on this. 'Perhaps you *should* stay,' she observed instead. 'I gather that you've got a good deal further with her than anybody else ever has.'

Fran shook her head. 'I've done what I came to do; now it's time for her to learn to trust her family.'

They walked in silence for a while, except for the panting of the dogs, who alternately rushed away into the mist and then came hurrying back to make sure they were still being followed.

'Do *you* ever think of going home . . . still miss England?' Fran suddenly asked.

'I can't go home while the Condesa needs me. I've kept her company for thirty years and we'll stay together now till one or other of us dies. But yes, I still find myself missing a strange mixture of things . . . like standing in the Mall and watching the Royal Standard fluttering in the breeze, or fat golden primroses under the hedge at home, and my father agonising over whether or not the first asparagus should be cut!' A capable hand swept the air in front of her, brushing memories away. 'I'm not complaining, and I've never regretted coming to Spain. I might have done, I suppose, if the Estebans had been less interesting.'

Fran thought there were other adjectives with which to describe them, but the one Miss Entwhistle had chosen hadn't been unfair – interesting they undeniably were. She found nothing more to say until the circuit of the castle wall had nearly been completed; then she found that, of its own accord, her mind had settled on a decision. It was time to go home, but first there was something to ask the woman at her side.

'Can you get the Condesa to help Juanita? She's the one who really ought to be involved. Apart from kinship, she's supremely elegant and worldly – just the person to restore Juanita's pride in herself. But it has to be done gently. Will she understand that?'

They were nearly back in the courtyard before Maud replied. 'You're asking a lot, because the Estebans aren't what *we*'d call gentle people; but don't judge the Condesa by normal standards. She loved her children and grew to hate her husband – with good reason, I think. The late Count was a selfish, unkind man who would have broken her spirit altogether if she'd stayed. I went with her when she left because she was in desperate need of me, but giving up Luis and Mercedes was terrible – for both of us.' Maud was silent for a moment; then her large hand patted Fran on the shoulder. 'I'll see what I can do for you about Juanita.' Then she whistled to the dogs and walked away.

It hadn't been much reassurance, but Fran's conviction was that, unlike most people, Maud Entwhistle probably accomplished more than she was inclined to promise.

Nine

J uanita was already up when Fran went in to see her, about to explain the decision she'd just come to outside on the castle wall; but Juanita looked up from the shirt she was fastening and spoke first.

'I came looking for you, but Constancia said you were out. We're going to Coruña with Pascal, provided we can be ready in time. He won't wait for us because he has to see someone there for Luis, but if we're punctual we can go with him.'

Fran agreed to swallow her coffee and roll, and postponed in her mind the moment when it would be possible to talk about her plans. They were downstairs by the time Pascal walked into the hall to say that his car was at the door, and suddenly all three of them were infected with the light-heartedness of children unexpectedly let out of school. Esteban came out into the courtyard just as they were leaving and Fran suddenly felt less like smiling. In the sunlight beginning to seep through the mist his face looked not only drawn but regretful, and she knew an absurd longing to say, as children did, 'We're going out to play; *you* come too.' Then Juanita remembered that she must fetch her St Christopher to charm evil away from the journey, and it seemed necessary to find *something* to say to the man who was waiting to watch them drive away.

'It's a miracle she can bear to get into a car, with or without St Christopher, after what happened.'

It was Pascal who answered. 'No miracle, Francesca; When she first came out of hospital, Luis spent hours driving her about until she'd lost the fear of being on the road again.'

It was a disconcerting sidelight on a man she'd accused more than once of doing nothing to help his niece, and she was relieved when he abruptly reminded Pascal not to be late for his appointment and strode away.

They parted company in the busy port, with Juanita prophesying immediately afterwards that he would be back with them before the cat could lick its ear! She had, Fran now knew, an assortment of odd English phrases in her vocabulary, and nothing gave her more pleasure than to bring them out.

'The poor man's in love with you,' she went on. 'I don't know why, because, apart from smiling at him nicely, you don't give him any other encouragement.'

'I was warned not to,' Fran said lightly. 'He's a charming but impressionable man whose job is to make a success of working with your uncle; he's not supposed to imagine that I'm the one woman he can't do without.'

'Inez!' Juanita unerringly guessed the origin of the warning. 'What a cow that woman is. Luis might be all right without her tied round his neck.'

'It's obviously not a view he shares,' Fran pointed out. 'In any case, try make a faint attempt at being fair. You may not like her, but she is beautiful, intelligent and a credit to him in the world at large. What more can a man ask?'

Juanita looked unimpressed. 'She's still a cow,' she repeated, but there the argument had to rest because the Marquesa's brother was coming towards them.

Half a dozen times during the day Fran hovered on the verge of confessing to both of them that she was planning to go back to England, but drew back from spoiling an outing that was giving Juanita so much pleasure. Pascal treated *her* with a perfect blend of affection and teasing, and to Fran herself he was caressingly attentive and kind. Allowing for a little Latin exaggeration, she had to accept that Juanita was probably right about him. When he helped her on with a jacket because the wind was cool, she felt his hands linger on her shoulders simply for the pleasure of touching her. The truth was that he scarcely needed the encouragement she was being so careful not to give him.

They ate a long, leisurely luncheon at a restaurant overlooking the bay, at the very point on the coast of Spain, said Pascal, from which the Armada had sailed for England four hundred years before; but he smiled when Fran promised not to harp on the subject. Flurries of rain kept sweeping a silver curtain across the sea that the sun dissolved again a few minutes later, reminding her of an April day at home. With the thought came another one: in outward appearance Pascal Vargas was quite unlike a slight, fair-haired Englishman, quiet of speech and slow of smile; but the reason she felt so comfortable with him was probably that he reminded her of Richard Weston. The two men shared the same sweetness of temper, and the conviction that life should be lived with kindness given and received. Richard's only unkindness, if that was what it could be called, had been to fall out of love with her when he caught sight of Felicity. Fran didn't expect him to recover from that change of heart. It surely behoved her, therefore, to value what Pascal seemed anxious to offer.

When Juanita left them to talk to a group of young people chattering in Italian together at a neighbouring table, Fran asked a question about Pascal himself.

'Shall you get used to working for Don Luis? Can you enjoy becoming a businessman, or would you rather be poor, proud, and happy in the sunlit south?'

Pascal smiled at the question but chose to answer with unusual seriousness. 'It's not my métier, you're thinking? Well, in a way that's true. I don't feel about Cantanzos as Luis does, and I'm a pleasure-loving Andalucían who enjoys many things more than honest toil! But the fact remains that I've discovered in myself a streak of ambition I didn't know was there. I don't want to make a fortune, but I *am* determined to become useful to Luis and share some of the responsibilities for other people that he accepts so uncomplainingly.'

Fran smiled at him more warmly than she meant to. 'I think you'll be very good for him. He's not a born communicator with the rest of the human race, but you *are*; that's more important than anything you can't yet do.'

Pascal's hand reached out to touch hers lying on the table. 'It was a good day for us when Luis found you in London. Stay, please, Francesca – we need you. George and Henry know that already; I tell them so every day!'

She thought she was about to hear what else he confessed to the dogs, but Juanita's conversation suddenly ended and she came back to sit down with them again. An announcement about going home seemed to be getting ever more necessary and ever more difficult at the same time.

Fran insisted on sitting in the back of the car on the journey home, making the excuse that lunchtime wine made her sleepy, but she was awake enough to overhear Pascal encouraging Juanita to make plans for the rest of the summer that all, it seemed, required the presence of Francesca Brown, if they were to be properly enjoyable.

They got back to Cantanzos late in the afternoon and knew as they drove under the last archway that changes had again occurred in their absence. An unfamiliar car was now parked in the courtyard, and a pile of luggage was on the flagstones, waiting to be carried inside.

'Oh God,' said Juanita, forgetting the man beside her. 'Inez is back!' Then she smiled in unaccustomed apology. 'I'm sorry, Pascal – that sounded rude; but it's no good pretending that I like your sister.'

He answered only to say that he didn't recognise the car, so it couldn't be Inez who'd arrived; but in the hall they found the Condesa talking to her and the friends who'd driven up with her from Seville.

'You're back earlier than we expected,' Pascal said, greeting her first.

'The impossible happened,' she explained with her brilliant

smile. 'We found the Feria *dull* – can you imagine it? Even gloomy Galicia seemed preferable, and then we got here to find it not so gloomy at all!' She managed to ignore Fran without seeming to, merely reminding Juanita that she knew the other guests. Pascal insisted on making an introduction, but Fran was equally firm in excusing herself afterwards. She climbed the stairs, thinking that her departure from the castle was now more necessary than ever; tomorrow, come what might, she must speak to Juanita and then to Luis Esteban.

She was writing a letter to her friend Anita in London when there came a knock on the door. Inez de Castro stood there, faintly smiling.

'You disappeared very quickly, señorita, no doubt tired of the way we Spaniards talk!'

Fran made a sound that neither agreed nor disagreed and waited for what might come next.

'Miss Entwhistle has insisted that she'd enjoy a quiet meal this evening,' Inez explained. 'It occurred to me that you'd much rather join *her* than us. I hope I'm right, señorita; she would be so happy to have your company.'

Fran smiled very sweetly. 'I shall look forward to it; we might even indulge in a little English silence! Thank you for the kind thought.'

She closed the door, knowing the truth: that she and Maud had been relegated to the place in which the Marquesa thought they belonged. Her only anxiety was Juanita's reaction to their absence from the dining room; but no doubt Inez would have her explanation ready: the two Inglesas had wanted a quiet dinner by themselves.

Not sure where to go downstairs, she decided to call first on Miss Entwhistle, who was allowed the grander surroundings of the floor below in order to be included in the Condesa's suite of rooms. It was an ill-timed visit, though, because she met Luis Esteban walking along the corridor from the tower.

He stopped to inspect the cotton dress and cardigan

she was still wearing, then frowned – his most frequent expression when looking at her, she realised.

'The dress is charming,' he said, 'but we have guests of my mother's this evening and dinner will be a little more formal than usual. Obviously no one has warned you of that.'

Fran offered him her sunniest smile. 'My evening is going to be very *in*formal with Miss Entwhistle.' It was clear now that the rearrangement was the Marquesa's idea, not his, and she felt obscurely comforted by the fact. The expression on his face wasn't promising, but she hoped he'd accept without argument the situation Inez had created for them.

'You share our meal in the dining room as usual; go and change, please.'

The 'please' was meaningless; it was an instruction she was being given. Her anger rose to meet it, and they stood glaring at one another, watched by a knight in full armour, who stood unconcernedly in the corner of the wide corridor. It was another moment of truth, Fran realised; life at Cantanzos seemed full of them.

'May we get something clear?' she suggested, trying not to shout. 'I am *not* going to change my clothes; Maud and I are going to eat together. That is what has been arranged.'

She didn't feel like smiling, but in some small corner of her brain lurked the knowledge that, since this confrontation was absurd, it would be better for both of them to be amused by it. She managed to produce a smile as she made her last effort with him. '*We* shall enjoy ourselves discussing the oddities of the Spanish, and you can feel free to do the same about us!'

It seemed a long time before he finally nodded and walked away. She watched him go, with no pleasure in having won her small battle; she felt exhausted instead, and sadly sure that he wouldn't be humanised by his marriage to Inez.

The following morning Juanita was knocking on her door long before the time at which they normally breakfasted together. Fran was up, but staring out of the window instead of getting ready to go out for her usual early-morning walk. The day had dawned fine again, but with a more delicate, uncertain beauty than it would have done further south. She understood now how lovely Galicia was, how loth anyone born there would ever be to leave it. Inez de Castro might persuade the Leopard to go travelling occasionally, but she might as well ask the tide to stop coming in as ask him not to return to Cantanzos.

Juanita's voice spoke from the doorway behind her: 'Good, *amiga*, you're up; I thought you'd still be asleep after talking till all hours with Maud.'

Fran turned to smile at her. 'We parted company at the sober hour of eleven thirty! How was *your* dinner party?'

'So boring I can't describe it.' Juanita frowned over that and then tried again. 'Well no, not boring, in fact; Granny didn't say much – I think she felt tired – and my dear uncle was in a thoroughly bad mood. For a change, it was Inez he was angry with, not me!' Juanita suddenly grinned at the thought. 'He was very polite, of course; with her he always is. But I know when he's smiling from the heart and when he's not. I suppose she *was* behind you and Maud not being there? It was a stupid mistake for her to make.'

Fran refused to be drawn into a discussion on the subject, but knew the moment was upon her that she must take. 'I'm glad you're here, *chiquita* – I need to talk to you. It's about going back to London.' She saw the storm gather in Juanita's face, and held up her hand in a little gesture of authority. 'Listen to me first, please. I haven't a real job here any longer. My training is in helping people who've been physically damaged; you no longer are. You were kind enough to suggest my going with you to Italy, but I suspect it was an idea you threw out to cause a little stir!'

'It's a brilliant idea; I want it to happen,' Juanita shouted.

'It *can't* happen until you're a good deal older than you are now,' Fran pointed out quietly. 'When the time comes, your uncle won't stand in your way; but for the moment you must be patient and stay here.'

'All right . . . all right, but please stay *with* me.' Tears gathered in Juanita's eyes and overflowed. 'You said you'd help me . . . be my friend . . . you promised, Fran.'

It was even harder than she'd expected and she was close to tears herself. 'I *am* your friend, my dear, and always will be; but it's time for you to trust your own family. Don Luis will see to it that you needn't waste the months you have to spend here; he'll find people to help you now in ways that I'm not fitted to.'

Juanita stared at her across the room with a kind of desolation in her face. 'I shan't be able to do anything right with Inez here. You're only going because of her. Pascal gives himself away every time he looks at you, and she isn't stupid – she'll have noticed that.'

'He'll forget me soon enough, I'm quite sure,' Fran insisted. 'What *you* must do is put a little faith in your uncle. Cantanzos ought, heaven knows, to be able to hold you and the Marquesa, but you might get on better with her if you didn't always have your fists up, ready for a fight.' She bent forward to kiss Juanita's wet cheek. 'You'll have a friend in Maud Entwhistle if you need one, but the person you must really get on terms with is your grandmother. She's forgotten more about elegance and fashion than I will ever know and, given half a chance, she'll share your dream with you.'

There was a little silence in the room; then Juanita smeared away her tears and spoke in a grave and adult voice Fran hadn't heard before. 'You may be right about my grandmother and, if I have to, I'll try to put up with Inez until I can get away. But you're wrong about Pascal – it comes of being English, maybe: you don't seem able to recognise when a man's in love with you. I dare say even Maud missed chances too, for exactly the same reason.'

Torn between a desire to laugh or weep, Fran agreed that not being Spanish had its disadvantages; then she pulled herself together and tried to smile. 'You ought to be able to guess what's coming next – too much emotion before breakfast isn't good for us at all. What we need now is a stroll in the fresh air!'

Juanita's face broke into a reluctant grin. 'With heaven falling about our ears I can still hear you and Maud recommending a bracing walk; no wonder we can't understand the English!

Ten

The walk had been taken and breakfast was over when Constancia brought in a letter for Fran delivered in the morning's mail. The scrawl on the envelope belonged to the last person she expected to find writing to her from London. Watching her expression change as she skimmed through the letter inside, Juanita ventured a question.

'Bad news, *amiga*? Has something happened?'

'I don't exactly know what it is,' Fran answered with a puzzled frown, then spread the sheet of paper out to read again. The style of its message was as unmistakable as Felicity's handwriting.

Dearest Fran,

We're back in London, but *you* aren't here, just when I badly wanted to talk to you. The New York thing was marvellous in a way, but not *entirely* satisfactory. Nothing ever is, is it, but I had such hopes this time! I loved Manhattan, but Richard was longing all the time to get back to London. Now he's all upset because you've gone rushing off to Spain in place of me. Darling, I'm sure you didn't *have* to – it was only a *job* I turned down. Anita showed us your letter, and Cantanzos sounds so like Dracula's castle that Richard now has the mad idea you need rescuing! He's probably looking for an excuse to get back to his beloved España, but I expect I'll talk him out of it.

One way and another we seem to be in a bit of a
muddle, don't we, but we love you very much!
Adios!
F

Fran laid the letter down again and tried to smile at
Juanita's anxious expression. 'Nothing serious; just a muddle, as my dear sister says. She and Richard are back in
London, rather put out not to find *me* there. They've also
seen the letter I wrote to a friend, giving my first impressions
of Cantanzos!'

'Shall I guess what they were? Winds howling round a
grim, grey castle's walls and a bunch of mad people locked
up inside!'

'It was written before I got to know you better,' Fran
pointed out with a smile, 'but that *was* the gist of it, I'm
afraid.' Then her face grew sober again. 'There seems to
be a chance that Richard will come looking for me; it's not
like him at all to be so impulsive, but Felicity seems to have
had an extraordinary effect on him all round.'

'He's got a guilty conscience about you, and so he should
have,' Juanita pointed out. 'Still, at least it means that you can't
go home until he gets here.' She considered the matter for a
moment and then smiled brilliantly. 'I know what it is: he's
had enough of your sister and wants *you* back again; but he's
unreliable, Fran – I think you should choose Pascal instead.'

'Well, my own thought is that you should stop romancing
and get on with some useful work.' She saw the amusement
in Juanita's face and spoke more sharply. 'Listen to me,
please. Richard will stay my dear friend – I've loved him
too long for that to change – but we can't return to where
we were; Felicity isn't forgotten as easily as that. Pascal,
whatever he thinks now, will recover the moment I go
back to London, and you might remember that I'm nearly
another Maud Entwhistle, *not* one of today's free-living
young women who are supposed to be feverishly on the
prowl for sex and adventure!'

Juanita shook her head, suddenly seeming older than her years. 'I don't know about the Englishman, of course, but you're wrong about Pascal Vargas, Fran, and *all* wrong about yourself. Compared with Maud, you're like Mount Etna waiting to erupt!'

Fran smiled wryly. 'You mean it as a compliment, no doubt, but let me tell you that we pride ourselves in England on our sangfroid! And right now, I intend to be very *froid* indeed and seek an interview with your uncle.'

She was nearly at the door when Juanita's wistful voice halted her. '*Must* you go home, Fran? I don't know if I can manage without you.'

'You'll manage very well. If I didn't believe that, I wouldn't leave. Now it's exercise time, *chiquita*. Start, please; I'll see you later.' But she walked very slowly down the stairs, considering what Juanita had said.

The assessment of herself had been shrewder than was comfortable. She wouldn't admit to the volcano – that was mere Spanish extravagance – but there'd been changes all the same that she was ready to blame on Cantanzos; something in the air, something in the people she'd met there, had had a strange effect on her. Richard had once explained to her Spain's frequent habit of affecting its visitors; it was a country where emotions weren't only intensified but laid bare. That accounted for her need to escape; she couldn't be comfortable in an atmosphere that was both supercharged and abrasive, all at the same time.

Downstairs in the hall, Marilar was polishing the floor, as usual. She answered Fran's question by pointing to a corridor – *el Señor Conde*'s office was along there; but he was never disturbed until lunchtime.

'A business matter,' Fran said gently, 'but thank you for the warning!'

She was aware of being watched as she walked away, but had no idea that Marilar was remembering her first arrival at the castle. They'd despised her quiet voice and manner, and shared Señora Fernandez's opinion that a poor foreign creature

like that would stand no chance against the termagant upstairs; but the Inglesa had stayed, and now the señorita
was walking again like anybody else. She was even known to
smile and laugh at the servants, something unheard of before.

A door opened as Fran reached the end of the corridor
and the middle-aged woman who came each morning to
work for the count emerged with a pile of folders in her
hands. Don Luis was there, she said pleasantly, but must
leave soon to keep an appointment.

'Five minutes?' Fran suggested, and the woman smiled
and held the door open.

The Leopard's den was a pleasant room, book-lined
except for the estate maps filling one wall. The windows,
to Fran's surprise, overlooked the rose garden; she'd have
expected him to choose a sterner view. The Count stood up,
polite but unwelcoming, and making an effort not to glance
at his watch, she thought.

'You're about to go out, I know, but this won't take long,'
she said hurriedly. 'The time has come for me to go home –
the sooner, the better, I think.'

There was a little silence before he spoke. 'It's a very
sudden decision. Does Juanita know?'

'Of course – I had to speak to her first. But what you asked
me to do has been achieved; now I think she must learn to
trust and rely on her family. That is the right thing . . . the
best thing for her.'

The man in front of her seemed intent on fidgeting,
untypically, with some papers on his desk, and didn't look
at her. 'She was hoping you would stay – for ever, as far
as I can make out, but at least until she's old enough to be
independent of me.'

'I know, but the Milan idea was a spur-of-the-moment
thing, not serious – not workable either, I think you probably
agree.' Fran hesitated for a moment, seeing that she must
choose her words carefully. 'What she needs most is the
company of people her own age, as well as some definite
training for the career she's after. A college of design in

Seville, if there is such a thing, would be ideal – her grandmother and Miss Entwhistle would be there to keep an eye on her.'

'And, as you're tactfully not pointing out, she refuses to like Cantanzos or – perhaps with the exception of Pascal Vargas – the people who are here.'

She could sense some emotion beneath the words, but not identify it; was he angry again? Or just tired to death of the problem his niece represented? 'We've had this discussion before,' was all she could find to say when it seemed impossible to point out what in any case he already knew: that it was Inez de Castro his niece most firmly refused to like. 'I think that, once I leave, Juanita will make friends with her grandmother; but in any case I should like to go home, please.' There was a tell-tale tremor in her voice, born of too much strain. She heard it herself and prayed *he* hadn't noticed. Sangfroid seemed to be lacking just when she needed it most.

He took a long time to answer, but at last he did and she was aware of something she *could* identify: a kind of despairing sadness. 'I'm afraid the truth is that you don't like Cantanzos either. But Juanita will be seventeen next week; can you at least bear to stay for her birthday?'

She tried to smile, to lessen the weight of emotion that now seemed to fill the space between them. 'Of course, but I'll go after her birthday as soon as it can be arranged.'

The next moment she'd walked out of the room; he was free to leave it himself, to keep his appointment, but he stayed there, seeing in his mind's eye the pale, strained face of the girl he'd brought so unthinkingly into their lives. He knew the reason for the anger he'd had to struggle to control a few moments ago; against any probability he could have foreseen, she'd become part of Cantanzos without the slightest effort, it seemed. He didn't mind that, but Cantanzos had made no impression on her in return. She had no right to make herself so necessary and then calmly leave again, unaffected by *them* in any way. He'd watched her sometimes when she was unaware – walking along the castle wall, laughing at the dogs' antics, the wind blowing her soft, brown hair. She'd looked as if she belonged there, so it was just a shock – that was all – to be sharply reminded that her own life was elsewhere.

The door opened behind him, and he heard Pascal's voice. 'Luis . . . still here? I thought you were going to Pontevedra?'

'I'm leaving now, a little later than I should have done. You might ring and say I'm on my way.' He smiled briefly at the man who'd come to stand beside him. 'Will you also tell Inez that I expect to see both our English guests in the dining room tonight? They've had time enough to decide what strange people we are.' Then he walked out of the room, leaving Pascal watching him and wondering what had happened to disturb his usually impassive friend.

With Juanita sitting outside in the warm May sunlight, dutifully studying a French grammar found in her uncle's library, Fran went in search of a telephone. The housekeeper indicated one she could use, and left her making a call to London. No one answered – Felicity wasn't in the flat – but it came as no surprise. The agency might already have lined up another job for her; if not, she wasn't a girl who took kindly to staying at home in the middle of the day.

Fran crossed the hall again just as Maud Entwhistle came down the staircase.

'You look worried,' said Maud. 'Anything wrong?'

'Not really; I was just hoping to speak to my sister in London, but she isn't in. I'll try again later.' She looked round the deserted hall, and then at Maud. 'Where *is* everyone?'

'Gone out to lunch with friends at Baiona. The Condesa shouldn't have done; she'd have been better resting at home.'

'Is she not well? Juanita mentioned that she seemed tired at dinner last night.'

95

Maud gave a little shrug. 'Too much racketing around at the Feria, I expect; she won't admit that she hasn't the stamina it requires any more. If I grumble, she smiles at me and just says she'd rather die dancing than in her bed!'

Fran smiled at her companion. 'You're deeply fond of her, I think, even if she isn't very easy to look after.'

'What about you?' Maud suddenly asked. 'Come to any decision yet?'

'I thought I had, but it seems that I must stay for Juanita's birthday next week. It's settled that I leave after that, but I'd have preferred to go sooner. Now there'll be time for her to discover how shaky is my hold on French irregular verbs!'

Maud's long face broke into a smile; she doubted if she'd been given the true reason for Fran's anxiety to leave Cantanzos but didn't press the subject. 'I gather that we're allowed back in the dining room this evening. What a funny, mixed-up lot the dear things are!'

'It's how they probably think of us,' Fran pointed out. 'We're well known for being awkward and out of step. Naturally everyone else can't be wrong, so the fault must lie with us, and quite often it does, of course!' She waved a hand at Maud before going back outside. 'See you at lunch, no doubt.'

After the meal, shared happily with Juanita and Pascal as well, she set out alone with the dogs and spent the afternoon trying to persuade George and Henry that they needn't come back and kiss her each time they'd been in the sea. Back at the castle, she handed them over to Pepé to be dried and brushed, and went indoors to make another attempt at ringing Felicity. It was the time of day when she was likely to be getting ready for an evening out, but there was still no reply. It would have to be an early-morning call, she decided, before a late riser was even out of bed. For no good reason that she could think of, the more elusive Felicity remained, the more necessary it became to talk to her. For the moment, though, there was the immediate ordeal ahead of dinner downstairs.

She was careful this evening to time her arrival for a moment when everyone but the Condesa was already in the salon. Marganita Esteban followed her in, pausing in the doorway as usual to 'compose' the entrance they expected; but, watching her, Fran thought Maud had been right: it required an effort now for her to take the lead, to sparkle and enchant, and beneath the flawless make-up the Condesa looked drawn.

With several more women than men at the dinner table, Inez laughingly apologised – in the hope, Fran supposed, of making two of them feel *de trop*. She grinned inwardly at Maud's wink across the table, but the Marquesa soon saw to it that the conversation stayed centred on Seville; there was little for the Inglesas to do but smile occasionally and try not to nod off during the long, elaborate meal.

Back in the salon afterwards, Fran promised herself a swift retreat upstairs once coffee had been served, but the plan was thwarted by the Condesa beckoning to her across the room.

'Forgive us for talking about people you don't know, señorita,' she said with a charming smile, 'but I expect you realise by now what gossips we are!' She glanced for a moment at Juanita, involved in a heated discussion with Pascal and one of the other guests. 'I congratulate you, by the way. That poor child is never going to be the equal of her beautiful mother – there's too much of Gino Fiocca in her for that! – but she isn't the wreck of a girl Luis brought me in Seville.'

It was meant, Fran supposed, to sound congratulatory, but all she heard was a careless judgement that made her hackles rise. The Condesa was able to deal in standards of perfection that ordinary women couldn't aspire to. Worse than that, Juanita as a person didn't count; she was merely regarded as an unsatisfactory replacement for someone no longer there.

'Any trained physiotherapist could have got her walking again,' Fran said briefly. 'It's more difficult to restore her confidence in life and her faith in herself; but it's beginning to happen – perhaps thanks to qualities she's inherited from her father!'

On the receiving end of this little speech, the Condesa looked at her with such astonishment that Fran was obliged to apologise. 'I'm sorry if that sounded rude, but her family *must* help now, instead of blaming her for not being someone else.'

It was unfair of the Condesa, she thought, to choose that moment to smile with a warmth that seemed genuine. 'Luis *said* I wouldn't quite know what to make of you; I think he was right!'

Fran knew even less what to say in return; an airy, self-deprecating wave of the hand might do if she could manage it, but she was too anxious for Juanita and too intent on making Marganita Esteban realise that it was her own granddaughter she must understand, not some visiting hired hand.

'Forgive me for labouring the point, but I shall be going back to London soon. She's truly talented, and she knows what she wants to do. All she needs is encouragement from someone who believes in her, and sympathises with her ambition.'

Fran looked at the face of the woman beside her, startled by what looked for a moment like despair. Then, as if aware of being watched, the Countess forced herself to smile and pat Fran's hand; but what she might have said was interrupted by Pascal coming back into the room, carrying a guitar. Marganita leaned back against the cushions behind her with a little sigh of relief and the murmured comment that they were about to hear something worth listening to.

A few moments later there was no doubt that she was right. Suddenly rapt and serious, Pascal was no longer the easy-going, cheerful companion Fran was familiar with. He seemed now a different man, possessed by the music that poured from the instrument in his hands. She recognised at once what she listened to: Albéniz's wonderful evocation of Cordoba. Then came the opening bars of something even more hauntingly beautiful: 'La Maja y el Ruiseñor'; but even as she remembered that Granados had written it as a song, Inez de Castro strolled over to stand beside her brother. There was a tiny moment of anticipation and then the golden stream of her voice poured over them. They performed well together, had obviously done it often before, Fran tried calmly to decide; but she was adrift now in a sea of emotion where rational thought stood no chance at all – entranced, confused and achingly aware of every current of emotion in the room. What else had she still to discover about these complicated people? And how could she bear Luis Esteban's expression as he stared at the woman who offered him her song? No concealment now; all that he felt, all that he was being made to feel by this compellingly beautiful and intense woman, was written on his face. Shaken by the discovery, Fran looked instead at her own trembling hands.

The song ended and, in the flurry of applause, she got up and quietly left the room. She must escape at once or break down and weep in front of these alien people, who would certainly despise tears. Emotion seemed to be in the very air they breathed; nothing here was veiled in the softer, mistier atmosphere she was used to. She went blindly up the staircase, ignoring for once the lonely knight in armour to whom she usually said goodnight. There was only one piece of comfort to cling to: she was going home as soon as Juanita's birthday was over.

Eleven

At seven o'clock the next morning, after a rather sleepless night, Fran was back in the little lobby off the hall again. At last, in answer to her ring, she heard the little click that said the call had been accepted at the other end.

'Felly, it's me, Fran. I've been trying to reach you since your letter arrived. I just want to be sure you're all right, and to tell you and Richard not to worry about me. I'll be home next week, in any case.'

'Then I wish we'd known sooner,' said Felicity, sounding aggrieved and miserable. 'Richard's already left for Spain. I *told* him how silly it was – I mean it *is* the twenty-first century we live in, and Cantanzos isn't exactly the centre of the white slave traffic. But he got very cross and so did I, and we parted bad friends. Now, of course, I'm thoroughly miserable here without him and deeply fed up.'

It was a sequence of events lived through before, Fran thought tiredly, but this time her sister couldn't see the usual ray of hope in what the future might bring next. For once Felicity was staring at the possibility of a mistake she might always regret.

'What did your letter mean – about New York not quite working out?' Fran asked. 'Leaving the present row aside, are you and Richard still together or not?'

'Of *course* we are – at least, I hope we are. I'm actually rather proud of him for not doing exactly what I want . . . but I need the chance to tell him so. This mad Don Quixote sort of behaviour isn't like him at all, sweet though he always is! I just want him to come back.'

A Rare Beauty

Sitting in her little cubby-hole, Fran took a firmer grip on the receiver and promised herself she wouldn't shout. She could prick even her sister's scatterbrained self-absorption by pointing out that she knew what Richard Weston was like because she'd been going to marry him herself. She could insist that if he came to Cantanzos she'd do her damnedest to get him back again; she could even destroy Felicity entirely by bursting into tears of bitter reproach. But none of those things was possible; instead, as so often before, she heard herself sound like a kind and elderly maiden aunt.

'Felly dear, there's no need to get upset. If Richard comes here at all, it will only be to make sure I'm all right. He'll then see the feudal splendour in which I live and drive away again feeling deeply envious! If he takes too long to arrive, dawdling to inspect every Romanesque church and chapel on the way, I shall already have left for London before he gets here.'

'He *does* do that – dawdle, I mean,' Felicity agreed, sounding a little more cheerful. 'It's funny how he loves *old* things so much; no wonder he wasn't very happy in New York! Darling Fran, I feel better for talking to you – I always do. Give Richard my very fondest love, if you see him, and *both* of you come home soon, please; I'm getting lonely.'

Fran agreed that they would, and replaced the receiver thoughtfully. From wanting very much to miss seeing her one-time lover, she'd now come round to hoping that he *would* arrive before she left; there were things to talk about. The situation as it stood might make an interesting storyline for a novel, but in real life it was becoming a mixture of the very painful and the very absurd.

Breakfast upstairs with Juanita was a more silent meal than usual, once they'd agreed that the previous evening had been different and *muy interesante*. Beyond that, Juanita didn't seem ready to elaborate, and Fran was equally untalkative. Her conversation with Felicity had merely pushed aside for the moment the pictures from the night before she was still seeing in her mind's eye. With a vividness there was no accounting for, memory replayed for her the images that had disturbed her sleep: Pascal's absorbed face as he touched the strings of his guitar; Inez, insolently but rightly confident of her power to mesmerise the rest of them; and, among her bewitched audience, the Leopard himself, captured at last. There wasn't any doubt about it, Fran knew – his longing and need had been too plainly visible; but so splendid a creature ought to have been left free. That, she decided, was undoubtedly what explained the sadness she was struggling to hide.

'You didn't tell me you were about to have a birthday,' she said suddenly. 'I'm to stay for it, if that's all right with you.'

Juanita's preoccupied face broke into a smile that held an echo of the Condesa's. 'Of course you've got to stay – it's all arranged, silly! A sort of family party, Luis says.' While Fran registered the fact that her uncle had suddenly become 'Luis', not 'Esteban', Juanita grew serious again. 'He was so nice about it that for once we weren't glaring at one another . . . more like friends. If it didn't mean putting up with sodding Inez, I wouldn't mind quite so much now having to stay here without you.'

Fran refused to be enticed into another argument about the Marquesa. '*Where* did you learn the expressions you use?' she asked instead.

Juanita smiled sadly this time. 'Papa's manservant got them from the English soldiers he knew as a child during the war! Giorgio and his wife Graziella looked after us, and I loved them both. They're getting old now, but Papa would want me to take care of them, and I shall.'

Fran looked at her with real affection. 'Good for you! I think your parents would be proud of you.'

'They might now; they wouldn't have been before you came to Cantanzos. *Couldn't* you bear to stay and marry Pascal?'

102

'I'm afraid not, aside from the trivial unimportant fact that he hasn't so far asked me to!' Fran stood up abruptly and headed towards the door. 'Now I have a rendezvous with two more of my admirers! Why don't you come too?'

Juanita shook her head, and Fran went outside alone, expecting to see Pepé there with the dogs; but it was Pascal waiting with them, not the servant, and although he gave the courteous little bow with which he always greeted women, the smile she was accustomed to didn't appear.

'Good morning, Francesca. You went away very suddenly last night; didn't you like the music? I was playing it for you.'

He sounded so grave – hurt almost – that she realised the conversation was to be a serious one; it wasn't by chance that he happened to be there, and now another moment of truth was upon her – the one she'd most wanted to avoid.

'Shall we walk as well as talk?' she suggested gently. 'It's what George and Henry think we're here for. The music was beautiful, as you must know. Doña Inez would grace any concert platform, and Don Pascal Vargas the musician I scarcely recognised at all!'

She had tried to speak lightly, but his sad expression didn't change. 'You mean you only recognise him when he's playing his usual role: the happy-go-lucky, well-meaning but rather frivolous fool who's trying to make himself useful here.'

Fran gave a little inward sigh: Spanish gloom was quite as thoroughgoing as Spanish gaiety, and Pascal was hell-bent this morning on being melancholy.

'You're usually *happy*,' she pointed out firmly, 'which isn't the same thing at all; and speaking for myself, I'm deeply grateful that you are. Let's face it: the Galician nature isn't exactly joyful! Maybe Andalucíans could do with a dash of northern sternness, but they're like yeast in bread up here! I suppose you all learn to sing and dance and play the guitar before you leave the nursery.'

She'd done her best to distract him from his 'great matter', but the grave expression on his face warned her that she'd failed. He hadn't even heard her last remark. Juanita had been right about him after all, and she must let him say what was in his heart and mind.

'I told you the music last night was for you, Francesca. Everything I have is yours, if you will take it.' A glimmer of a smile touched his face for a moment. 'I should manage this so much better in Spanish, *querida*; I'm afraid our English lessons didn't cover proposals of marriage!' His hands on Fran's shoulders gently turned her to face him. 'The Spanish way of doing things would be to sweep you into my arms and kiss your lovely mouth until you'd agreed to be my wife; but something tells me that it wouldn't work. You've been so careful to give me no grain of encouragement that I think the reason is another man. Am I right?'

'There *was* another man,' she agreed slowly. 'In fact we were going to marry in the autumn – by then we thought we'd be absolutely sure, after some previous mistakes! It turned out to be only another mistake for Richard. He met my sister and fell in love with her instead.' Despite the seriousness of the moment she smiled at the expression on Pascal's face. 'Thank you for looking so astonished, but you wouldn't be if you saw Felicity; she's as beautiful as the dawn, and just as irresistible as the Condesa must have been at the same age.'

'So you came here hurt and unhappy, to be faced with Juanita at her worst, not to mention the rest of us.'

'Señora Fernandez *did* seem like the last straw,' Fran admitted ruefully. 'Things got better though; for one thing, *you* weren't ever unkind, and this is a good moment to say thank you.'

His hand under her chin forced her to look at him. 'But not a good moment to repeat the question I asked you? Will you not marry me and let me love you for ever?' His eyes searched her face, seeing only sadness and regret. 'I already know what it is you don't like to say, but you mustn't go back to London thinking that what Inez has almost certainly told you is true. I *don't* fall in love afresh with every woman

I meet, although I often enjoy their company. I *am* in love with you, now and for ever, I think. Will you believe that, please, despite my sister?'

Fran nodded, almost too touched to speak. 'Dear Pascal, I'm not saying no because of anything Inez has suggested . . . it's just that, leaving Richard out of it, I don't belong here; she was right about that!'

'I know Juanita hates her, but *you* mustn't, please,' he said earnestly. 'She's always loved Luis, just as he's loved her; but he wouldn't give in over Cantanzos and so she rushed into marriage with a man twice her age. She got wealth and the life she wanted in the south, but had to manage without happiness. She won't make the same mistake again; she'll marry Luis this time.'

'But you are needed here to hold things together, so that she can persuade the Leopard to leave his den occasionally!'

'Something like that,' he agreed with a faint smile. He leaned forward to leave a gentle kiss on her mouth, then framed her face in his hands. 'Go back to London, Francesca, but don't think for a moment that you'll have seen the last of me. One day you'll forget the fool of a man who should have married you when he had the chance, and I shall teach you that you *do* belong here.'

She nodded again, now entirely unable to trust her voice, and turned to walk back to the courtyard in time to see Maud Entwhistle hurrying towards them.

'Fran dear, there you are – I've been looking for you.' Then her glance went from Fran's pale face to the man beside her. 'You can tell me to go away, though, if I've interrupted something.'

Pascal managed a smile that was as affectionate as usual. 'Our conversation was just over. Now the dogs are going to take me for a walk while it's your turn to talk to Francesca!'

His hand touched her cheek in a fleeting, tender gesture, and then he went away, with George and Henry dancing beside him.

'Nice man,' Maud said briefly.

'Very,' Fran agreed, struggling not to burst into tears. She swallowed the lump in her throat and tried again. 'You were looking for me,' you said.

'It's Marganita. Backache's an ongoing problem, but she can't move at all this morning. I know you aren't here to mend the entire household, but I hoped you'd agree to take a look at her. Will you, Fran?'

'I will, of course,' came the answer after a small pause, 'but not if it's just your own idea. The Condesa must be willing for me to examine her, on the understanding that I'm trained in certain things but not in others. If I think she needs to see a doctor, I shall say so.'

'Say it firmly enough and she'll listen. She's too accustomed to *me* trying to tell her how to behave sensibly.'

'I'll go and get into my white coat,' Fran said. 'It didn't impress Juanita, but it's supposed to make me look professional.'

Maud gave way to a rare moment of embarrassment. 'Sorry if I barged in just now.'

'George and Henry were very glad you did; they can never understand why human beings need to talk so much!' She smiled cheerfully at Maud. 'I'll see you in the Condesa's room.'

Five minutes later, looking at the white-faced but unwelcoming woman who stared at her, she couldn't help thinking that the Esteban family were remarkably hard to help.

'You don't have to accept my services, Condesa,' she said with more calmness than she felt. 'I'm afraid this is Maud's idea.'

'I realise that; the wretched creature can never resist interfering. She knows I hate being mauled about.' But a tremor in her voice gave her away; because she was already in pain, she was fearful of more hurt.

'Just *looking* at your spine will tell me whether I can help you or not,' Fran suggested. 'May I at least do that?'

The Condesa gave a reluctant nod and, with only one

stifled exclamation, allowed herself to be turned face down-
wards. 'Oh, touch me if you must, so that Maud can see me
suffer; but I warn you, I shall make a great fuss.'

In fact she made no fuss at all as Fran's hands gently
explored her spine. Half an hour later the painful session was
over, and Marganita lay back exhausted against her pillows,
saying nothing at all when Fran walked towards the door.

'What now?' asked Maud, going with her. 'A rest followed
by a reviving cup of tea?'

'I think so. The Condesa will still feel tired and sore tomorrow, and one treatment won't be enough – the misalignments
have been in place too long to be corrected quickly – but
there'll be a definite improvement after that.'

Maud leaned forward and surprised herself by leaving a
shy kiss on Fran's cheek. Then, when the door closed behind
her, Miss Entwhistle went back to the bed.

'I expect you heard what was said. Perhaps next time
you'll feel strong enough to thank the girl who is trying to
help you.'

'I may even feel strong enough to fire *you*,' the Condesa
snapped. Then she caught hold of Maud's hand in a sudden
gesture of remorse. 'You know I didn't mean that, *cara*.
Forgive me, please. I *will* thank Francesca, I promise you.
The strange thing is that, even when she was hurting me,
there was healing in her hands – I could feel that as well.' And
she smiled so sweetly that Maud's grim expression relaxed.

'You may not be dancing at Juanita's party, but Fran will
see to it that at least you're on the mend. Now I'll go away
and leave you in peace.'

She went out, hoping that Fran was also being left in peace
– the interlude with Marganita must have been tiring for her
as well, and she'd looked strained; but on the floor above
Juanita was half-jokingly complaining at being left alone
all the morning when there were things she was longing to
discuss. Fran's heartfelt reply came as a surprise.

'If *you*'re going to be difficult too, I shall run screaming
from the castle and throw myself into the sea.'

She managed to smile at Juanita's startled expression but felt bound to explain. 'Between my sister, dear Pascal, and your grandmother's unhappy spine, I've had a trying morning. All I need now is for Richard to take it into his head to appear and my cup will overflow!'

Juanita smiled impishly at her, ready to return the advice she'd often been given. 'What you need now is a nice walk before luncheon. I shall see that you get it, *querida!*'

The walk *was* calming, and luncheon, shared only with Maud because the Condesa was asleep and everyone else was out, was peaceful. The only urgent matter, they agreed, was to decide what to wear at the birthday party, now only two days away.

'I'm losing weight, am I not, Fran?' Juanita asked with touching pride. 'But I still don't fit into my old dresses. In any case, I want something more . . . more *sophisticata* now. Where shall we go shopping tomorrow – Santiago? I shall buy beautiful dresses for all of us.'

'Thank you for the generous thought, but I shall buy my own,' Fran said, smiling at her, 'and Maud's wardrobe may already be immense, for all we know.'

'Maud,' said that lady, 'will wear what she always wears: a long black skirt of immemorial age and a silk shirt of irreproachable cut and *very* discreet colour! But I don't mind shepherding the two of you to Santiago, if Marganita doesn't need me here.'

Still smiling at the idea of an outing together, they parted company after lunch, even Fran for once welcoming the idea of a siesta in her room. She slept almost immediately and only awoke to the sound of someone knocking on her door. It was Constancia standing there, glad to report that the Señorita was being asked for in the hall – a *señor inglese*, who spoke Spanish most beautifully, had called and was extremely anxious to see her!

Twelve

A breathing space was needed before she went down-stairs. Five minutes, she told the image staring at her in the mirror, to change her crumpled skirt and tidy her hair; Richard didn't like disordered women. The truth not acknowledged to herself was that she needed time to face the moment of seeing him again. Perhaps he was similarly nervous, wondering what they would find to say to each other, now that he was here.

When she got as far as the first floor she could see him down below. He was talking to the housekeeper and, miracle of miracles, the grim Galician woman was smiling. As she passed the armoured sentinel at the corner of the stairs, her signet ring tinkled against his mailed hand and the small sound made Richard look up. Señora Fernandez went away, and he was free to walk towards her as she came down the last flight of stairs. Just the same Fran, slender and graceful, he thought at first; but he wished that she would smile at him. There was something else to notice as well: he felt rather overawed himself by the castle's massive grandeur and the austere beauty of the hall they were in, but Fran seemed so unconcerned by it that it was as if she'd become a stranger to whom he could think of nothing to say.

'Dear Richard, I'm impressed! Five minutes here and Señora Fernandez is eating out of your hand. I've been around for three weeks without wringing a smile out of her!' It sounded like Fran, and she was her familiar self again, but he hadn't reckoned that it was how their conversation would begin.

'You don't look very surprised to see me – did you guess I might come?'

'No, but Felicity wrote to me, and then I telephoned her in London. She said I was to give you her very fondest love, by the way; she sounded lonely.'

Richard glanced round the hall, and then tried to smile at her. 'There are things to say, but this strikes me as a very public place; is there something smaller we could hide in?'

'Let's go outside. You've come to Galicia when it's basking in a very untypical heatwave.' She led him along a maze of corridors, as easily as Ariadne guiding Theseus through the labyrinth, he thought, and they finally emerged into a charming rose garden.

'Not what I expected,' Richard commented with a smile. His hand gestured to the grey tower of Cantanzos behind them, shouldering its way into a cloudless blue sky. 'I suppose none of it is, except for its sheer size and solidity.'

'Yes . . . well I did rather let imagination rip in my first letter to Anita,' Fran admitted. 'But you *are* seeing Cantanzos at its most benign and unusual best. Come when a storm is driving in from the Atlantic and it makes a rather different impression.'

'But you've even got used to that, I think?' Richard suggested.

'Yes, I have; in fact, on a really quiet day I miss the sound of the sea! Earls Court Square will never seem the same again.'

She would have been content to let the conversation remain on this trivial level, but Richard led her to a seat and she could see him steeling himself for more serious matters.

'I *had* to come and see you, Fran – had to find the words to say how sorry I am. I treated you so abominably, and I really don't know why; we were looking forward so much to . . . to the autumn.'

'I know why,' she answered quietly. 'We weren't mistaken about our affection for each other – that was real, and

I hope it always will be. But Felicity doesn't deal in gentle, undemanding relationships; for her it's the *coup de foudre*, the thunderbolt from heaven that lays an unsuspecting man low! Come to think of it, *she* would be happy in Spain – it's enough of a *todo o nada* land even to satisfy her!' Fran reached out a hand to calm her companion's agitated fingers. 'Don't be agonised about *me*, please, if that is what you are. You didn't mean to hurt me, nor did Felicity, and that's the only thing that can't be forgiven, my father used to say: the deliberate intention to hurt.'

There was a little pause, but at least now, she thought, he might be able to relax. In a moment or two he'd begin to talk about himself and Felicity; the need to do so was probably what had brought him there.

'Felly is upset about quarrelling with you,' she said, to help him along the way. 'It isn't like her to cry over spilt milk, but at the moment she'd like more than anything to kiss and make up. If it still matters to you to know, I think she loves you very much.'

'Yes, it does matter,' Richard answered slowly. 'I'm not sure whether we shall be able to manage together as a couple – no man and woman were probably ever more ill-matched than we seem to be; and yet we need each other so badly. Can you explain that, my dear, all-knowing Fran?'

'Chemistry, I think they call it,' she suggested, smiling at him. 'All I can recommend is what our school reports used to say; you'll both just have to try harder at understanding each other.'

He touched her cheek in a little tender gesture, and at the same moment the postern gate behind them clicked open and Luis Esteban walked into the garden. They both stood up, looking, Fran feared, like delinquents caught out in some petty crime. She took a deep breath and spoke with what she reckoned was heroic self-control.

'A friend from London has called to see me, Don Luis – Professor Richard Weston. Richard, this is Count Esteban y Montilla, the owner of Cantanzos.'

While the two men shook hands and exchanged conventional courtesies, she tried to recall what that first letter to Anita had had to say about the Count – probably nothing that Richard could reconcile with the urbane, charming aristocrat who was now enquiring what had brought him to Galicia. The little scene Luis Esteban had just interrupted wasn't alluded to; they could imagine, if they liked, that it hadn't even been noticed.

Richard did his best to meet smoothness with smoothness. 'I'm on a sabbatical from London University at the moment, trying to complete a book about the pilgrim route to Santiago. With Francesca so close by, it seemed a pity not to call and see how she was enjoying Galicia.'

Luis Esteban nodded. 'I think I remember being told that you had written a book about our Civil War. You're obviously something of a Spanish expert, Professor.'

'I'm deeply interested in Spain, at least,' said Richard, not to be outdone in civilities; but it was time to call a halt to them, Fran decided: the conversation was becoming too much of a strain.

'I was just about to tell Richard that he would have missed me but for Juanita's birthday party.' She turned to the man beside her. 'My patient is walking well again and my job is finished, but I'm kindly being invited to stay here until after the weekend!' About to take Richard's arm and lead him firmly towards the gate, she was halted by the Count's deep voice.

'Francesca seems anxious to hurry you away, but I'd like to hear more about your book, Professor. What stage have you got to – initial research, or are you at the end of the pilgrimage?'

She suspected the sincerity of the question and wondered if Richard suspected it too, but it was more necessary to register the sound of her name on the Count's lips. He'd never used it before. Did it amuse him now to pretend in front of Richard that they'd done anything but snap and snarl at each other?

'The first rough draft is nearly complete,' Richard was saying. 'I *have* travelled the route on a previous visit – in fact, I spent the whole of one long vac doing the walk from Cluny, in France. It was unforgettable, but only to be tackled once! Now I just need to do a little more work in Santiago itself. I'm going back there now to check into a hotel.'

'If you need somewhere to stay, why not be my guest here?' Esteban's hand indicated the massive pile behind them. 'We aren't short of space, as you see!' His glance skimmed Fran's forbidding expression and returned to rest on Richard Weston. 'Really, I insist that you stay over the weekend at least, if only to add to Francesca's enjoyment of our party on Saturday – it's my niece's seventeenth birthday.'

'It's kind of the Count,' Fran put in hurriedly, 'but wouldn't it seem more sensible, Richard, for you to be in Santiago?'

He smiled his sweet, gentle smile. 'I don't think so, Fran; but in any case I can't resist staying in this wonderful place. Thank you, Don Luis; I accept with the greatest pleasure.'

'*Muy bien!* Señora Fernandez will look after you indoors, and Francesca can acquaint you with our rather complicated household! Until this evening, then.' He smiled and strolled away, leaving silence behind.

'Charming man,' said Richard when it seemed safe to do so.

'Viper, you mean,' she corrected him bitterly. 'For some reason that I fail to understand, it's amusing *el gran Condé* to play the part of an urbane, generous and welcoming host. We've done nothing but disagree violently since I got here; now, suddenly, butter wouldn't melt in the Leopard's mouth.'

'Leopard?' queried Richard, faint but persistent. 'Darling Fran, aren't you rather mixing your metaphors?'

She pointed to the flag flying above the tower, its bright

113

leopard leaping across the scarlet cloth. 'That's him – your amiable host!'

Richard looked from the flag to her flushed face – he hadn't seen her looking like this before, huge eyes more green than hazel now, nose and cheekbones dusted with freckles from the wind and sun. She didn't possess Felicity's golden beauty, but she was lovely in a quieter way that was all her own, and not forgettable once it had been properly noticed.

'Fran dear, it isn't *you* I usually have to tell to calm down!' he said gently. 'I think you've had a strange time here after all, but you *are* soon going home, don't forget, and I shan't get a splendid chance like this again. Why don't we just enjoy the next day or two?'

She nodded, and finally smiled. 'You can make yourself very useful by letting Juanita and me come to Santiago with you tomorrow – it will let Maud off a day's shopping! But now we'll walk along the wall where we *may* not be disturbed, and I'll "acquaint" you, to use Don Luis's lordly word, with the odd creatures you're going to meet here. I'll begin with George and Henry, I think!'

One way and another it had been an eventful day. With Richard handed over to Señora Fernandez to bestow in some corner of the castle, Fran retreated to her own room. Given a choice, she would have foregone dinner altogether and stayed there, but she could remember her own first night at Cantanzos too vividly; Richard would need support in his ordeal of trial-by-Spanish-stare.

She met him by arrangement at the top of the staircase and was glad to see the unusual care he'd taken with his appearance – fair hair neatly brushed for once, college tie carefully knotted.

'You look quite a swell,' she said with a smile. 'Keeping England's end up very nicely!'

'I'd say you've been doing that yourself, pretty well. Spain seems to suit you.' He waved his hand at their surroundings. 'You certainly chose a splendid spot to come to. This is just about the most perfect example of a fifteenth-century castle that I've ever seen. No wonder Count Esteban is immensely proud of it.'

Fran agreed, trying not to feel some absurd pride in it herself as she led him across the hall to the salon. Luis Esteban detached himself from the cluster of other people and came to meet them. 'Forgive me for deserting you this evening, Professor. Some of us are committed to dining out, but my cousin Pascal will take care of you. I have just time to make some introductions.'

He began with the Condesa, sitting in a majestic armchair that she knew perfectly framed her fragile beauty. She held out her hand and smiled approvingly as Richard bowed to kiss it, just skimming it with his lips – quite to the manner born, Fran reckoned, watching the little scene. In his progress round the room he also won a friendly smile from Juanita, and a more challenging one from the Marquesa, but Pascal's welcome was as brief as courtesy would allow, and Fran suspected that she knew why. Her Spanish friend had identified the newcomer correctly and felt himself deceived. He thought she should have warned him that her erstwhile lover, who was probably not erstwhile at all, was about to arrive.

It was easier when the Count had taken the diners-out away and Pascal had led the rest of them into the dining room. Fran could explain what she referred to as the chief reason for Richard's visit – the book about the Camino de Santiago – and suggest indirectly that *she* had very little to do with his being at Cantanzos. Richard talked well, and not for too long, about his hobby horse, and then returned the conversation to the Condesa's preferred hunting ground, Andalucía. They found an acquaintance they had in common and from then on Fran could relax; the Professor was doing well, and his pleasure at being back in Spain was so sincere that even Pascal began to smile at him.

The following morning she paid an early visit to the

Condesa, and taught her the exercises that could safely be done, now that her spine and pelvis were properly aligned.

'I'm afraid you'll still feel tired today, and I shall want to check you over again tomorrow; but your back is looking better already.'

'Clever and gentle but firm,' Marganita said, smiling at her. 'No wonder my granddaughter is a changed creature!'

'Well, we're now off to Santiago – a little shopping spree for us while Richard prowls about the cathedral.'

'Good! Pascal might be able to keep his mind on work if he doesn't have to watch the Professor smiling at you. You were doing your best to pretend you weren't there last night, but two men can always recognise an opponent in each other!'

Fran smiled at her, wondering why she'd ever found the Condesa hard to like. 'You're confusing me with some dangerous Spanish beauty, Doña Marganita; the Marquesa, now, *would* be worth a duel!'

'That is true, I have to admit, but so is what I said, Francesca. Enjoy your shopping spree, but prevent my granddaughter, if you can, from choosing something suited to a world-weary divorcee of thirty-five; at her present age she's certain to have the curious ambition to look much older than she is. I've told her the shops to go to.'

Fran promised to do her best, but later in the morning, when they'd parted company with Richard in the city, she discovered that Juanita's taste was quite as sure as her grandmother's. The outfit selected with no indecision at all was a clove-pink chiffon skirt and matching beaded tunic that charmingly concealed a still slightly too-plump figure. Fran's own choice was a simple dress of jade-green organza that won Juanita's careful approval, and the pair of them met Richard for lunch feeling extremely pleased with themselves.

On the walk back to the *hostal*, Fran suddenly announced that she would catch them up; she had one more thing to buy but didn't need their help in doing it. She rejoined them ten minutes later with two small parcels hidden in her bag, and found them sitting at a lunch table on the terrace. Beside her own plate sat another little package, beautifully wrapped, and labelled from Juanita '*con mucho amor*'.

'*Querida*, it's *your* birthday tomorrow, not mine. What is this?' Fran asked, suddenly near to tears.

'A little present . . . to say a big, big thank you and please not to forget me when you go back to England.'

With the gift carefully unwrapped, the sunlight fell on a necklace made up of strands of tiny, glinting brilliants, as fragile and beautiful as a cobweb with the dew on it.

'It's the loveliest thing I've ever been given, but I'm not sure that I shall ever dare wear it,' its bemused owner managed to gasp.

'Of course you'll wear it,' Juanita said firmly. 'It's to go with the green dress, which is very good but a little too plain on its own.'

'Mamselle la couturière has spoken,' Fran said unsteadily to Richard. 'You don't know it yet, but she's going to set the fashion world alight one day.'

'Well, I think I probably am,' Juanita agreed, quite certain of it, in fact, but anxious not to brag. Then her smile wavered as she turned to Richard herself. 'I shall be very, very sad tomorrow because my parents aren't there; but this afternoon I shall go to the cathedral by myself and thank the Holy Mother of God for sending me Francesca when I needed her so badly.'

Much less dismayed by this display of emotion at the lunch table than might have been expected, Richard patted her hand with the kindness of a compassionate academic who had been comforting anguished students for years. It was the moment when they needed a waiter to appear and, as if conjured up by magic, there he was, grave as a grandee, as all Spanish waiters are.

When the leisurely meal was over, Juanita went to make her private little pilgrimage to Saint James. She returned to the *hostal* to find Fran sitting lost in thought while Richard slumbered peacefully in a chair beside her. Afraid of saying the wrong thing, Fran merely held her hand instead. Juanita had tear-stains on her cheeks, but she was more serene than Fran had ever known her.

'I wouldn't pray after Mama and Papa died,' she said quietly, so as not to wake Richard. 'I hadn't been inside a church, even, until the day we came here with Pascal. But suddenly today I wanted something I'd lost that I knew I could have again.'

'I'm glad, *chiquita*,' Fran said simply, and leaned forward to kiss her cheek. Then she pointed at their sleeping escort. 'What shall we do – leave him here and stroll out by ourselves?' But even as she spoke he woke up and confessed to a small sartorial anxiety of his own. He hadn't set out for Spain expecting to attend a future couturière birthday party; would a suit of dark-grey flannel do, or should he hire a *traje de luces* and pretend to be a visiting toreador? Trying hard not to smile, Juanita gave the question consideration: not the *traje*, but perhaps something to cheer the flannel suit in the way of a new tie? Richard agreed to this, and half an hour later had been firmly guided to the purchase of a crimson-silk bow tie and an exceedingly expensive shirt to go with it.

'Now we can go home,' Juanita declared, and Fran mentally recorded another victory for the day – Cantanzos was at last being thought of, for the moment at least, as home – but all she said was that Richard had been so kind to bring them, shouldn't his reward be a recital of Spanish music, if they could persuade Pascal to play it for them?

'I'll let you ask him then,' Juanita said pointedly. 'He's been known to refuse what I want him to do.'

Thirteen

It was soon clear the following morning that Juanita's birthday would be different from any other day Fran had spent at Cantanzos. Even her early walk along the wall showed her Maud out with the dogs instead of Pascal. When their routes converged and the Great Danes' joy at meeting Fran allowed them to make themselves heard, Maud explained that Pascal was in charge of preparations for the party and already hard at work.

'Your nice man is helping him,' she added. 'When last seen he was trying to explain to Pepé the best way to hang fairy-lights along the terrace – a tricky assignment, because although Pepé doesn't really know what to do, he can't bring himself to admit that an Inglese can teach a Galician anything!'

Fran smiled but grew serious again. 'I hope it stays fine, and that today will be a time Juanita remembers with happiness as well as grief; above all, I hope her family can make her understand that she is still loved.'

Maud's face looked thoughtful. 'Pious hopes I'd have said those were a month ago, but now everything somehow seems possible.' She whistled to the dogs, who obeyed the summons for once. 'They'll be quite well behaved by the time we leave and that's another, smaller miracle.' Then her large hand gave Fran a friendly pat. 'Time we went indoors – I expect you know that breakfast is in Marganita's sitting room this morning for the privileged few!'

Gathered there a little later Fran found the few that she

expected, apart from Luis Esteban; but Richard Weston was unexpectedly included as well.

'I was told that you were hard at work,' she murmured to him. 'You can't have conquered Pepé already.'

Richard's gentle smile shone for a moment. 'We're getting on quite well now. Fortunately he gave himself a small electric shock doing things *his* way, so now he's prepared to listen!'

Fran was about to ask him if they were waiting for the Count to arrive when Juanita spotted her and came running over to be hugged.

'*Feliz compleaños, querida,*' Fran said warmly. 'I hope it's going to be the loveliest of days for you.'

'It already is; look what Luis has given me.' She pointed to a gleaming Ramirez guitar from Madrid, propped against a chair. 'Someone must have told him I wanted to learn, and Pascal says he'll teach me.'

'It's beautiful,' Fran agreed, 'but why isn't your uncle here himself?'

'He had to go out, but he'll be back later.' She turned a glowing face to Richard and smiled at him. 'I expect you want your breakfast!'

'Well, the day did begin rather early, but I can hold out easily enough if you want to tackle the rest of your parcels.'

She hurried away to consult her grandmother and the Condesa agreed that present-opening might come first. There was a moment's hesitation while she decided on the correct order, and Fran watched with interest as she opened the Marquesa's first – it seemed that Juanita was starting with the ones she valued least. Nevertheless the gift was beautiful: a fringed, silk shawl in all the colours of the rainbow. Next came Richard's parcel, selected for him by Fran in Santiago: a glass rose in a vase, each pale, translucent petal deepening to rose colour at the tip. Maud's present was a lace mantilla, Pascal's a carved ivory rosary. Juanita's flushed face was becoming tremulous with emotion, but she tried to deal calmly with the intricate wrapping of the Condesa's present. Inside the box lay a string of perfectly matched seed pearls, so beautiful a choice that Juanita was weeping when she went to kiss her grandmother. Only one small package remained: Fran's gift – a ridiculous anticlimax, she feared, after what had come before; but what nestled in the box released Juanita's pent-up emotion in a gust of delight. She held it up for the rest of them to see: a smiling, entrancing cat fashioned out of shining black glass. Squatting on its haunches, it surveyed them with an expression of sublime, ineffable contentment. It was as absurd as it was beautiful.

'Oh, Fran – I *love* him,' Juanita gasped, torn between tears and laughter. 'I shan't part with him *ever*.'

'He needs a name, but I thought I'd leave that to you,' Fran said, smiling at her.

Pascal suggested Alfonso, and Juanita was still considering it when breakfast arrived, brought in honour of the day by Señora Fernandez herself as well as Constancia.

When the breakfast party broke up, Fran stayed behind to examine her patient again. The adjustments she'd made to the alignment of the Condesa's spine were all in place and she pronounced herself satisfied; it was now looking in good shape.

'It *feels* in good shape,' Marganita confirmed, smiling at her. 'I can't describe the relief, only thank you for it, which Maud tells me I didn't do before! Dear Francesca, may I dance at my granddaughter's party?'

'Sedately, I think, Condesa; a tango *might* be a mistake!'

She agreed reluctantly to avoid a dance at which she particularly excelled and, still smiling at the thought, Fran left her to Maud. It was time to rejoin Juanita, already at work in one of the many small rooms leading off the kitchen corridor. A row of vases was lined up, and flowers seemed to be everywhere.

'An arrangement for each supper table, Señora F. says,' Juanita explained anxiously. 'Twenty of them, and it's not a job I'm good at. The bloody flowers fall out as fast as I put them in.'

'Persevere,' Fran recommended. 'Meanwhile, do I detect more of Giorgio's English lessons?' She asked the question with a grin, but changed her tone of voice at the sight of Juanita's suddenly stricken face. 'Darling, I was only teasing.' But the huge eyes staring at her were now full of sorrow.

'I haven't heard from them, Fran – Giorgio and Graziella, I mean. I shouldn't grizzle when I've been given so many lovely things, but I didn't think *they* would forget my birthday – just a little card would have done.'

'Dear girl, I'm sure it's on its way,' Fran insisted with all the certainty she could offer. 'You know how chaotic the postal services can be here, and they're probably, as Giorgio would say, a bloody sight worse in Italy.'

Juanita smeared her wet cheeks and tried to smile. 'I should have thought of that – perhaps a card will come tomorrow.' But she heaved a little sigh before going back to the task in front of them.

They'd just finished it and were congratulating each other on their handiwork when Pascal came hurrying in. Juanita was wanted in the courtyard and, no, she couldn't stop to wash her hands because he needed her there *now*, if he wasn't to be fired for failing in his duties. Mystified, she allowed herself to be towed outside, followed by her fellow flower-arranger, who she insisted must come too. Expecting to find estate people gathered there for some small presentation, Fran was disappointed to find the courtyard deserted, and Juanita looked at Pascal a trifle impatiently.

'This is silly, isn't it, when we've got so much still to do indoors?'

'*Paciencia por favor, chiquita . . . un momentito!*' He glanced anxiously up at the tower, saw an arm wave aloft, and then smiled as Luis Esteban's car turned in quietly under the archway. A moment later Fran heard the sound Juanita made, half-sob, half-laughter, as she saw who was being handed out of the car; the next moment she flung herself at the small, round woman who stood smiling at her.

'Graziella! *Dios mio* . . . and Giorgio too! My bad ones – I told Fran that you'd forgotten me!' A less small but equally round man had now reached them from the other side of the car, and the three of them hugged and kissed each other and wept and laughed together.

Waiting with Pascal, Fran made a brave attempt to keep her voice steady. 'How in the world did they manage it?'

'They didn't; Luis arranged it all – sent the tickets, and collected them this morning from the airport. He was anxious in case it might upset Juanita too much, but when the three of them have had a private little lunch together, I think she'll be all right, don't you?'

'They're the best present anyone could have thought of giving her.' Fran was silent for a moment, considering something else that she now knew for certain; the evening's party was to be what Luis had referred to as a 'family affair', by which was meant that everyone connected with Cantanzos was invited to share Juanita's birthday. It had been planned in that way, Fran realised, so that Giorgio and Graziella could fit into it with no awkwardness at all. Each person there would be a servant of the estate in one way or another.

'They're staying here, I take it?' she asked huskily.

'There's a little self-contained apartment on the ground floor of the tower. It's all ready for them and they and Juanita are to lunch there so that they can talk nineteen to the dozen in Italian!' Fran nodded and would have turned away, but Juanita was leading her guests towards them, and Giorgio's eye kindled at the chance to practise on a real *Inglesa* – his English words were blooded rusted, he said cheerfully.

'Never mind; Juanita remembers very well everything you taught her!' Fran commented solemnly, and smiled as his face split in a grin of pure pleasure. Then it was Pascal's turn to be introduced, and she was free to look at the tall man patiently waiting to escort them into his home. She wanted to thank him for what he'd done, wanted more than anything in the world to apologise for so often having misjudged him; but the closed expression on his face said that he wanted neither thanks nor apologies from an opinionated outsider who'd been fool enough to get him all wrong. *El gran Condé* didn't give a damn *what* Francesca Brown thought of him. Realising it, she said nothing at all and simply walked away, back to the flower room.

By eight o'clock the guests were beginning to assemble; by nine they were being invited to serve themselves from the huge buffet supper set out in the dining room. Those who preferred to could eat at the tables in the hall, but the evening was so beautiful and serene that many people chose one of the tables set around the terrace. As the daylight faded, Pepé's fairy-lamps came on, and then magically the flambeaux along the castle walls began to glow as well.

'It's pure enchantment,' Richard murmured to Fran. 'I shan't forget Cantanzos as long as I live, and it's thanks to you that I'm here at all.' He stared at her across the small table they shared, knowing that he wouldn't forget her either, whatever happened to them in the end. In her softly coloured dress, with Juanita's present sparkling at her throat, she was lovely enough for any man to be content with, but she could offer him more than that: intelligence, kindness and courage would come with Fran. He wanted to say these things, but Felicity was waiting for him in London, and some residual grain of common sense insisted that he wouldn't be allowed to love them both at once. Nevertheless, knowing it didn't stop him feeling resentful when Pascal Vargas came to sit down at their table with a well-turned Spanish compliment on his lips.

'Darling Francesca, I suppose Richard has already told you that you look like a dryad strayed in from some enchanted forest!'

'Not quite,' she said, smiling at him, 'but we *have* agreed that we're in the middle of a fairy tale. Juanita looks so transfigured by happiness that it's as if she feels her parents are here.'

Pascal nodded, but before he could say anything more, the musicians grouped at one end of the terrace struck up an opening dance. At the same moment Luis Esteban walked across to where Graziella was sitting, bowed, and led her on to the flagstone floor; then it was Giorgio's turn to offer Juanita a beaming grin and escort her into the dance. Pascal watched them for a moment or two and then smiled at Fran.

'The solos have lasted long enough; it's time for us to join them, I think. Ricardo, my friend, *your* privilege is to partner the Condesa; she's still the best dancer in Seville, not to mention Galicia!'

From then on the night grew merry but not raucous. Handed from one unknown partner to another, Fran marvelled at the innate good taste that taught these unsophisticated people how to behave; there was no doubt that they were enjoying themselves, and the Count's hospitality was very liberal, but no one was intent on getting drunk, or over-boisterous. She said this to Maud when they were sitting together, resting from their labours on the dance floor, and Maud nodded thoughtfully.

'It's not quite as true as it was, I'm afraid. When I first came here, I never saw a drunken Spaniard, and a woman the worse for drink would have been unthinkable. That has changed now, sadly; Spain isn't immune from today's social ills. But in a backwater like this part of Galicia the old habits die hard, and Luis is rather good at holding the community together.'

Fran smiled at her companion's typical understatement. 'In other words, you think he's God's gift to everybody here!'

'Something like that,' Maud agreed, calmly sipping the chilled white wine in front of her.

Fran watched the throng of dancers for a moment, picking out Juanita in her beautiful pink outfit, gliding by with the young man who managed the castle's home farm; Pascal was dutifully piloting Señora Fernandez round the floor, and Richard was being taught a new step by a laughing, bright-eyed Constancia. For most of the night Luis Esteban had spent his time circulating among the guests, offering a pleasant word here and there to each of them. He hadn't greeted Fran, but she refused to feel ignored; it was understandable that his concern was for his own people. At last, though, he'd decided to abandon the duties of a host and was now simply enjoying himself, dancing with Inez de Castro. They made a couple it was impossible not to watch, perfectly matched, together at last after the Marquesa's mistaken marriage.

'They've forgotten that the rest of us are here,' Fran murmured suddenly, unaware that she'd spoken aloud. Maud glanced at her face, registering its sudden infinite sadness and the note of desolation in her low voice.

'You've become very involved with the people here,' she said gruffly. 'It must make life rather wearing if it happens wherever you go.'

'Usually not,' Fran managed to explain, 'but I haven't been sent to a place quite so . . . so compelling as Cantanzos before!' It was the castle itself and its setting, she intended Maud to understand, that had made so deep an impression on her. She forced herself to look away from Inez, dazzling in fringed white silk tonight, held in the arms of Luis Esteban; she must concentrate on Juanita instead.

'Can you fix it so that Doña Marganita takes Juanita with her to Seville? Our birthday girl is much less contrary than she was, but nothing will change her opinion of the Marquesa. If Inez is to be here for good from now on, Don Luis's only hope of a quiet life will be to let Juanita leave.'

Maud's hand descended on Fran's shoulder for a moment as she stood up. 'I'll see what I can do; but right now I've got another difficult trick to perform. Marganita's looking very tired, but I shan't be allowed to say so. I shall have to suggest instead that an elderly companion who can't keep pace with her needs to go to bed!'

'Will the trick work?' Fran asked curiously.

'I expect so – she doesn't go to sleep unless I read to her. It's a habit started many years ago when we first left Cantanzos and she was in such terrible distress.'

There was a little silence before Fran spoke again. 'She's lucky to have you as a friend, but I'm sure she knows that.'

Maud just smiled and said goodnight, leaving Fran still sitting there, grateful to be left alone. She was aware that something about the long, eventful day and night had made a change that she would eventually have to acknowledge and accept, but she wouldn't allow her conscious thoughts to delve now into what it was. The truth lay just below the surface of her mind, but as long as she could keep it hidden there, it wouldn't hurt her.

She wasn't aware of someone coming towards her until the Count's deep voice spoke just behind her. She swung round, ready to smile again, not ready at all for the sudden spring of delight she felt at finding him there. He wasn't going to avoid her completely after all; she *was* about to know what it felt like to be held in his arms. It might make another memory she'd never be able to forget, but her whole recollection of the past few weeks would be a mixture of pleasure and pain.

He hadn't come to lead her out into the crowd of dancers, though. Instead, he asked politely if he might sit down. She stilled the erratic beating of her heart and nodded, then had to wait while he signalled to a passing waiter to serve them more wine. His long-fingered hand, brown against the whiteness of the tablecloth, was gripped round the bowl of his wine glass. It looked tense, she noticed, and wondered why that should be so. If he still doubted the happiness the day had given his niece, she must say something to reassure him.

'It's been a wonderful birthday for Juanita – I hope you

127

know that.' Without realising it, she spoke to him for the first time as if they were on equal terms; she wasn't an employee stepping out of line again. The alterations that the evening had made included this most significant change of all.

As if aware of it himself, his dark brows were drawn together in a sudden frown, but instead of responding to what she'd said, he deliberately led the conversation away from Juanita. 'My mother tells me that she wouldn't have enjoyed it at all without your help. I'm very grateful for it, but you weren't meant to do extra work.'

She could read nothing in his impassive face; there was only the impersonal coolness of his voice to go on. Was he, dear God, about to offer her money for attending to the Condesa? Feeling slightly sick, she tried to smile above the renewed thumping of her heart.

'It's a very small quid pro quo for Richard Weston's welcome here. He won't ever forget Cantanzos.'

This was acknowledged with a courteous bow – the sort of gesture a fencer would offer an opponent who'd just made a shrewd hit. She would have liked to think it was an absurd game they were playing, but knew it wasn't true; whatever they were engaged in was serious, not a game.

'You asked to go home now that your work is finished,' he said next. 'I've booked a seat for you on Monday morning's flight to London. It gives you a day to recover from the party. I hope that's convenient.'

She tried to remember how much she'd wanted to escape back to normal life; told herself she'd asked that it might be sooner, not later. It made no difference to the coldness at her heart and the taste of nausea in her throat. She saw in her mind's eye the stone leopard carved above the archway entrance; in her first glimpse of it she'd identified the unicorn it was about to maul as being Juanita. The truth was that the poor creature had turned out to be herself.

'*Is* Monday convenient, Francesca?'

128

The cool, repeated question demanded a reply, and she prayed to all the gods at once that her voice wouldn't tremble when she gave it.

'Ideal, thank you. Richard will be leaving then – he can take me to the airport and save Pepé the trouble.'

'The Professor will be anxious to fly home with you perhaps? I didn't think of that, I'm afraid. I should have done, seeing that his hackles rise whenever Pascal looks in your direction! Cantanzos will have to settle down again without Francesca Brown's disturbing presence.'

His formality was bad enough, but this slightly contemptuous raillery she found impossible to bear.

'I dare say Cantanzos will manage easily enough; it's had long centuries in which to learn to survive.' She drew round herself the last vestiges of strength that she possessed and looked at him. 'It's been a long day. I think I shall follow Maud's example and give up trying to compete with Spanish stamina. Say goodnight to Juanita for me, please – I don't want to interrupt her dancing.'

She stood up so quickly that, even as he got up himself, she'd walked away; he could see her, slender and graceful in her beautiful green dress, threading a path through the guests, removing herself from his life.

'Darling, why are you standing there as if you can't remember what the next dreary duty is that you have to perform?' Inez's laughing question made him turn round to look at her, and she was startled into seriousness by the expression on his face.

'*Querida*, you look tired to death, but I suppose we have to endure this boring party to the bitter end.'

A strange smile twisted his mouth, then faded again. 'We Spanish are renowned for our stamina – Miss Brown has just told me so!'

'Miss Brown should go home before she forgets entirely that she's been employed to do a job of work here. Pascal has been partly to blame, I'm afraid, by making a friend of her, but now your mother seems to think she's indispensable as well. Really, one wonders how Cantanzos will manage without her!'

'She also assures me that it will,' he said gravely. 'She and the Professor are leaving on Monday.'

Inez stared at him for a moment, for once not sure that she could gauge his state of mind . . . was he amused, angry, hurt? She could only be sure that *something* was being kept in check that put a huge strain on his usual self-control. Her beautiful face looked soft with concern for once, and she smiled at him with ravishing sweetness.

'Marganita is talking of taking Juanita back with her. Encourage her, please, my dearest, so that we can be on our own again. What a joy that will be after the past few months!'

The promise of comfort and delight to come was clear, and he made the gesture that was expected of him by leaning forward to kiss her mouth. Then he held out his hand and led her back into the crowd.

Fourteen

There was a sea change during the night: the clear skies and sunlight of the previous week might never have been; Galicia was its damp, silver-veiled self again. Fran set out early as usual and found the alteration a comfort in her present state of mind. She wanted no brightness exposing the muddle of relief, sadness and regret that she floundered in; better by far this soft grey mist that blurred even the outlines of the castle itself and left the salt taste of the sea on her lips.

She was sitting on a smooth lump of rock, watching the tide advance to meet her, when Richard clambered up to where she was perched.

'I spotted you from the top of the wall,' he explained. 'Everyone else still seems to be asleep.' She didn't answer and a sidelong glance at her showed him an expression so withdrawn that he wondered whether she'd even heard what he said. 'Fran, are you all right? You look like the forsaken mermaid longing to return to the sea!'

She looked blankly at him – Luis Esteban had once compared her to a mermaid, too. Then she shook her head and answered, 'I was saying goodbye to it, as a matter of fact. Living and working in London, I'd forgotten how I missed not being within sight and sound of the ocean; now I shall have to get used to doing without it all over again.' She dug cold hands in the pockets of her jacket and turned to face the tumbling sea. 'I'm leaving tomorrow, too. Could you drop me off at the airport when you go?'

'So soon? Juanita didn't mention it last night.'

'She doesn't know yet; I didn't know myself until the party was nearly over. I see now, though, that it's the best arrangement: she won't miss me at all with Giorgio and Graziella still here. No doubt Don Luis worked that out as well.' She fell silent again, then remembered that Richard was still there. 'What are you going to do – stay a bit longer in Santiago?'

'Perhaps one more day; then I'll drive back over the pilgrim route – just to make sure the things I've written about are still there. Spain is changing so fast that I can't be sure unless I check. A week at the most, though, and I'll be back in London.'

'What are you going to do *then*?' Fran might have asked, but she chose not to put the question. She hadn't missed what the others had noticed too: the warmth in his face when he looked at her, the spark of admiration and desire; but it was only because in this different setting he'd seen her differently, that was all. Once back in London with Felicity he'd be in thrall again to her beauty and bright laughing spirit.

Fran stood up suddenly, but Richard caught hold of her hand. 'There's nothing odd happening, is there? . . . Nothing wrong, I suppose I mean, for you to be going so suddenly.'

'Nothing at all,' she answered steadily. 'Juanita's known for some while that I reckoned it was time to leave; she'll take it in her stride now.' A tremulous smile touched her mouth. 'The truth is that I *want* to go home; I've been here too long already.' Then she began to pick her way over the tumbled rocks to the steps that led up to the castle wall, and after a moment Richard followed her.

The day was spent largely as Fran intended, talking about the party; but she wasn't able to prevent Juanita's first outburst of anger and grief.

'It's sodding Inez, isn't it? *She*'s behind your going, Fran. I *like* Luis now – why does he let her wind him round her little finger?'

132

'It's nothing to do with her, and very little to do with your uncle,' Fran insisted firmly. 'I promise that we'll keep in touch, and come the day when your first dress show is unveiled in Milan, I shall be there, sitting in the front row!'

Juanita blinked away the angry tears glistening on her long lashes and began to talk about the future. It was arranged that Giorgio and Graziella would continue to look after the palazzo in the Via Manin, and there, a few years from now, Juanita Fiocca intended to open her elegant atelier.

Dinner that evening was something of a strain: the Count and Pascal had little to say, Fran even less, and Juanita's tongue was bridled by the memory of the kindness she'd received the previous day; but between them Richard, Inez, the Condesa and Maud kept the conversation going. Fran said goodbye to *them* that night, but early the next morning Juanita and Pascal were out in the courtyard, with George and Henry there to provide a little light relief. She'd scarcely exchanged a word with Luis Esteban since they parted company on the night of the party. It seemed hard to believe that a man who set such store by Spanish punctiliousness would fail to appear now, at least to say goodbye; but the moment came when she was hugged by a weeping Juanita for the last time, and handed into the car by Pascal, and there was still no sign of the man who'd brought her there.

'I shall see you again, Francesca,' Pascal said, leaning in to kiss her on both cheeks and then, because he couldn't help himself, on her lips as well. 'I shall come to London if I have to.'

She managed a smile but couldn't see his face for the tears that now blinded her as well. Then Richard mercifully put the car in gear, and a few minutes later they passed under the last archway and turned onto the Santiago road. Her stay at Cantanzos was over.

Thin, early-summer rain was falling over London. There was never much in the middle of the great metropolis to mark the changing of the seasons, except in its precious green parks; but Fran was suddenly conscious all the same of time lost while she'd been away. A small ornamental cherry tree in the tiny patch of front garden outside her house had budded and bloomed, but the pink blossom was over now.

She'd tried several times to telephone Felicity the day before to say she was coming home, but there'd been no reply. The flat was still empty when she let herself in, but signs of her sister's untidy occupation made it clear that she was still staying there. Unwashed dishes littered the kitchen sink, and discarded underclothes were heaped in the bathroom. Fran took a firm grip on a sudden spurt of rage, but promised herself the laying down of some house rules when her sister appeared.

She'd unpacked, tidied the rooms, and started the washing machine when Felicity let herself in. At the first sight of her, irritation died, as it usually did, and it was impossible not to smile at her.

'I did try to ring yesterday,' Fran said, 'but you weren't here.'

'I was on my way back from checking up on Mummy in Cornwall. Darling, it's lovely to see you, but where's Richard? Isn't he home too?'

'Not for a few more days; he's retracing his pilgrim route backwards from Santiago. Didn't he tell you he planned to do that?'

'He's told me very little since we left New York,' Felicity pointed out with a hint of complaint in her voice. 'Even when he did ring, he sounded quite unlike himself; you were both having a marvellous time in that ridiculous castle place, and he didn't seem to mind a bit that I was all alone here.' She stared at her sister, registering some change that she couldn't define. 'I don't know what it is about you that's different, Fran, but something is. I'm beginning to feel sorry that I didn't take the Spanish job myself; I think it must have turned out to be fun.'

'It turned out to be an unhappy, damaged adolescent

who'd made up her mind that she couldn't walk again after the car crash that killed both her parents. Does that sound like fun?'

Felicity's cheeks turned a faint, becoming pink. 'Perhaps not, darling, but you're being so utterly angelic about Richard that I'd feel better if you *had* enjoyed yourself in Spain.' She hesitated a moment before going on. 'We couldn't help falling in love, Fran . . . it just happened; and I knew that it was serious, not just a fling, because he isn't at all the kind of man I usually imagine that I could settle down with.'

'I had noticed that,' Fran agreed soberly. She watched her sister's face, noting that its normal bright confidence was missing; perhaps for the first time in her life Felicity was either not sure what she wanted or no longer sure that what she wanted could be had.

'We're in a bit of a muddle,' she said truthfully. 'That's why I need Richard to come back; so that we can get ourselves sorted again.' Then her lovely smile finally reappeared. 'What about you – back to the agency tomorrow?'

'Yes, but I shall ask for some hospital work. I'm tired of eavesdropping on other people's lives, especially among the over-privileged!'

'No problem about that; they'll give you your pick. My own clients aren't very jolly at the moment: mostly middle-aged gents suffering from their past athletic glories! There's also a rich pop singer who's jiggled and heaved her spine into a total mess. I might be doing the rest of us a favour if I left her as she is. The girl can't sing – she just strips beautifully on stage.'

'Well, straighten the poor thing out anyway,' Fran recommended, then she smiled at her sister. 'I'll cook supper if you promise not to strew disorder everywhere while I'm in the kitchen.'

'Sorry – I know I left things lying about this morning, but I overslept. New leaf turned over as of now, cross my heart!'

Her enchanting smile that always earned forgiveness shone
again. 'I'll pour us delicious drinks while you cook and tell
me about castle life. I've a feeling it might have produced
a dashing Spanish creature who fell in love with you.'

'I did find an admirer,' Fran admitted primly. 'In fact,
two or three, if I count George and Henry as well, although
I suppose they weren't Spanish, properly speaking!'

She was launched now on the things that could be safely
talked about; there'd be no need at all to mention that the
flat seemed unbearably cramped after Cantanzos, that she
longed to look out on the tumbling sea instead of London
street traffic, and that her heart was very sore. She could
pretend that she was angry to have been sent away like
a dismissed housemaid, could even pretend that she was
simply disappointed in a man whose ways had sometimes
seemed splendid; but the truth was that she was deeply,
lastingly hurt, and that couldn't be talked about.

Richard Weston returned to London a week later. Fran came
home late one evening after seeing a film show with Anita to
find him sitting in the kitchen with Felicity over the remains
of supper. She hoped she imagined a faint coolness in the
air, but was careful to greet him casually, because her sister
seemed to be watching them intently.

'You're back then,' she said too obviously, to fill a pause
that felt awkward. 'Was everything still where you wanted
it to be along the *camino*?'

'Pretty much unchanged, thank heaven. I've a bit of
rewriting to do, but nothing to hold me up too much. I've
been describing Cantanzos to Felly instead; she's rather
bored with hearing about my pilgrim route!'

'She's probably rather bored with Cantanzos as well by
now,' Fran pointed out. 'In a week's time you'll be like me,
looking back on an exotic little episode that you almost seem
to have dreamed up – not real at all!'

He thought, looking at her, that unusually for Fran she
wasn't being entirely honest – she'd lived the episode too

136

intensely by far for it to seem anything like a dream. But he smiled at her and suggested that it was time he went back to his own flat in Bloomsbury. She took what seemed to be a hint and left them to say goodnight to each other, but went to her own room wondering how soon Felicity would move out of Earls Court Square into Richard's roomier apartment – soon, she hoped; however much they pretended that it wasn't, three was an awkward number in the situation they were in. She wanted them to get on with their lives together; wanted even more to regain some peace of mind and sense of purpose for herself. It had been a pathetic lie to say that Cantanzos was already relegated in her mind to some never-never land of dreams and fantasies; there was nothing about it and its inmates that she couldn't vividly recall, no moment of her stay that she couldn't relive. The memories would fade in time – she clung desperately to that article of faith – but until they did, she would go on lying as she'd done just now.

Juanita's first letter arrived quite soon. They'd agreed on correspondence as the means of keeping in touch so that her written English would be given some practice; but it was phrased exactly as she spoke: no words wasted and opinions very freely expressed. Giorgio and Graziella had gone back to Milan, and life at the castle without her dear *amiga* as well was bloody boring – not even Inez to spar with because she and Luis were visiting Madrid. Pascal was lovesick and dull, so it was something to be thankful for that her grandmother and Maud were still there. It was raining more often than not, but she was working hard, as her *Inglesa* had instructed, and she was still losing weight! Fran was comforted to know that Juanita was managing so well, but the Condesa's continuing stay at the castle was a surprise, especially with her son not there.

She showed the letter to Felicity, thinking it would amuse her, but it only drew forth one brief comment.

'The lovesick Pascal was your "admirer", I suppose; he sounds rather wet to me.'

'Well he shouldn't,' Fran said crisply. 'He's a charming, gifted man as it happens.'

'Sorry – but I'm scarcely in a position to know.'

She was right, of course, but Fran felt disinclined to apologise for snapping at her. They were often at odds with one another now, tempers frayed by living at such close quarters and by griefs they chose not to share. Richard's visits only seemed to make things worse, and when he'd gone home one evening, Fran finally decided to clear the troubled air.

'Felly dear, I don't think I'm very easy to live with at the moment. Wouldn't you be better with Richard? It's obvious that *he* isn't happy either, so why not move in with him?'

'Because he hasn't asked me to,' Felicity suddenly shouted. She could never be less than beautiful, but pent-up anger and fear were disfiguring, even for her. 'He was glad enough to have me go away with him – flattered to show me off to his dreary academic friends who couldn't land a lover if they tried – but that was before a guilty conscience about *you* sent him rushing off to Spain.'

'He's back from Spain. What difference can it have made?'

Felicity stared at her, blue eyes sparkling with sudden angry tears. 'Why ask *me*? You know better than I do what the answer is. That little stay at the castle changed things, didn't it? You were suddenly someone more interesting – not the girl he'd taken for granted that he was going to marry before I came back to London and he discovered what wanting someone really meant.'

'So what are you saying?' Fran asked hoarsely. 'That I've tried to entice him back again? That he doesn't now know which of us he wants? You're wrong on both counts. I thought – a long time ago it seems now – that we could make a companionable, comfortable marriage. It wouldn't work now because *he*'s in love with you and, although I'm not in love with anyone else, *I*'ve glimpsed what love between a man and a woman ought to mean. Anything less won't do.'

Despite the miserable turmoil she was in herself, Felicity was sidetracked for a moment into staring at her sister. 'Something *did* happen to you at Cantanzos – I knew it the moment you came back. You aren't like me, ready to throw your bonnet over any reasonable-looking windmill, so of course I thought it was Richard you still fancied.'

Fran managed a shaky laugh. 'What a dreadful word! No, I do not fancy him any more than he fancies me, but you could make us sound less like little iced cakes on a tray!'

Her sister's blue glance still lingered, sad now and unconvinced. 'You're probably right about yourself, but I'm a better judge of men than you are; let's face it, darling, I've had more practice. Richard enjoys going to bed with me, but he rather thinks it's *you* he needs to live with! What do you imagine that does for a girl's self-esteem?'

She asked the question with a brave, wry grimace that couldn't hide the extent to which it mattered. For some reason that no expert would ever be able to explain, Felicity's wayward heart had fixed itself on a serious-minded, shy historian whose only unconventional piece of behaviour in his life had been to jilt one girl in favour of her sister. Fran hesitated over what to say, longing to give comfort but afraid to offer what might turn out to be quite the wrong advice.

'Couldn't you marry your Spanish admirer?' Felicity suddenly asked. 'That might settle all our problems and, Fran, you *are* nearly thirty-one. I know it isn't the end of hope nowadays, but you haven't exactly made a career out of being a femme fatale.'

It was only fair to agree that she had not, but then Fran made up her mind what else to say. 'I like Pascal Vargas very much, but I'm not going to marry anyone just so that Richard can decide who it is he wants. We talked about you once at Cantanzos and there wasn't any doubt that he loved you; but he's afraid as well of not being able to keep you happy. You must either persuade him of that or make a fresh start somewhere else. Does that sound reasonable?'

A glimmer of amusement lit Felicity's sad face. 'It sounds

like my kind elder sister trying yet again to straighten me out!' But she remembered, after they'd said goodnight, something that hadn't sounded like Fran at all. There'd been a glimpse of love, it seemed, bright enough to rule out not only Richard but the Spanish admirer as well.

The following evening Felicity rang to say that, after a visit to the theatre, she'd be going back with Richard for the night. Persuasion was obviously under way; having made up her mind, she never hung about.

The next day, after strenuous sessions in two hospitals, Fran got home to find the flat still empty. A letter lying on the hall table took the place of her sister's voice calling out that restoring drinks were being poured. She was suddenly reminded of a previous occasion when an unexpected letter from Felicity had changed her life; this note couldn't announce anything so dramatic, but she sat down at the kitchen table to read it.

Dearest Fran,

I *did* try, but even my powers of persuasion weren't enough, and *you*'re the fly in our ointment, as I suspected. I'd hate you if I could, but we aren't very good at hating each other, are we?

The agency offered me a rush job this morning – New York, which I loved; so I jumped at it. Forgive the mess, but I had to pack in great haste. I should be airborne by the time you read this scrawl.

I'll write to Richard from NY. It's a truth universally acknowledged by everyone except him that a man can't successfully love two women at once!

I promise to be in touch soon. Don't fret about me, and take care of yourself.

Your loving
Felly

The letter *was* another drama after all, but its tone this time was very different: sober, sad and mature. Fran even

140

smiled briefly at the passing nod in the direction of Jane Austen – not one of Felicity's preferred novelists – but she felt weighted down by frustration and regret. Lives had gone awry that shouldn't have done, and in the process something of great value had been lost. Felicity wouldn't stay cast down for very long; optimism and hope were in her blood and bones, but Richard was a different matter. Fran feared she could foresee without the slightest doubt what he would think should happen next – not immediately, but when the dust of failure had settled.

The telephone rang while she was making a pretence of eating supper. The call was repeated twice later on and, feeling ashamed of her own cowardice, she decided each time not to answer it. The following evening Richard was waiting on the doorstep when she got home; cowardice now was no help at all.

Settled in the sitting room, with wine poured in an attempt to make the visit seem normal, she made herself begin.

'You won't have heard yet, but Felly has gone back to New York. The agency offered her an urgent job and she decided to take it.' Fran looked at Richard as he sat nursing his wine glass; unlikely as it seemed, she thought she could see relief uppermost in his face, as well as shamed regret. He said nothing, however, and she had to go on herself.

'The note she left for me wasn't one of Felicity's usual breezy apologies for having made a mistake. Failure has hurt this time, the more so because she doesn't know why she failed.'

'The mistake and the failure were mine, not hers,' Richard said slowly. 'She's so sweet and easy to love that I nearly convinced myself that I should let things ride – pretend that we weren't certain to come a terrible cropper in the end. But we *were* certain to, Fran. The kind of life I lead would have bored her to madness before long; and when the delight of loving her had worn off, I'd have understood the extent of

141

the error we'd made.' He looked across at Fran. 'And you were caught in the middle of the mess – that's my worst regret of all.'

He was hell-bent, she could see, on being tragic and guilt-ridden; a little breast-beating would have to be allowed because he wasn't a man who could carelessly damage other people; but she had to reduce what had happened to its real proportions.

'We've all got hurt,' she finally agreed, 'but good's come out of it as well. Felicity won't make another mistake: in future she'll measure any man she meets against you; you'll be her indispensable yardstick. You, having loved her, now know the full extent of what is possible.' She shook her head as he started to intervene. 'Let's be honest and admit that it isn't how you and I loved each other.'

He didn't argue or protest; it was scarcely the time to suggest that the future needn't be the same as the past. However, he thought his ultimate grief might be that he wouldn't be allowed to prove it to her. She'd made discoveries of her own in the past few months, and in her quiet and self-reliant way had travelled away from him, for the time being out of reach.

'What about our Spanish friends?' he asked, accepting that that conversation was over. 'Have you heard from Juanita?'

'We exchange letters regularly. The gist of hers is that the weather's awful, she's working hard, and the Marquesa doesn't improve on prolonged acquaintance! The only surprise is that her grandmother and Maud are still there. She doesn't say much about it, but I get the impression that the Condesa isn't well.'

'Or she finds Seville in high summer too hot and crowded,' Richard suggested. He looked at Fran, wondering whether he imagined that her face looked thinner. With her hair tied back for ease of working he could see the little hollows now at temple and cheekbones.

'You still miss that lovely place – and perhaps the people

there as well,' he added, suddenly remembering Pascal Vargas.

She nodded, but smiled to show that the missing didn't amount to much. 'I defy anyone to forget Cantanzos in a hurry – even Señora Fernandez made an impression! I promised Juanita I'd visit her in Milan one day, but I don't bank on her remembering her English "bully" by the time she's ready to sail under her own steam.'

Richard stood up, aware that it was the moment for him to leave. 'You look tired, Fran, and I've got work I need to finish. If I promise not to be a nuisance, may I call round sometimes . . . take you out and feed you now and then?'

'Why not? We're friends . . . best friends!' she said, smiling at him. 'Of course you may.'

He leaned forward to plant a gentle kiss on her cheek, and then let himself out of the flat.

Fran considered the supper she ought to go and prepare, resisted the temptation to just pour herself another glass of wine instead, and finally telephoned Anita upstairs with an invitation to share her spaghetti Bolognese and a threatening dose of acute melancholia.

Fifteen

Felicity's first effort at keeping in touch arrived the following week: a letter posted not, as Fran had expected,
in New York but from the Connecticut seaboard. Here,
she explained, was where the disabled children she was
working with had been taken to escape the city's summer
heat. There was a wealthy family hinted at as the provider
of the children's escape route, but the letter didn't even
mention the philanthropists by name.

Fran read the letter with growing astonishment. An assortment of children, white, brown and black, from the slums
of New York, sounded the sort of patients Felicity would
normally have gone far out of her way to avoid – it was
a measure of her need to get away that she'd taken the
job at all. But the tone of what she wrote was the really
astonishing surprise: no hint of boredom, regret, or self-pity
– Felly's usual reaction to the taking of another wrong step;
instead, the letter breathed contentment. For the moment, at
least, she was glad to be where she was.

It was a piece of unexpectedly good news to chalk up,
and to share with Richard.

'Not quite Felly's scene, you're thinking,' he suggested
after she'd given him the letter to read. 'A novelty that will
wear off before long?'

Fran shook her head. 'It might be that, but somehow I
don't think so. Her patients up till now have been the sort
of people she imagined she wanted to be among: rich, smart,
and famous – today's celebrities, in fact. The trouble was
that it always turned out that she didn't like them, often

144

reasonably enough! But I think she's discovering that she does like these deprived children. Whether she stays or not, they'll make a difference to her.'

'And she to them,' Richard slowly commented, seeing in his mind's eye the lovely, laughing, generous creature who was Felicity when she was happy. Then he smiled at Fran. 'Now will you promise to stop worrying about her? I think that's what you have been doing. You also work too hard, and you're getting very thin. Dr Weston recommends a holiday – a long lazy break with warmth and beauty guaranteed. What about Amalfi, or some unspoiled Greek island?'

'Are there any left? Anita's just come back from visiting her grandparents, and even lovely Mykonos is getting tarted up and tourist-ridden, she says. I think I'll stay here! Anyway, my weeks in Galicia *were* a sort of holiday; I certainly can't pretend that I was overworked there.'

She regretted the sentence immediately she'd said it; harking back to Cantanzos was as pointless as it was painful, like touching an aching tooth with one's tongue. The time had come to dredge up a cheerful smile instead and move the conversation away from herself.

'Tell me about the book. Will it be finished before a new term starts and you're back in harness again?'

The invitation was all he needed; they'd come full circle to where they'd been before Felicity played havoc with their lives: Fran the patient, intelligent listener, Richard the enthusiastic rider of whatever hobby horse currently absorbed his attention; but there was a difference that she realised very clearly, even if he did not: no love affair, however passionless and uncompetitive, was in prospect now; she couldn't travel backwards to that extent.

Not aware that her attention had slipped away from him, he had to repeat a question he'd asked already.

'Is it such a rotten idea that you don't even want to consider it?'

He sounded a little hurt and she hastily apologised. 'Sorry,

145

Richard; try it on me again. I wasn't quite following what you said.'

His idea, it seemed, was to commission some pen-and-ink drawings to accompany the text of his book. 'You see, Fran, it's not going to be a heavy, academic rehash of thirteenth-century European history, or even a guide to every Romanesque church and chapel along the way from Roncesvalles to Santiago. It's a book about the people who've chosen to become pilgrims and earn the right to wear their cockle-shells – the mixed bag of people who continue to make that choice even now. It's a book for them, as well as for students of history.'

'I think the drawings are a splendid idea,' she said, answering his question at last. 'Will your publisher suggest an artist?'

There was a little pause. 'I thought of suggesting the artist who springs to mind: Juanita! Do you reckon she could do it . . . or would even want to try?'

Fran took time to consider this new question carefully before she answered. '*You*'d have to be the judge of whether she's skilled enough, but I'm quite certain that she'd love to be asked, and it's true that line drawings *are* what she excels at. Richard, write and ask her to send you some trial sketches – better still, ring up; you'll be able to explain better what you want.' From her initial moment of doubt, she was rapidly getting excited by his idea, seeing it as Juanita herself would see it: as a vote of confidence that she still needed.

With the castle telephone number in his pocket, Richard went home promising to report whatever happened next. The following evening he rang to confirm that Juanita had been persuaded at the end of a long conversation to try her hand at sketching in the Plaza del Obradoiro any of the pilgrims who caught her eye. If the trial drawings were successful, the job would be hers.

'Did she sound pleased . . . happy with the idea?' Fran wanted to know.

'She sounded terrified, as a matter of fact, but very pleased as well.' Richard sounded pleased himself, Fran thought, obviously reckoning that a mixture of terror and delight would call forth the best that Juanita was capable of. 'What other news from Cantanzos?' Fran finally felt obliged to ask.

'None to speak of, apparently. Juanita didn't complain, but it can't be very lively for a seventeen-year-old, to be stuck on that windswept promontory, with a grandmother and her middle-aged companion for company. The Count spends a lot of time in Madrid at the moment, and Pascal often has to be away, too, in Oviedo and Bilbao – Esteban's business interests are pretty far-flung, I gather.'

'Don Luis hasn't married the Marquesa yet, I take it? That would certainly have been considered news.'

'No, and Juanita was her customary forthright self about it; the day Inez settles in for good as the new Condesa is the day she reckons to kiss Cantanzos goodbye. It's *todo o nada* with Juanita all right; she either loves you or she hates you.'

'What do you expect? She isn't half Spanish for nothing. The hating *is* thorough, but the loving is also very wholehearted when it comes!'

It was a comment that reminded him of Pascal Vargas: not a typical Spaniard in some ways, but surely wholehearted in loving Fran. He still did, according to Juanita; the Knight of the Doleful Countenance himself had nothing on the quiet, thoughtful businessman Pascal had become. It wasn't an opinion that Richard chose to pass on to Fran; the sooner she forgot the charming, guitar-playing Spaniard, the better. But he felt sadly sure that she hadn't forgotten Pascal yet; more time and *paciencia* were needed before the spell faded. His only hope was slowly, gently to regain the ground he'd lost with her, and convince her in the process that he wasn't a man to make the same mistake twice. The fever that had been Felicity in his blood was over now, as if it had never troubled him at all.

*　　*　　*

A wetter and cooler summer than usual was merging into autumn when Luis Esteban brought his mother back from a visit to Madrid. She looked very tired and pale, but smiled at him when he handed her out of the car.

'Home at last! How very odd for you to hear *me* say that, *querido*, but I shan't want to go away again. I should like to stay at Cantanzos now, please.'

He answered with a little kiss on her cheek and then led her indoors; but later that evening, when she'd been helped to bed, he waited in the firelit salon for Maud Entwhistle to come downstairs.

'She's told me what the consultant said,' Maud began quietly. 'Then I heard what *she* said: no pointless surgery, just to postpone what must happen in the end. It's her choice, my dear, and we have to allow her the dignity of making it.'

He nodded without speaking, and she watched him hold out his hands as if he needed the warmth and brightness of the fire. She knew his age precisely, of course; he'd been a child of ten when she and Marganita had left Cantanzos thirty years before. She knew the huge responsibilities he'd inherited when his father died; but he looked older than years and responsibilities should have made him; she thought sadly that she watched a man who'd forgotten what happiness felt like.

'She wants to stay here,' he said at last. 'I'm very glad about that; it heals a wound that wouldn't ever quite go away. But I think I must find Juanita somewhere to visit for . . . for the next few months – somewhere less sad than we shall be here.'

'She won't go,' Maud insisted gently. 'It took a while for it to happen, but she and Marganita understand one another now. Juanita is older than her years, not surprisingly, and she'd deeply resent not being allowed to help. Marganita will make it as easy for her as she can . . .' Maud's voice broke a little, and she abandoned what else she was going to say.

'Thank God for Richard Weston and the pilgrim route,'

Luis said to fill the silence. 'He seems delighted with the sketches Juanita is sending him.'

'So he should be. Fran was right to say months back that the child could draw, and she's getting better all the time – sharper and more confident. It was her idea to go with Pascal on his present trip. I don't know how much business he's getting done: she set off with a list of places she'd fixed on with Richard to visit!'

Luis pushed a log back into place on the hearth before he spoke again. 'Juanita's letters that she left out to be mailed were still addressed to Miss Francesca Brown. The Professor may be an excellent historian, but no one could call him a forceful lover. Wouldn't you have expected them to be married by now?'

Maud was silent for a moment, but her expression gave away, as usual, what she was deciding she wouldn't say.

'You're struggling not to point out that I'm being very unforceful myself!' Luis suddenly suggested.

It was also so unlike *him* to touch directly on his own affairs that Maud could gauge the extent of his distress about his mother; just for the moment, in the quiet firelit room, his usual defences were down and he needed the relief of talking.

'We're bedevilled by the past, Inez and I,' he went on slowly. 'She can't help seeing herself becoming, as my mother was, starved of the warmth and colour of southern life. Cantanzos for her is something to be endured. For me it *is* my life; I belong here; it's where I'm needed.'

'The irresistible force and the immovable object,' Maud agreed wryly. 'All I can suggest is something that doesn't spring naturally to the Spanish mentality.'

'The old English remedy of compromise!' He smiled at her with deep affection, and then reverted to where the conversation had begun. 'The next few months are going to be hard for you – harder than for anyone else.'

'I'll manage,' she promised. 'I shall even smile, because that's something my dear friend will insist on.'

He nodded, and they both abandoned the painful conversation.

Pascal and Juanita returned the following day, and soon afterwards Inez came back from visiting relatives in France. The household gradually adjusted itself to the knowledge that the Condesa was gravely ill but, with much help from Maud, she managed to insist that life went on normally at Cantanzos. She still made her evening entrance into the salon, elegant and entertaining as ever, and only her companion knew what the effort cost. Juanita's work was inspected and praised, and Pascal was almost always asked to play for them afterwards – more beautifully, Maud thought, than he'd ever played before.

The pretence of normality was hard on all of them, but when Pascal made a suggestion one day that he believed would help, Luis Esteban flatly turned it down.

'I'd agree to a trained nurse; in fact, it's what my mother must have before long. But Francesca Brown isn't that. Her expertise would be of no help to us now.'

'It isn't her expertise Marganita needs; it's Fran herself, someone she trusts completely.'

'She has that in Maud – who'd be deeply hurt, I think, at the idea that anyone else is needed.'

Pascal persevered, for once blind to the opposition clearly visible in Esteban's face. 'I'm *thinking* of Maud – God knows *she* needs help, and Francesca was her good friend.'

'You'll tell me next that the dogs miss Señorita Brown as well,' came the biting reply. 'Why not admit that you're thinking of yourself, too? Stop pining, *amigo*, for a girl who'll end up marrying the Professor as soon as he can spare the time from writing his blasted book.'

White-faced and equally angry, Pascal managed not to shout. 'I'm aware of that. I've nothing to gain myself; Francesca refused what I offered her. For my own peace of mind I'd do better not to see her again, but what's best for me doesn't seem to matter very much at the moment.'

There was a long silence; then Luis leaned over to touch his friend's hand in a little gesture of apology. 'Forgive me, please. It was a monstrous thing to say.' Another silence fell and he carefully arranged some papers on the desk in front of him, as if the task was more important than what he said next. 'The truth is that I don't want Francesca back. She helped Juanita more than we could possibly have expected but . . . but for someone so quiet she managed to disturb Cantanzos quite thoroughly! It's your sister's strong opinion that we're better off without her, and it's mine, too.'

Pascal realised that the heart of the matter had now been reached. In the battle he was fighting to save his own future with Inez, Luis couldn't afford the hostage that Francesca represented. The sleeping arrangements in the tower remained unchanged and Pascal knew why: Luis wanted a wife who would share his life at Cantanzos; he would refuse Inez as a lover until she made up her mind to accept what he offered. The tension between them was fierce and destructive, and it could only end in one of them submitting to the other. Unable to do anything to help, Pascal felt deeply sorry for both of them; it seemed a struggle that could only now occur in this remote part of Spain, between two people of rare principle and pride.

At last he remembered that it was his own turn to say something. 'You're the boss,' he agreed gently, 'but I think you might have to change your mind.'

'There'd be no point in doing so,' Luis said with finality. 'Francesca Brown wouldn't come. She went home feeling, rightly, that she'd been dismissed. I'm ashamed to say that I wasn't even here when she left, to say *vaya con Dios*. I think you can be sure she's had enough of Cantanzos.'

Pascal left the argument there, but a week later the Condesa herself settled the matter. She pushed away the uneaten food in front of her and put out a small, thin hand to touch Maud's arm. 'Dearest, shall we ask Luis to bring back Francesca for a little visit? She'd be a comfort to both of us, I think.'

Pascal watched the strained face of the man sitting opposite him. It seemed to be turned towards Inez, as if insisting that *she* must be the one to speak; but she said nothing at all. More surprisingly, Juanita was equally silent for once, but her large, dark eyes were fixed on her uncle. At last Luis smiled at Marganita, and broke the silence himself.

'Why not?' he said gently. 'We can invite her at least, and see if she will come.'

The following day he asked Pascal to drive to Santiago and board the afternoon flight for London.

Sixteen

It was Anita, climbing to her flat on the top floor, who found a stranger on the point of turning away from Fran's front door. She returned the polite 'Good evening' he offered her and then added something more.

'If you're hoping to call on Francesca Brown, I'm afraid she isn't there.'

'She's away from London at the moment?' The question was quiet but anxious, as if the stranger's visit was urgent. 'You're wondering why I ask,' he went on. 'My name is Pascal Vargas, and I've come from Cantanzos, in Spain, to see Francesca.'

Anita's expression cleared. 'You play the guitar very beautifully, Fran said. She's around, Señor Vargas, but tonight is her choir-practice night; she'll be home about nine.'

'I shall come back then,' Pascal said; but Anita suddenly smiled at him. 'I could offer you a drink and a seat upstairs. Fran would do the same for any friend of mine.'

He accepted the offer with a charming bow and followed her up a flight of stairs to the attic floor.

'It's very charming,' he was quick to say a moment later, looking round the combined kitchen, sitting room and bedroom contrived out of the roof space of the Edwardian house.

'But not much like a castle in Galicia!' Anita pointed out with a grin. 'I heard about that as well from Fran. She found it hard to settle down again in Earls Court Square, and *her* flat's bigger than mine.'

Pascal considered his hostess with the due care that any true-born Spaniard always devoted to a woman – not English, surely, with her black hair and strongly marked features.

'Half-Greek,' Anita confirmed obligingly, 'but London accommodates half-breeds like me very easily.'

'Lucky London,' said Pascal, sounding sincere. 'Have you known Francesca a long time?'

'Since I arrived here, three years ago, and we fell over one another on the stairs one morning; we've been friends ever since.'

'Professor Weston also paid us a brief visit. Are you acquainted with him?'

Anita nodded, but her thick eyebrows drew together in a frown. 'Yes, I know Richard Weston. He comes quite often again now.' Disapproval faintly tinged her voice, but she left the subject there, and busied herself with putting wine and crisps and olives on the table.

They talked easily for a while of Greece, but after a glance at her watch, Anita went to the telephone. Her call was answered and Pascal was able to follow her side of the conversation.

'You're back early, Fran – what a pity! I've got a very nice Spanish visitor up here, but I'm afraid he's really come to see you. I'll send him down – at least, I will if you're all right. You sound a bit odd to me.

'Hoarse from singing too loudly, she says,' Anita explained to Pascal as she put down the telephone. 'It doesn't sound much like Fran to me.'

Then she escorted her guest to the door and sent him down to the floor below.

The door that he'd knocked at earlier now stood open, and Francesca was there . . . not seen for several weary months, but not forgotten in any particular, except that the freckles painted on her skin by sun and sea wind had faded in London's unhealthier air. She was smiling at him but, as her friend upstairs had said, her voice sounded hoarse when she spoke.

154

'It's lovely to see you . . . come in, please. Anita didn't mention who the Spanish visitor was; I thought it might be Juanita who'd taken it into her head to dash over here.'

She thought she was talking too much, but Pascal seemed to find it difficult to say anything at all.

'I didn't know you sang,' he finally managed to remember. 'You kept very quiet about it at Cantanzos.'

'I can warble in tune in a crowd! I don't claim to sing as the Marquesa understands the word.' She looked at the clock on the mantelpiece and then smiled at him. '*You* won't have eaten yet, and nor have I. I can offer you paté, salad and cheese here, or do you need more than that?'

'Of course I need nothing more; but may I not take you out, Francesca?'

She shook her head. 'It's been a longish day and I'd truly rather stay here.' Then she smiled at him. 'But put all thought of the castle dining room out of your mind; we eat in the kitchen here!'

'I like your home,' he said, looking round the pleasant room. 'I envy you those watercolours, especially.'

'They were my father's,' Fran explained. 'He had very little money to spare for his own pleasures, but his eye was keen when it came to spotting something of value. These were painted by an artist called Garman Morris, who rather specialised in these East Coast seascapes. My mother didn't want them, nor did Felicity; so they became mine.'

With their supper laid out in the kitchen, she finally asked the question that occupied her mind.

'How is everyone at Cantanzos? Juanita has been failing as a correspondent recently, but I assume it's because her work on Richard's drawings has kept her very busy.'

'She's well and, as you say, *muy occupado*. We all are, with the exception of the Condesa. She's the reason I'm here, Francesca . . . she is ill, I'm afraid.'

'How ill?' Fran asked quietly, prepared by the sadness in his voice.

'The diagnosis is cancer of the liver. She's chosen to let the disease run its natural course rather than pretend that drugs or surgery could do anything but prolong matters a little. Marganita sees no value in a half-life.'

'No, she wouldn't, of course.' Fran looked at him with eyes full of regret. 'I'm so sorry, Pascal . . . sorry for all of you. Is she with you at the castle?'

'Yes – her other decision is to stay there; it's as if she couldn't leave a second time. Luis finds some comfort in that, I think.'

Fran nodded, certain that he would. 'Poor man, and poor Maud; *she* must be broken-hearted.'

Pascal hesitated over what to say next. 'You haven't asked why I'm here,' he said finally. 'Luis thinks it's a wasted visit because you won't agree; but Marganita is hoping you'll come back to Cantanzos – partly for her own sake, but partly to help Maud as well.'

'Why does Don Luis think I won't agree?'

'Because professionally you don't normally tend dying patients, but also because he has the feeling that you weren't treated well in his home. I know you found him arrogant and autocratic, but it isn't his usual way to be careless of other people. I can't explain what went wrong, except to say that the past months have been a very big strain in one way and another.'

Fran looked across at Pascal's troubled face, seeing in it all the concern and affection he felt for his friend. 'I don't have to be made welcome, by him or by Doña Inez; but I can't come even to help Maud if they really don't want me there.'

'Luis wants whatever will help his mother. Come, please, if you can bear to, Francesca.'

'Then I will,' she agreed. 'It may take a day or two to find someone to fill my place here, but I'll come as soon as I can.'

He let out a long sigh of relief, and then leaned across the table to kiss her cheek. 'Thank you, *mi amor*. I shall fly home tomorrow and wait to hear from you.' Then, in an effort to lighten the atmosphere, he smiled at her. 'I enjoyed meeting your friend upstairs; she reminded me of Juanita – both of them opinionated girls! Was I right to think she reckons Richard Weston has been forgiven too quickly?'

Fran didn't take offence, but she sounded firm. 'Richard only concerns me and my sister. Felicity is truly happy at last, working in New York, while Richard and I are the friends we were long before she appeared on the scene. That's all that anyone else needs to know about us.'

'Put in my place so gently but so firmly,' Pascal commented with a rueful smile. 'It isn't the time to talk about myself, and you mustn't fear that I'll be a nuisance when you're back at Cantanzos. *One* day I shall try to make you understand that, given the chance, I'd take care of you and love you for ever; but for the moment I'll go away and leave you in peace, because you look very tired and sad. I shall go back to the hotel to ring Luis and say that our dear Inglesa is coming home again! *Buenas noches, querida.*'

He left the lightest of kisses on her mouth and then let himself out of the flat before she could even get up to go with him to the door. She heard the slam of the downstairs door, and his voice hailing a taxi outside in the street; then there was only the silence of the flat to listen to, and the confused murmurs in her head. Grief for Marganita and Maud was uppermost, but beneath that aching sadness lay something else that needed to be faced; now, tired as she was, was the moment of truth to end all such moments.

It had been a pathetic little lie to pretend that she'd half-expected to find Juanita at the door. Anita had made it clear that her Spanish visitor was a man. The truth was that it was the Leopard himself who'd come once before; it was he who might have been in London again and decided in passing to deliver something for Richard from Juanita. That possibility had made it hard to speak to Anita on the telephone, and bitter disappointment a moment later had forced her to smile at Pascal like a wound-up doll. He was her dear friend, just as Richard was; either of them would make her a kind and devoted husband, but neither of them would do. That almost unmanageable truth had been hidden in her heart for too long and it was a kind of relief to accept it now. She must face at last the reason why her abrupt departure from Cantanzos had hurt so much.

She was almost certain that the Count didn't want her back, and fully certain that Inez de Castro didn't. She need only remember that and she'd be able to manage well enough. Love fed only on slights and hurts must eventually shrivel and die; no self-respecting heart could go on ignoring such punishment. She might even be well again, sad but cured of madness, by the time she returned to London.

This time it was Juanita's smiling face she could see as she walked out into the foyer of the airport three days later. Then she was being hugged and kissed, and a little wept over as well.

'Oh Fran, I'm so *glad* you're here. Luis made it clear that he thought you'd have had enough of us; but I knew you'd come because we needed you.' She waved to Pepé, standing by the door, to come and collect Fran's luggage, and then they followed him out to the car.

'We'll talk in English,' she muttered, 'then Pepé won't understand. I can't talk about Granny at all; you'll see for yourself how wonderful she is. Maud gets thinner day by day, but she's the one who holds us all together.'

Fran turned to look at the girl beside her, now scarcely recognisable for the sulky, pudding-like adolescent who'd first awaited her at the castle.

'No more losing weight now, *chiquita*; you're quite slender enough.'

Juanita's eyes suddenly filled with tears again. 'I know – even Granny says so.'

Fran held her hand for comfort, but said quietly, 'I've all sorts of messages for you from Richard. He *knew* your sketches were good, but even he was surprised by the publisher's reaction to them. "Illustrations by Juanita Fiocca" will figure boldly on the title page. Richard just manages not to say so, but I can tell he thinks you've chosen the wrong career; anyone can design the strange garments that women choose to wear!'

Juanita's tragic expression gave way to a smile, but only for a moment; then she remembered another cause for grief. 'Imagine it: I actually forgot something awful that you don't know about. It happened the very day Pascal left for London. Do you think *that* could have had something to do with it?'

'I might make a guess, if you tell what it is,' Fran pointed out.

'The thing I've always dreaded: Luis and Inez are planning to marry as soon as possible. It's a very great disappointment; I thought he'd have learned more sense by now.'

'You happen not to like her,' Fran said after a moment spent commanding her voice to sound normal, 'but she's stunningly beautiful, seductive as hell, and talented in more ways than I can call to mind. Your uncle would be a blind fool if he *didn't* want to marry her.'

Juanita turned to her companion, looking unexpectedly sad. 'You left something out. I don't think she'll give him a moment's true peace; my parents always said that's what makes a marriage last.'

'They were right,' Fran admitted, 'but you can't know what the relationship really is between Don Luis and the Marquesa; you're only judging it by the way she affects you. There's one other thing: I'm quite sure the announcement was made to give your grandmother the comfort of knowing that their future is fixed – she's been waiting a long time for that.'

Juanita thought for a moment and then nodded reluctantly. 'I hate to admit it, but it's probably true. She sees Inez as the next Condesa.'

It was a fact to silence them both, and they scarcely spoke

again for the rest of the journey. Pepé turned the car off the road and into the castle drive, but Fran was careful not to look at the carving above the archway, nor at the flag flying above the tower. She had no intention this time of letting Cantanzos wind itself into her imagination; it was going to be just a place that she must stay in for a while and leave again without a backward glance when the time came to go.

Deposited by Pepé at the great front door, she was met by Señora Fernandez, unsmiling still but no longer hostile, and led to the bedroom she'd been given before. The windows were open because the October afternoon was mild, and a nearly high tide beyond the castle wall brought its remembered background noise into the room. For months past, in London, she'd told herself that Cantanzos had been dream-inspired, like Kubla Khan's pleasure-dome at Xanadu. Now she knew what the truth was: her life in London seemed to be the dream-like chimera; the reality was here after all. However, things weren't quite as they'd been before: roses scented the room, to make her welcome, and she smilingly accepted the tray of tea and biscuits that the housekeeper had instructed Constancia to bring. She was unpacking when Maud knocked on her door an hour later, and enfolded her in a most untypical hug.

'Very glad to see you, Fran – and so will Marganita be. I hope it wasn't too unfair to ask you to come.'

Fran shook her head, trying to conceal the shock of seeing Maud's exhausted face. 'I'm just thankful to have been sent for; you look as if you haven't slept for a week.'

'I catnap during the day when Marganita is dozing. She resists all but the bare minimum of drugs, so the nights are the worst times for her. I read to her or we talk, and slowly the hours pass. When daylight returns, she finds courage again. She's the most remarkable woman I've ever met.'

'I think you make a good pair,' Fran said truthfully. 'But we'll share the night watches from now on.'

Maud smiled and didn't protest. 'Juanita wanted to do

that, but she helps during the day, and that's quite enough of an ordeal for her. Luis comes in at night, but I don't let *him* stay too long – he must work all day.' Maud's tired eyes examined the face of the girl who was now leaning against the window sill, watching grey-green sea meet grey-mauve sky on the horizon. 'We missed you when you went away. Did you miss Cantanzos?'

Fran turned and smiled at her. 'Very much, to begin with, but I got over hankering for feudal splendour! Once I stopped bumping into things in my rather small flat, it seemed a cosier place to live in than a medieval castle.' She was silent for a moment, then made the comment that Maud was probably expecting. 'Juanita told me about Don Luis and the Marquesa. I hope Marganita is pleased.'

'She'd have them marry tomorrow if she could; Cantanzos needs something to celebrate, she says. But the world at large wouldn't think it very appropriate, and I don't blame Inez for wanting to wait for a grand affair when the time comes: the setting demands it.'

'Juanita will still be here then, not in Seville. Is that going to work out?'

Maud's haggard face was suddenly lit by a gleam of pure amusement. 'I couldn't understand why Inez had suddenly become my friend and admirer, but finally the penny dropped: she's going to persuade Luis to let Juanita go back to Milan, with me – at a loose end by then – to keep an eye on her!'

'From everyone else's point of view it isn't a bad scheme,' Fran was forced to admit. 'But what about you – would you mind it?'

Maud gave a little shrug. 'I shan't care what I do once Marganita no longer needs me. A scattering of distant cousins aren't enough to draw me back to England. I'd rather help Luis by taking Juanita off his hands, and it pleases me to see her growing more and more like Mercedes day by day.' Maud glanced at her watch. 'I'd better go – siesta-time is over. My poor lamb doesn't eat enough now to make the effort to come down to dinner worthwhile; but she likes to appear afterwards. Pascal plays for us, Inez sometimes sings, and somehow we pretend that life is normal.'

'If the Condesa knows I'm back, perhaps I should come with you to say hello? The sooner she accepts that I'm here to help, the better.'

Maud nodded, and they went down to the floor below together. The Condesa's lamplit room was the enormous one Fran remembered from her previous visits. The ornately canopied bed was empty and she felt a little stab of alarm until a voice faintly called her name. Marganita was lying on a day-bed in front of the fire that flickered in the hearth despite the mildness of the evening.

'Pascal *said* you'd come if he asked you very nicely!' A small, skeletal hand reached out to hold Fran's, and the Condesa's wasted face smiled at her. 'We wanted you back, Francesca.'

'So here I am,' she managed to say steadily. The tears that pricked her eyes had to be blinked away, because there was no place for them here. 'Richard sends his greetings, Doña Marganita – to the lady against whom all other females will be measured in future. Pity the rest of us, please!'

The ghost of the Condesa's old smile lit her eyes for a moment. 'I *was* worth being measured against, it's true. Darling Francesca, take care of Maud for me. Juanita can manage now, thanks to you, and Luis has Inez; but all I've brought Maud is sadness.'

'She wouldn't agree with you. Who would she have had to love but for you and your children?'

Marganita nodded, thinking back over their life together. 'Yes, love *is* the important thing. I ran away from Cantanzos all those years ago because I couldn't bear it here with a husband who didn't love me. With Luis to love her, Inez won't notice the solitude and the Atlantic storms.' The frail voice faded, then grew stronger again. 'Is it all right for you to have left Richard? He doesn't mind waiting?'

'He'll wait,' Fran assured her calmly. 'He's a very patient man.' Then she bent down to kiss the Condesa's cheek. 'I'll leave you with Maud now, but I'll be back later.'

Seventeen

O nly Pascal was in the salon when she went downstairs before dinner. He greeted her with an engulfing hug instead of the formal kiss on each cheek, and then held her at arm's length.

'Thank you for coming, *querida*. We shall be able to manage the next few weeks better now. Even Señora Fernandez has been heard to say that she's quite glad you're back.'

'Damned with faint praise?'

'On the contrary – the lady's greatest compliment! I would have come to meet you this afternoon, but Juanita so clearly wanted to be the one to welcome you that I didn't insist. A gypsy solemnly assured my mother years ago that her son showed signs of having a noble soul! I'm beginning to think it might be true.'

'No doubt of it,' Fran agreed, trying not to smile. 'My father apart, you're the kindest man I've ever known.'

She was being kissed again for the tribute when Inez and Luis Esteban walked into the room. Fran was offered the Marquesa's hand in a brief greeting, and then her glinting smile.

'Good evening, señorita. We must ring a little bell in future to warn you and my brother that you're about to be interrupted!'

'You could have come in sooner without "interrupting" anything very significant,' Fran replied calmly. Then it was necessary to say something to her gaunt-faced host. 'I'm so very sorry about your mother, but glad to share in looking after her.'

'Thank you,' he said, but stayed where he was, just inside the door. There, no touch of the hand need be offered; her arrival back at the Leopard's lair was obviously meant to match her earlier departure from it in terms of warmth and cordiality. She was glad of it; she would soon be able to see him as nothing more disturbing than a nearly-absent host – a man so determined to withdraw himself from any kind of contact with her that he might as well not be there at all.

She was debating whether congratulations on his engagement to the Marquesa would be accepted or ignored when Juanita caused a diversion by ushering into the room a tall, bearded man wearing the black soutane of a Catholic priest. Inez made the necessary introduction; Father Ignatio was now a frequent visitor to the castle, she said.

With the priest at the dinner table, and Maud as well, the conversation was easier than Fran had feared it might be. Pascal's social grace was enough to steer them safely past any shoal that looked threatening, and Inez now had about her the indefinable authority of the hostess, whose duty it was to keep her guests happy. Saying little herself, Fran had ample opportunity to watch; there was a different air about the Spanish woman now. With some long-drawn-out period of uncertainty over, she was entirely sure of herself and sure at last of the tired-faced man who smiled at her from his place at the head of the table. The word 'mistress' inevitably came to mind to describe a beautiful woman who matched her setting so superbly. Fran saw her not only as the mistress of Cantanzos in all but name, but surely already Luis Esteban's lover. There was the conscious awareness of being desired and loved, and even at last an unusual air of contentment. The Marquesa had made her choice and was clearly not regretting it.

Fran watched them, aware that her own indifference to pain was due to the anaesthetising effect of Marganita's illness; when that no longer protected her, she would be free to leave Cantanzos and never come near it again.

With dinner over, Father Ignatio got up to leave. His host

went out with him, and so did Maud; but when they returned, a few minutes later, Luis was carrying the Condesa in his arms, as gently as he might have cradled a wounded bird. Lowered on to a huge sofa, she smiled at them – still making her entrance, still the one the rest of them watched.

'My dears, wasn't it clever of Pascal to lure Francesca back?'

If there'd been going to be an awkward pause, Juanita filled it by walking at once to kneel beside her grandmother. 'She wouldn't stay for us, but she's come back for you, Granny darling; you're the lure!'

Marganita smiled at the vivid face close to her own and, watching them, Fran tried to remember what Juanita in her worst days had once said: that she and her grandmother had agreed not to like each other. They'd both travelled a long way since then.

Without waiting to be asked, Pascal quietly tuned his guitar, then swept his hand over the strings: the Condesa's evening pleasure was about to begin. He looked across at Fran with a questioning smile, but she shook her head. As if the brief exchange had been noticed, Inez went to stand beside her brother, for once not needing to be asked to perform. She chose to sing love songs and she sang them of course for Luis – an open gift to her lover.

Beautiful as it was, Fran longed for the recital to end; the anaesthetic wasn't working after all, and the firelit room held more emotion than she could bear. At last, though, Marganita sent a tiny signal to her son; he kissed the singer's hand, and the recital was over. By the time he returned from carrying his mother upstairs Fran had said goodnight herself, and quietly left the room.

She set her alarm for three a.m., woke and dressed, and went down to relieve Maud. The Condesa, feverish and in pain, accepted some pills and finally slept, holding Fran's hand. Grey dawn light slowly crept into the room, and another long night was over.

Released by Maud's return, Fran walked out into the

damp morning air, heading by sheer force of remembered habit for the tumbled rocks that were the castle's first line of defence against the encroaching sea. Offshore she could see small flecks of white on the grey water, but where she found a place to sit, protected by the wall, there was no wind at all.

Twenty-four hours ago she'd been part of the great, noisy, bustling ant heap that was London; now there was this empty, peaceful world that she seemed to share with no one else at all. It remained so for a moment or two longer; then peace was suddenly shattered as George, always just ahead of Henry, came bounding along the wet sand left by the retreating tide. Their heads went up as she whistled; ears pricked, they saw her perched on her rock and made a dash for their remembered friend. She emerged, distinctly damp from their embrace, to find that it wasn't Pascal who'd brought them out. The taller, leaner figure of Luis Esteban stood waiting for them to calm down.

'They're easily excited, I admit, but you have a deplorable effect on my dogs,' he observed as if it was somehow her fault.

'They have loving natures,' she pointed out, trying to resist Henry's attempt to climb into her lap. 'I missed them very much in London, and we're pleased to see each other.'

He stared down at her, noticing that there was a faint sheen of moisture on her hair, and that George's enthusiastic kiss had left a damp, sandy trace on her nose. She seemed not to care that it was there, although no other woman that he knew would have ignored it. He tried for a moment to imagine Inez sitting there, with one hand stroking the dog's warm fur, but imagination wouldn't carry him that far. He told himself that it was this unemphatic girl who didn't belong, and that his beautiful Marquesa did; but the effort it took made him sound stiff and cold.

'You shouldn't have come back. Pascal had no right to inflict this ordeal on you.'

It confirmed what she thought she already knew; the unyielding man in front of her would have left her unsent for.

'Pascal didn't "inflict" anything,' she said quietly. 'I *chose* to help Maud and Juanita take care of your mother. We can manage the heartbreak better together.' She realised too late that she hadn't mentioned Inez at all, much less his own sadness; but they had each other and could do without her sympathy. The conversation was becoming more of a strain than she could bear, and she cast about desperately for something so banal to say that he would take the dogs away and leave her the empty world again. Her hand gestured to the sea and sky in front of them.

'It looks different from when I was last here – autumnal already. "Summer's lease hath all too short a date," I'm afraid.' That would surely send him away, but he astonished her instead.

'"And every fair from fair sometimes declines,"' he went on calmly, '"By chance, or nature's changing course untrimmed."'

She was betrayed into staring at him, then understanding dawned and made her smile. 'It was Maud, I suppose, who got you learning Shakespeare's sonnets!'

'She certainly introduced us,' he agreed. 'One of the many gifts I have to thank her for.' There was a little pause before he spoke again. 'The doctor who comes to see my mother every few days doesn't commit himself about the . . . the progress of her illness. Are you able to stay? Or perhaps I should ask instead if you can bear to stay until she no longer needs help?'

'Of course I'll stay,' Fran said briefly, 'provided you and Doña Inez don't mind putting up with me.'

She sounded so doubtful that he was forced to smile. 'You aren't as difficult as all that to put up with.' It might have sounded grudging, but it didn't, and she thought for a moment that some kind of truce had been achieved. Then he shattered it again.

'I don't suppose Pascal thought to mention what the agency in London has been told: you're here on the same terms as before. You must be paid for the time you spend here.'

It had been a fine truce while it lasted. Now she leapt to her feet, impelled by the anger running like fire through her body; but beneath its heat was the cold despair of knowing how he really regarded her. She tried to keep her voice steady but failed; she could hear it shaking.

'I had the foolish idea that I was here as the Condesa's friend; but to quote the indispensable Bard again, I'm afraid it was "vaulting ambition" o'er-leaping itself! Thank you for making matters clear. Will the Marquesa let me know if she'd prefer me to eat with the other servants?'

Thoroughly wound up, she might have gone on in this vein, but he suddenly closed the gap between them and clamped his hands on her shoulders. His face was full of anger to match her own, but there was something else that in the danger of the moment she couldn't identify; the word 'desolation' floated in the turmoil of her mind, but of all the words she could have found it seemed the most unlikely.

'I'd *shake* some sense into you if it would do any good,' he shouted, 'but my stupid dogs would think that I was hurting you.'

'They'd be right,' she answered fiercely. 'You *have* hurt me. It's an old Spanish custom that I ought to be getting used to by now. Before we end this conversation, there's one more thing to say: I absolutely refuse any payment for the time I stay here – it's my gift to Marganita. Whatever you send to London will be returned.'

She had no idea what would happen next; Spanish male pride was a formidable thing and this particular Spaniard had it in spades, as today's expression went. A dagger in her heart, perhaps; or a seat booked on the next flight back to London? They came to the same thing, more or less. But what did happen was much more unlooked for. As if anger and the threat of violence had never

been, the corners of his mouth lifted in a smile, rueful
and sweet.

'Oh, Francesca, what am I going to do with you?' His
hands released their grip on her shoulders and gently framed
her face instead. 'Could you, please, stop being Britannia
on the warpath for a moment and listen to what *I* have to
say? Hurting you just now was the thing furthest from my
intention. What you are doing for us here *can't* be paid for;
but at least I must ensure that you aren't losing what you'd
be earning in London. Is that something to berate me for
like . . . like a Galician fishwife cheated out of a bargain!'

She shook her head, still sure of having been wrongly
treated, but wanting to weep as well for the effort he was
making to mend her hurt, like a parent trying to kiss a
wounded child better. It was a side of the Leopard not
seen before and scarcely guessed at, given his own bleak
childhood once Marganita had run away.

'Do what you want,' she said tiredly at last. 'It doesn't
matter now.' All that did matter was to bring this conversation to an end and have him go away. 'The poor dogs
were expecting a walk, and it's time I joined Juanita for
breakfast.'

He released her, but brushed the grains of sand off her
nose with gentle fingers. 'Very becoming in an odd sort
of way!'

She smiled because he seemed to want her to, but still he
didn't move away.

'Forgive me for hurting you in the past, Francesca. It's
too difficult to explain – in fact, so impossible that another
of your poets will have to help me out:

> I will but say what mere friends say,
> Or only a thought stronger;
> I will hold your hand for as long as all may,
> Or so very little longer.'

Then, as if this was how they normally conversed together

or passed the time of day, he smiled faintly and walked away with the dogs loping beside him.

Fran sat down on her rock again, because her trembling legs wouldn't support her. She wouldn't think about Browning's poignant words, except to insist to herself that a man who liked to disconcert her had quoted them for no other reason at all. With that effort made, she just sat watching the slow ebb of the tide until the dampness of the morning seeping through her sweater made her shiver. Then she got up and walked back to the castle.

A routine established itself that would see them through the difficult days and nights to come. After breakfast with Juanita, Fran would try to sleep for an hour or two; then they'd go walking or shopping together. After lunch she'd change places with Maud in the Condesa's room, and Juanita would be there as well to show her grandmother some new sketches, or the progress she was making with her guitar. Maud returned to the sickroom after dinner, and Fran took her place at that dead hour of the night when the human heart was 'sore in doubt concerning spring' or any other sign of hope. Sometimes Marganita was too drugged to do anything but drift in and out of a shallow, restless sleep, and Fran sat holding her hand, watching the strange shadows thrown by the fire's flickering light. More often she was awake and asking to be read to, or wanting to talk. It was the distant past she talked about, the time when she'd first come to Cantanzos as a bride.

'I wasn't in love with my husband,' she murmured sadly, 'but the Montillas were poor as church mice, so everyone said it was a splendid match. It wasn't a "match" at all, of course, and the castle I'd begun by thinking so romantic became a prison in the end.' She lay quiet for a moment, listening to the wind that was rising outside with the incoming tide. 'I hated that sound then, but the strange thing is that it doesn't frighten me now at all. Does it you?'

Fran smiled, shaking her head. 'No – I rather like the idea of the wind prowling round these immense walls. Anyway, it isn't Nature's unkindness that frightens me; it's the cruelties that people inflict on each other. If you feel the same way, you can't possibly be frightened here: everybody loves you too much.'

Marganita's smile shone for a moment. 'Thank you, dear Fran, but I'm not sure that's true of Father Ignatio. He does his best, poor man, but he can't help thinking that repentance has come rather late in my case!' Her voice faded into silence and Fran was just thinking that she'd fallen into a doze when her faint voice came again. 'I was a worse mother than I was a bad Catholic, but Luis hasn't stopped loving me.'

'Nor have the Virgin Mary and her Son,' Fran promised gently. 'Father Ignatio knows that as well as we do.'

Marganita gave a little nod, but her eyes were suddenly full of tears. 'I did want to see Luis's children before I died . . . I wanted to see *him* completely happy . . . oh, I wanted so many things that I'm not going to have.'

Unable to answer, Fran bathed her flushed face and then sat stroking her hair until she slept again, and slowly the faint light of another dawn filtered into the quiet room.

The weeks that followed grew wild with wind and rain. To walk along the castle wall was to invite being blown off, and the rocks below them seemed to be always drenched in spray. Even Marganita's rose garden wasn't sheltered enough to stay out in for long, as one storm after another drove in from the Atlantic and the days scarcely seemed to grow light at all.

Luis and Pascal worked as usual, and came and went about their affairs, but it was Pascal now who under-took anything that required a night away from the castle. Immersed in the final stages of the Condesa's illness, Fran was scarcely aware of either of them, or of the woman who was to fill Luis's life in future. Looking at his ravaged face across the dinner table, it was enough to pray that in easier times to come Inez would be able to make him happy.

Her own life and Maud's now revolved round the doctor's visits and Marganita's failing attempts to remain herself; but the truth was that the disease was in control, and they only wanted for her the release that would come with its victory.

On a morning quieter than most, with a rising sun for once painting a line of gold on the eastward sky, Fran was able to walk out on to the castle wall again. The cold, salt air tasted wonderful after the overheated room she'd just left, and the sea splashed gently against the rocks, pretending that this playful mood was the only one it knew. She walked for a long time but finally turned to retrace her steps in time to see someone – Pepé probably – outlined against the sky on the top of the tower. She stood still, not needing to be told what his purpose was there. The Leopard's flag was being lowered; the bright, laughing, valiant woman who'd become her friend was dead.

Eighteen

The following days were sad and unsettling. Even Señora Fernandez was red-eyed from weeping, and Marilar burst into tears in the middle of serving a dish that the Condesa had particularly liked. Luis Esteban dealt with the formalities of death, but it was Inez who took charge of the needs of the living. Calm amid the confusion, she ran the household and dealt with an unceasing stream of visitors; efficient, composed and elegant, she was the perfect helpmate to an overdriven man.

'We ought to feel nothing but admiration,' Fran observed to Maud Entwhistle one afternoon when they were safely out of earshot. 'I'm afraid it says something about *us* that we find her harder and harder to bear.'

'It's mutual,' Maud answered with a certain relish. 'I've known Luis longer than she has and know more about him than she does; that's the black mark against *me*. I'm not quite sure what yours is. I'd like to think that she scents competition, but it can't be that. He pays more attention to an ancient of days like me than he does to you.'

Fran's brief nod said that this was true, before she offered an alternative. 'She's probably got a rich, well-connected wife lined up for Pascal and fears that he has the poor taste to prefer me!'

Distracted for a moment from the matter in hand, Maud stared at her curiously. 'Could you marry him if it meant living here with Luis and Inez?'

'Even if it didn't mean that, the answer's no, I'm afraid,' Fran said firmly. 'It's a great pity, because I'll never meet a

174

nicer man, and at going-on thirty-one I can scarcely afford to be choosy!' She smiled at her companion and deflected the conversation from herself. 'What about you? No wrong decisions ever made, no regrets?'

'There weren't any decisions to make. The only man I *would* have married chose someone else, not unreasonably. She was very pretty and biddable, and he could see from a mile off that I wasn't either of those things. Anyway, by then my path had crossed Marganita's and I knew where I was needed.'

'You may still be needed – to provide Juanita's escape route from Cantanzos. Will you go to Milan with her?'

'If Luis asks me, yes. On the other hand, if Inez tells me sweetly what my instructions are, I shall probably say no. There's Christian humility and grace for you!'

'I'd call it proper pride, and you're entitled to that,' Fran pointed out. 'I try to remember that Marganita wanted her for a daughter-in-law, but I can't forgive her for squeezing Juanita out of her uncle's life as she now does. It's touch-and-go whether she can restrain herself from asking me to leave before the funeral. One mourner the less wouldn't matter, but I'm ignoring the hints for Juanita's sake. She's lost parents and grandmother within a year and a friend the less for her now does matter.'

Maud nodded, still thinking of something else Fran had just said. 'Marganita wanted Inez here because she set a high value on beauty and style, and the woman has both, we're bound to agree; but what she hasn't got is generosity. All the years I've known her she's made me aware – as only a supremely seductive woman can – that I was the most pathetic of God's creations, a plain and totally undesirable female! It strikes me as funny now, but it hurt when I was half my present age.'

Maud's transforming smile rearranged the angularities of her face, but before Fran could say that the man who'd passed her by had been a fool, the conversation was inter-rupted by Juanita coming to catch them up. Because of the weight she'd lost, she looked taller now, an elegant, slender figure in her dark overcoat. Her face had thinned down too, increasing the resemblance to her mother in the photographs Fran had seen of Mercedes Fiocca. She looked older than her seventeen years – not quite a woman yet, but unrecognisable for the surly, unresponsive adolescent of their first meeting.

'There's no one to talk to indoors,' she said rather forlornly. 'Everyone's busy except me, getting rooms ready. Some relatives from Seville are due to arrive, Señora Fernandez says – Montilla relatives of Granny's.'

'They're your relatives as well, in that case, *chiquita*,' Fran pointed out thoughtfully. 'It seems to me that *you* ought to go and welcome them – Doña Inez can't be left to do it all, can she?'

The innocent query brought a grin to Maud's face, but it took a moment for Juanita to perceive the message. Then, for the first time since Marganita had died, her own expression brightened.

'Granny would have wanted me to help – of course she would.' She beamed at both of them, and then marched back towards the courtyard.

'A declaration of war, I think, and quite right too,' said Maud when she was out of range. 'Don't worry about her, if that is what you *are* doing now; for all that Mercedes looked so beautiful, there was some of the old Count's steel in her, and Juanita has inherited it as well.'

'Even so, it's an unequal contest,' Fran pointed out, 'between her and the Marquesa.'

'But not between her, supported by *Luis*, and the Marquesa.' Maud shot a sudden glance at Fran's face. 'You look unconvinced. You should have more faith in him. Besotted with Inez he may be, but that doesn't stop him thinking clearly about other people.'

It was Fran's regretful conclusion that it did, but she wasn't minded to argue with the woman beside her who, in a different way, was just as besotted about *him*.

'We'd better go back, I suppose,' she said instead. 'I've promised to visit Marilar's mother, who has a bad back, and when I get there I confidently predict that she'll suggest three other people with aches and pains that I ought to be able to do something about.' She smiled at Maud, but then suddenly reverted to the beginning of their conversation.

'I know that Juanita shouldn't have to be your problem, but I can't see any happy future for her here. I'd suggest inviting her to London, but what she longs to do with all her heart is to go home to Milan, and live there with Graziella and Giorgio – to take care of *them* in fact. But she can't quite do that yet on her own.'

Maud's capable hand descended on Fran's shoulder and gave it a brief pat. 'Stop worrying and leave her to me. I'm twice your age, with no exciting life of my own about to blossom in front of me. If you really can't see your way to marrying Pascal, you must go home and put the Professor out of his misery. I'd say he's been a very patient man!'

Fran agreed that he had, and on that amicable note they walked back the way they'd come, in time to see unfamiliar cars parked in the courtyard, and Pepé busy unloading luggage. They went in by a side door so as to avoid the bustle in the hall, and it wasn't until Fran returned from her visit to Marilar's home in the early evening that she had any inkling that a storm was brewing.

She'd barely walked into her bedroom when there came a tap at the door. The maid stood there, looking anxious even when Fran smiled at her.

'It's all right, Marilar; I think I've made your mother feel more comfortable, but I'll check up on her again tomorrow.'

Muchas gracias were murmured, but still Marilar hovered, and began hesitantly to explain that the Marquesa had been in '*mal humor*' at not being able to find the *señorita inglesa*. Fran got the impression that Marilar would have liked to suggest that she hide in a cupboard until the storm had passed, but didn't quite have the nerve for it.

'If the Marquesa asks again, you can say that I'm back,' Fran suggested calmly. 'But I shall see her later on in any case.'

She smiled in order to send the maid away looking more cheerful, but closed the door behind her suddenly, reminded of her conversation with Maud. If Inez was about to suggest another absence from the dining room for the two Inglesas, it would be a piece of pettiness that even Maud would find it hard to smile at. Unlike Fran herself, she probably knew the visitors from Seville as well as the Marquesa did, and would have found comfort in talking to them about Marganita.

Half-anticipating Marilar's return with another message or a pre-dinner visit from Juanita, it was a more unwelcome surprise to find Inez at her door when she'd just finished changing into her usual evening rig of skirt and fine cashmere sweater. The Spanish woman walked in uninvited and closed the door, a studied impertinence that made Fran's dislike of her suddenly boil over.

'You could have sent a servant to tell me not to appear in the salon this evening. I assume that *is* what you've come for?' Hostility was out in the open at last and she was glad of it; but they could meet on equal terms now, because she'd come back to Cantanzos as the Condesa's friend, not as Luis Esteban's hired servant.

'What I've come to say is this,' Inez answered coldly. 'You've outstayed your usefulness, Miss Brown, and I see no point in your remaining beyond tomorrow morning. By all means intrude on a family gathering this evening if you get pleasure from doing so, but don't stay beyond tomorrow, please. My brother will make the arrangements for your journey home.'

Sickened by the venom in the other woman's face, Fran swallowed the bitter taste of nausea in her throat and managed to speak calmly.

'I shall miss the Condesa's funeral if I leave tomorrow. Does Don Luis know what you're suggesting?'

The Marchesa's triumphant smile warned her of what was

coming next. 'Don Luis didn't want you to come at all; he won't in the least object to your leaving.'

It was true, Fran knew; the damned woman could smile because she was on firm ground now, and the only comfort left was to deny her the sweetness of seeing how much it mattered.

'I'll leave tomorrow then,' Fran agreed, hoping to suggest that it would be something of a relief to go. She stared at the beautiful face in front of her, shocked by her own desire to hurt its perfection in some way. Too much time spent in Spain was having a disastrous effect on her. Emotions that she scarcely recognised in herself were under control, but only just, and this all-or-nothing land would destroy her altogether if she stayed in it much longer.

'Juanita will expect to be told why I'm leaving before the funeral,' she decided to point out. 'I shall say what could be taken to be the truth – that I'm unable to stay any longer. At least she'll be angry with *me*, not you, whom she has to continue to live with.'

'Not for much longer, probably.' The Marquesa's eyes sparkled with hostility. 'It was you, I suppose, who encouraged her to behave as if she owned Cantanzos this afternoon when her uncle's guests arrived. Even Maud Entwhistle doesn't have quite your gift for interference in matters that don't concern her, but perhaps she'll be the next one to tell us what we ought to do.'

'If Juanita has annoyed you, it's probably my fault. She's deeply upset by her grandmother's death so soon after losing her parents, and it seemed to me that it would help her to be allowed to share the grief she feels – with her uncle and with her other relatives. She *needed* to be doing something for them.'

'She merely managed to embarrass them by trying to humiliate me.' Inez shrugged her slender shoulders. 'Well, the silly incident is over now and forgotten, and you and I have cleared the air between us – a relief for both of us, I think. I shall say *adiós*, Miss Brown.'

'Not quite, perhaps,' Fran said steadily. 'I shall take my usual place at the dinner table this evening, and I expect Maud will want to do the same.'

The Marquesa's brilliant, unamused smile was like the flick of a fencer's rapier against her skin. 'Until this evening then.'

A moment later she'd left the room, and Fran leaned against the closed door, too exhausted to feel anything but the futility of what she'd tried to do. Inez was quite right: she'd certainly outstayed her usefulness; but there was one last effort to make, and she pulled herself together sufficiently to go to the room next door.

Juanita had been weeping; there were tear-stains on her cheeks and her eyes were red.

'It's all my fault,' she said tragically. 'You're being sent home because of me. Inez and I had a set-to once the guests were safely out of the way. When she said I was being ridiculous, pretending I was important here, I got so angry that I shouted at her – told her what you'd said: that Granny's relatives were mine, not hers. At the time it was worth it to see her face, but I'm so sorry now, Fran.'

'Darling, it doesn't matter; I should have left very soon anyway.' Fran gave her a little hug and then tried to smile at her. 'She and I had a little set-to as well – pointless as quarrels always are, but I wanted to make sure she knew who to blame. You can't fight with her all the time: you still live here; and you must also think of your uncle. *He*'s grieving for Marganita too, and the last thing that would seem bearable to him now is to have to live with women who have different claims on him fighting each other.'

'Yes, I realise that,' Juanita agreed quietly. 'Inez does, too – she said something about me going back to Milan. I know it's only because she wants to get rid of me, of course, but I don't care as long as I can go home. Fran, you'll come and stay, won't you . . . you do *promise*?'

'Yes, I promise.' She smiled more easily this time, knowing that Juanita would be able to manage now. 'Bathe your eyes, *chiquita*, and look cheerful. I've foolishly insisted on going down to the salon with the rest of you, just to show the flag! But I shall need your help and Maud's if I'm not to fall to pieces and weep into the soup, like poor Marilar the other evening!'

Juanita's ravaged face broke into a smile that the Condesa would have recognised as inherited from Mercedes.

'Of course you won't fall to pieces. Maud and I will see to it that you don't, *amiga*.'

Nineteen

Of the evening that followed Fran found that she was left with only visual memories. What she or anyone else said faded into oblivion, but pictures remained in her mind's eye and they all seemed to include Inez, beautiful in her mourning black, smilingly attentive to the guests, and beyond any doubt at all the castle's undisputed hostess. Fran watched from an observation post halfway down the table and understood Luis Esteban's intention that the evening should make something clear to everybody there: the Marquesa, soon to change her name and rank to his, was the star he wished to see shine. In order that *she* might scintillate and dazzle and bewitch, he would minister quietly to his guests but offer Inez no competition. Fran doubted if it was something he could maintain for very long – the position of second fiddle wasn't his natural one – but for the moment, obviously, Inez was to be made to feel indispensable, to him and to Cantanzos.

There was no music afterwards in the salon when the long meal ended, only the subdued conversation that seemed appropriate among people brought together for a funeral. Fran took refuge with Maud and an elderly man, introduced to her as Juanita's great-uncle, who proved pleasantly easy to talk to; but when he was greeted by someone else, she was able to explain to Maud that this was her last evening at Cantanzos.

'A rather futile gesture of defiance,' she said wryly. 'I should have done better to waive my right to a seat at the dinner table!' She smiled at her friend, but Maud thought

182

it was the saddest smile she'd ever seen. 'Say goodbye to Marganita for me, and keep Juanita out of trouble with the Marquesa if you can. The idea of going back to Milan has been mooted, I think, and it might be enough to keep our firebrand reasonably docile!'

Maud smiled rather grimly. 'Docile – Juanita? I doubt it, my dear. I'd offer to do my best, but intentions and effects always seem to contradict each other! We encouraged Juanita to assert herself this afternoon, and the result of that is to have to watch Inez in this evening's starring role. I'm afraid I was wrong: the contest isn't Inez versus Juanita *and* Luis after all.'

'How could it be,' Fran suggested, 'when he's longing to marry Inez as soon as he can? And, hate her as I do, it's easy enough to see why.' She drew in a sharp breath – a gasp of pain, it sounded to Maud – but went on calmly. 'I can't bear farewell scenes, so I'll say goodbye now. Even if we don't manage to keep in touch, I shan't forget the past few weeks we've shared here.'

'Nor I,' said Maud, 'but we will keep in touch, never fear.'

Fran's fingers touched her friend's cheek in a little gesture of affection, and then she nodded towards the door. 'Discreet exit time for me; I've had as much of this evening as I can bear, and I've got packing still to do. *Adiós, amiga!*'

She went unobtrusively towards the door, in case the Count should notice and intercept her; but she needn't have worried. No one, least of all the Leopard, seemed anxious to keep her there.

A note from the Marquesa had been placed on her dressing table: Pascal had volunteered to take her to the airport, and they would need to leave at eight o'clock. Constancia would bring her an early breakfast, and Pepé would deal with her luggage. The Señorita was to take with her the Count's thanks for her services, and their joint good wishes for her future success.

Fran tore the note into small pieces and threw them into

the waste-paper basket. Then she dragged herself back and forth across what seemed to be the ever-increasing spaces of the room, collecting clothes and books and oddments and flinging them into suitcases. Nothing registered now except the weight of tiredness that she struggled with. There was no pain and no despair – just the fog of exhaustion in which she moved slowly about the room, occasionally blundering into things; but when she finally fell into bed, she lay awake, listening to the sounds of wind and sea that she was hearing for the last time. She slept at last, and only woke to the urgent pinging of the alarm clock beside her bed, and Constancia's knock at her door.

The late-November morning was barely growing light when she went downstairs. Pascal's car was waiting in the courtyard, but only Pepé was there, stowing her luggage in the boot. He didn't smile even now, but his grip on her hand was warm and firm as he wished her a safe journey back to London. She was left alone to wait for Pascal to arrive, thankful that there was no one she had to talk to. It was enough just to be able to stand there, quietly taking leave of a place she wouldn't see again.

Then a side door opened, but instead of Pascal it was Luis Esteban who walked towards her. The farewell scene she'd most needed to avoid was upon her after all. Her heart began to beat uncomfortably fast and she hid her hands in the pockets of her coat, but now her own distress suddenly seemed unimportant. Even in the dim light she could see the lines etched into his brown face by the strains and stresses of the past months. He looked beyond the reach of the comfort that anyone else might offer; temperament and the code in which he'd been reared insisted that whatever was to be endured must be dealt with privately. However, if she was to say anything at all, it must be said now.

'The road to hell is paved with good intentions,' she murmured sadly. 'I wanted to help Juanita but only made things worse. I should also have stayed out of everyone's way last night; it was a silly piece of bravado to insist on coming downstairs.'

Was it a glimmer of a smile that touched his mouth? It came and went so quickly that she couldn't be sure.

'Any more confessions, Francesca? Or are those all the sins you can own up to?'

She shook her head, silenced by the gentleness in his deep voice. It was a note she'd heard once before when, instead of being angry with her, he'd quoted Browning's lovely lines.

'It doesn't occur to you to chide *me* for ingratitude . . . for letting you go like this again after all that you've done for us?'

She had to find something to say that would make Inez's behaviour seem justified and reasonable; it had to be done for *his* comfort. 'I came both times to be useful, but now there's nothing more to do. It's the right moment to go home, knowing that I can leave Juanita to you and Maud.'

He stared at her, noting for the last time the things to be remembered about her – the things that had to be noticed before they could imprint themselves on memory, because they didn't clamour for a man's attention or insist on being admired. He hadn't ever touched her hair, but he knew that it would feel like silk against his fingers. Were her eyes more green than hazel, or was it the other way round? It seemed unbearable that he would never now be able to decide.

'Pascal very much wanted you to stay,' he said abruptly. 'It's a great pity that Richard Weston had a prior claim before you came here first of all; but our lives depend on timings, and most of them, I'm afraid, we manage to get wrong.'

She lifted her hands in a little gesture that said she didn't know quite what – yes to Richard's claim, per-haps he'd take it as. Then, in answer to her unspoken prayer, Pascal came hurrying out to join them, seeming to bustle untypically instead of being his usual laid-back self.

185

'Time to go, Francesca, unless we are to miss the flight and I'm allowed to bring you home again.'

She could even smile at him. 'Home is London, not here, so let us not miss the flight, please.' Now came the difficult bit: to put out her hand and have Luis's fingers close hard around it. 'I shan't forget Cantanzos,' she said hoarsely. 'Say goodbye to George and Henry for me.'

'*Vaya con Dios*, Francesca!'

The lovely, grave farewell was as much as she could bear. She turned blindly towards the car door that Pascal held open for her, and got in. A moment or two later they had turned under the last archway on to the Santiago road, and the tears she could do nothing about trickled warmly down her cheeks and clogged her throat.

Pascal said nothing, and simply conveyed his weeping passenger as if this was the way a woman sitting beside him normally behaved. At last Fran mopped her face, and prosaically blew her nose – a gesture so firmly unromantic that it made him glance at her and smile. She was about to apologise for being a trying passenger when he suddenly steered the car off the road into a deserted lane and cut the engine.

'I can't drive and talk at the same time,' he explained quietly, 'and we shan't have another chance to talk. I haven't been able to work out why you wouldn't marry me – you like me well enough, I think; and you aren't in love with Richard Weston, I'm fairly sure. But this morning I finally understood: it's Luis, isn't it? I couldn't miss the pain in your face when you got into the car.'

She sat silent for a moment, aware that she couldn't lie to him, but deeply reluctant to confess the truth instead.

'It isn't something I can't manage, but he gets in the way,' she admitted at last. 'That's why no other future I'm offered seems as if it will quite do. I'm hoping to grow out of it in time – which is what we say at home to small girls with a painful tendency to spots and hero-worship!'

'But you're not a small girl,' Pascal pointed out gently.

'That *is* a problem,' she had to agree. She'd sounded forlorn, she feared, and went on more firmly. 'If we happen to meet in a few years' time, we shall be able to laugh at the muddle we're in now. Luis and Inez will have settled down happily together at Cantanzos, you will have found a charming Spanish lady to marry, and I shall probably have done what was intended long ago and become Richard's wife!'

Pascal saw no point in saying that he had little faith himself in the predictions she'd just mentioned, least of all the one that ought to seem most likely. He hadn't only seen Francesca's face that morning; he'd seen his friend's as well. Luis Esteban had long been committed to another woman and there could be no going back on that. Codes of behaviour had changed elsewhere, but not in this remote and fiercely conservative corner of Spain. Luis would marry Inez for sure, but their happiness together was much less certain.

'Do you regret having come here?' Pascal asked suddenly. 'Would you have come if you'd known what was going to happen?'

'I think so,' she answered after a moment's hesitation. 'Yes, I'd always have wanted to help Juanita, and to know the Condesa and Maud.' She put out her hand to touch Pascal's in a little gesture of affection. 'I would have hated not knowing *you*. Meeting *el gran Condé* has been education rather than pleasure! I may be less satisfied in future with what I'm allowed to have, but at least I now know what the possibilities for happiness really are; I was a long way from having discovered them before.'

'You could say that of all of us,' Pascal said wryly, 'and it only goes to show that education is a dangerous thing! I was perfectly content for years, flitting along the surface of a very pleasant life; nothing about it had to be taken very seriously so nothing hurt. Look at me now, *querida*: serious *and* hurt!

He smiled as he said it so that she wouldn't need to feel guilty, but she couldn't be reassured as easily as

187

that; for his unhappiness she knew that she *was* responsible.

'I'm sorry,' she murmured huskily. 'Promise me you'll keep looking for the Spanish lady.'

He made no promise but leaned over to kiss her mouth instead. 'First things first, sweetheart; at the moment it's your flight to London we have to look for, and now I must concentrate on getting you to the airport.'

Two hours later, with the formalities of departure finally completed, the security checks survived, and the waiting about endured, she was loaded with the other passengers into an Iberia flight for London. There was the usual exhilarating roar along the runway, then the climb through swathes of grey cloud into the serene, empty blueness of the sky above. There was nothing she need do or remember; no pain she had to feel. For as long as she could stay up above the world, she was quite safe.

The sky over London was clear for once, tinged with the pink afterglow of a fine winter day. Santiago had been shrouded in rain when she left. Here the shop windows were beginning to look festive, a reminder that Christmas wasn't far away. She hadn't noticed the weeks slipping past at Cantanzos; time had played tricks with them, dragging or racing by according to the erratic final stages of Marganita's illness. But then castle life itself had been *full* of contradictions; serenity and turmoil there went easily hand in hand.

Her own flat, when she let herself into it, seemed stale and unused, even though Anita had been kind enough to water the plants and forward her mail. For the moment her own imprint on it had vanished; it required an effort to remember that here – this pleasant, small space – was her home. She sank into an armchair, aware that her feeling of isolation was the only important thing to struggle with. The sounds she could hear outside were London sounds; the interrupted life that she must stitch together would have no further connection with the sea-washed

walls of Cantanzos or the people who belonged inside
them.

She was surprised to find that the knowledge wasn't
painful; a certain degree of tiredness brought with it a
blessed euphoria. Without intending to do anything about
them, she could sit and vaguely consider the suitcases she
ought to unpack, the calls needing to be made, and even the
food she should go out and buy.

At last, stirred out of her trance of exhaustion, she climbed
the stairs to knock on Anita's door.

'Well hello!' said her friend, smiling but surprised. 'Did
I know you were coming back? Have I forgotten some
important telephone call?'

'You didn't know, because I only knew myself yesterday
evening, and I left Cantanzos early this morning.'

'Come in and tell me the story,' Anita insisted. 'But first
I'll pour you a glass of wine. You look as if you need it.
There's a *triste* air about you, as the French say. Sit down
while I get supper – I know there's nothing in *your* fridge.
What will you have, by courtesy of Marks and Spencer and
the microwave: chicken Kiev or chilli con carne?'

Fran smiled at her. 'One of these days, so help me, I'll
teach you how to cook! Meanwhile I'll have the chicken,
if it's all the same to you.' She sipped the wine that Anita
had poured, and considered what to say next.

'Start at the beginning,' her friend advised, as she came
to sit down at the kitchen table. 'The lovely Spaniard I
reluctantly sent down to you lured you back to that strange
place. What happened next?'

Fran briefly described the days and nights shared with
Maud in the Condesa's sickroom; it was easier to speak of
Pascal's recitals in the salon after dinner, and the pleasure
of seeing the affection that Juanita and her grandmother had
shared before it was too late. 'So it wasn't all sadness,' she
finished up. 'In fact, it was a privilege to know Marganita,
well or ill; she was one of those unique people you only
meet once in a lifetime.'

189

Anita nodded, then pointed out that the résumé hadn't mentioned the Count or Inez de Castro – both no doubt present while Marganita had gradually been dying.

'They were there, of course,' Fran agreed, 'but I saw very little of either of them. Their marriage is going to take place as soon as Cantanzos settles down again after the funeral.'

'So is that the end of your little excursion into Spanish high society? Or will you be invited back for the wedding?'

'The Marquesa would have to be desperate for guests to invite me,' Fran said with heroic calm. 'I left more suddenly than expected at *her* suggestion – she thought I was a bad influence on Juanita!'

'The woman must be mad. My guess is that she doesn't want you as a sister-in-law, though why that should be so I can't imagine.' Anita frowned at what she was eating and then repeated her question in a different way. 'No more visits to Cantanzos, then, since my impression is that you *aren't* going back to marry Pascal – something else I can't understand, by the way!'

'Nor I, when he's so very nice! But no, I shan't go back. I've promised to stay in touch with Juanita, but that will be when she gets back to Milan with Maud.'

Anita got up to make coffee and brought it to the table before delivering her final thought on the subject. 'I'd refuse any more work in Spain, if I were you, Fran dear; there's something about the place and the people that's much too unsettling.'

Not sure whether to laugh or burst into tears, Fran managed simply to agree that her friend was right; she'd stay well clear of the Iberian peninsula in future. Then she thanked Anita for her various acts of kindness and took herself back downstairs. Now she needed to do nothing but go to bed; tomorrow would be soon enough to let Richard know that she was home, to contact the agency, and to assure Felicity that there was nothing to stop her returning to London whenever she wanted to. The best part of a year had been used up since she'd walked into the

Connaught Hotel and met a man called Luis Esteban; it was long enough to have been involved in his very Spanish drama. Francesca Brown was on course again now, with her back firmly turned to *todo-o-nada* land, and her heart more or less under control.

Twenty

Her friends at the agency were pleased to see her back, and Richard Weston made no attempt to hide his relief, though it fell short, she told him, of her choirmaster's joy at seeing her in the front row of the sopranos again – they'd lacked her steadying influence, apparently.

'It's a serious matter,' she said when he looked unconvinced, 'a pre-Christmas performance of *"The Messiah"* in the town hall is going to stretch us to the utmost – if not even a little beyond!'

Richard smiled at her lovingly. 'Darling Fran, you're being very bright and brave, but you don't have to try so hard for my benefit. Admit you've had a gruelling time at Cantanzos – something they had no right to inflict on you. It needs recovering from.'

She knew that what he said was much more true than he realised, but he was wrong as well; and the assumption that she needed to 'recover', as if from some painful disease, she found very irritating.

'Nothing was inflicted on me that I didn't choose to accept,' she said sharply, stung by a sudden memory of insisting on the same thing to Luis Esteban. For a moment he was vivid in her mind's eye as he'd said goodbye, gently instructing her to 'go with God'. Instead of *him* looking at her there was only this man: kind, well-meaning, inadequate Richard; but her glance at him discovered that he was also looking hurt.

'No need to snap, sweetheart,' he suggested. 'I was only trying to help, and you're more tired than you realise.'

'Sorry – I didn't mean to sound cantankerous; it's the pre-Christmas frenzy that makes me ill-tempered. I swear I heard "Jingle Bells" played seven times today!' She smiled at him with deliberate cheerfulness, but something was wrong, he felt certain; or at least something about her was different, and he blamed the change on Cantanzos. It wasn't the superficial resentment of someone having to come down to earth after the splendours of castle life – Fran set less store by wealth and privilege than any woman he'd ever met – but *something* that she'd found at Cantanzos was being grieved for, and he was inclined to think that what she was haunted by was the memory of the place itself. She seemed often to be only half-attending to what he said, as if she still listened to other sounds that he couldn't hear.

'Term's nearly over,' he said suddenly. 'Let's go away, Fran – have Christmas in some fairy-tale, snowy, Austrian village, or go and listen to a feast of music in Prague.'

About to refuse, she suddenly changed her mind. Part of the intention was probably to underline his hope that they were a unit again, futures linked together for good at last. She couldn't share the hope, but she would be very lonely without him, and the idea of escaping somewhere for Christmas looked attractive.

'I think I'd like *you* to choose, and tell me what I'm going to do,' she said finally, 'bearing in mind my debut in the town hall! We can't leave London before that.'

He'd half-expected that she wouldn't agree, and caught her up in his arms in a sudden rush of gratitude for the fact that he hadn't lost her after all. It was what he deserved for being such a fool about Felicity; now, he couldn't understand the madness that had overtaken him. Every time he looked at Fran, every time he walked into her ordered, charming home, he tried to remember the chaos of the weeks in New York with Felicity, and the feverish, unreal excitement of it all that had even made work impossible. He felt now like a condemned man reprieved at the moment of execution, and it seemed necessary to say so.

'Dearest Fran, if I once did seem to take you for granted, I shan't ever again. I'll regret hurting you for as long as I live, and love you a little bit more with every day that dawns.'

He meant what he said; there was no reason, no excuse, not to feel very touched by it, and she was ashamed of the effort she had to make to sound grateful.

'That's positively the last time you're allowed to apologise for being bewitched by Felicity,' she said instead. 'It's in the past, along with some odd behaviour of my own that I'm not even admitting to! Shall we agree now that the present and future tenses are the only ones that concern us?'

'You're beautiful and wise and good, and I love you very much,' Richard said humbly.

She shook her head, trying to smile despite a wildly unreasonable longing to scream at him. 'Thank you, but I'd rather you loved awkward, stubborn, ordinary *me*, and not some lovely figment of your imagination; if you can't, you'll be disappointed again, and we shall end up with another failure.'

She didn't free herself when he kissed her. His mouth was comforting and warm, and if she tried hard enough, she needn't compare it in her mind with a kiss that could only be imagined. If she tried *very* hard, she needn't think at all of Inez de Castro lying in her lover's arms, with firelight dancing on the walls of a tower room and the sea whispering outside.

'We aren't going to fail,' she heard Richard say, and opened her eyes to find him staring at her anxiously. 'I think the Austrian Christmas is the one you'd prefer; that's what we'll have, Fran darling.'

She agreed, then said a firm goodnight and led him to the door. He never asked if he might stay, sensing that she would say no. The time would come, he hoped, when some tiny sign would be forthcoming that she was ready to be loved. Until it did, he must somehow be patient.

*   *   *

194

It was, of course, Felicity who managed to upset his dream of a carol-filled, candle-lit *gasthof* somewhere in the snowy Ahlberg. He was still trying to decide which village to choose when Fran telephoned, calling a halt to the scheme, at least for herself.

'Felly's coming back for a few days – the only time she can get away, just over Christmas. She rang last night, sounding very het-up and excited, *very* anxious to see me – you know how she talks, every other word underlined – and very certain that I *couldn't* go away just when she's due to arrive. I can't imagine what it's all about, but I'm afraid I must stay, Richard. There's nothing to stop you going, though, and I'm such a pathetic performer on the slopes that you may even enjoy it more on your own.'

'I shouldn't enjoy it at all,' he said resentfully. 'Really, Fran, it's too bad of Felicity. Can't she come some other time? Did you even say that we planned to go away?'

'I said it twice, but I'm not sure she was paying attention either time; Felly is always listening to what *she*'s about to say next!' Aware of his deep disappointment, Fran tried to make amends. 'I'm truly sorry, Richard, and I wouldn't have agreed to scrub our holiday if it hadn't really sounded important for me to be here. We'll do it together another year while I can still manage to clamber on and off a ski-lift! But *you* go now, please.'

'I shall spend Christmas here with you,' he said stiffly, 'and damn Felicity freely in my mind for the selfish, demanding creature that she is.' With that he ended the conversation, and Fran replaced her own receiver reflecting that his enchantment with her sister had finally been bludgeoned to death by sheer exasperation. There wasn't the slightest need to fear that Felly's golden beauty would dazzle him again; he was immune now to the virus and, like measles for most people, it couldn't be caught twice.

She was making lists of things needing to be done – a sure sign, she thought, that youth was over – when the next bombshell arrived. This time it was Juanita proposing

195

a Christmas visit for herself and Maud. If they could stay with dear Fran, only a bed for aged Miss Entwhistle was needed; she – Juanita – would enjoy sleeping on the floor! When the long conversation ended, Fran went upstairs to lay her problem in front of Anita.

'Send whoever you like to sleep up here,' her friend agreed immediately. 'I'm just sorry I shan't be here myself to meet them. What will Richard make of this fresh invasion, by the way? Or is he still sulking too much to care?'

'That's putting it rather harshly,' Fran suggested ruefully. 'Feel sorry for the poor man. He was all set to show me how dashing he is on skis – not a hint of the unadventurous, nearly-middle-aged academic about him! But he also wanted to give me a lovely holiday, and instead of that, we shall be working flat out.'

'And you don't really mind a bit,' Anita suggested. 'In fact, you haven't smiled so cheerfully since you came back from Spain.'

Fran thought about this for a moment. 'Well, it's because I want to see them all, I expect; and Richard will enjoy showing Juanita London when she gets here. He's at his very best sharing what he knows with someone as quick and appreciative as she is.'

Anita grinned at her. 'And all your ducks are swans as usual.'

'Well, my geese are anyway! Thank you, Ani dear; I'll lug up the necessary bedlinen for Felly and Juanita; Maud can have my spare room all to herself.'

She went downstairs thinking that it only needed her mother to ring and say she fancied Christmas in London with her daughters, but with courage plucked up to telephone to Cornwall she found that Melissa had plans of her own.

'Far too busy to come away now; all our arrangements will fall to pieces if I'm not here to take charge. But darling Felicity is coming down the day after Boxing Day, she says, and I'd rather have her all to myself, not shared with you and Richard and all these odd Spanish friends of yours.'

She made them sound, Fran reflected, as if they each had two heads; still, it was something to have her mother sounding cheerful, and much more to know that she didn't want to stir from home. There was nothing to do now except put the finishing touches to the flat, and await the arrival of her various travellers.

It was Felicity who reached London first – the same lovely, laughing girl whose smile had been enough to turn away wrath since she was a tiny child; yet *not* the same girl. Some extra Manhattan pzazz now defined the way she wore her clothes – denim jacket and trousers that had nothing countrified about them – and her hair was now a brief, blonde crop of pure gold. It was clear that Felicity and New York had taken to each other.

'You look wonderful,' Fran said as soon as they disentangled themselves from hugging each other. 'I've often wondered what a million dollars looked like; now I know!'

'Idiot! New York has smartened me up a bit, but it's the same old me underneath.' Large blue eyes were now fastened on her sister in a serious way that *wasn't* quite like the old Felicity. '*You*'re a bit too thin, Fran, though I have to say the cheekbones are lovely! It was harrowing for you, going back to Spain, and I don't think you've quite got over it yet. They sounded rather extraordinary people, too.'

'You can judge for yourself; two of them are joining us for Christmas! You'll recognise Maud and Juanita from my letters. The Count, his fiancée, and her brother were going to Seville, but *they* had the much better idea of coming here.'

Fran offered the explanation waiting for the remark her sister would almost certainly have made not long ago – that she'd rather have been going to meet the Count than his niece and his mother's elderly companion. Not only did the remark not come, but an expression of almost comical dismay spread over Felicity's face.

'Fran dear, now I've got news for *you*! I didn't come to

197

London alone. The dearest, loveliest man you can imagine is at the Hyde Park Hotel, just dying to meet you! He understands about me wanting to stay here with you, but I said there wouldn't be room for him as well.'

Fran examined her sister's face, understanding at last the combination of excitement and seriousness that had underlain her telephone call from New York; but she'd been here before at this same stage of breathless, delighted happiness.

'I'm about to meet the new love of your life,' Fran guessed with a smile. 'He's rich, he's good-looking, and he's even kind to the children you're looking after. You're quite mad about him in fact, and he, of course, is equally besotted with you!'

'Nearly right, Fran dear. Most of it fits, but he'd be the first to insist that he isn't good-looking at all. He's also twenty years older than me, and he limps from having a diseased hip as a small boy. The children I help look after are his, by the way – I mean it's his money that provides for them, and it's his Connecticut home we take them to in the summer.' She grinned at her sister. 'I think I've managed to surprise you!'

'Gobsmacked would describe me better,' Fran suggested faintly. 'Why is he so anxious to meet me?'

'Because you're going to be his sister-in-law – he said he needed to vet you first! Then I'm going to whisk him down to Cornwall to meet Melissa.'

Fran stared at her radiant face a moment longer and then held up her hands in a gesture of defeat. 'It seems quite pointless to ask if you're sure, Felly dear, when you look and sound so happy.'

'And you're trying not to remind me of all the times when I've been in this state of bliss before; but it *is* different now, Fran, and *I*'m different as well.'

'Yes . . . I do believe you are,' her sister agreed slowly. 'Well, I can't wait to meet my prospective brother-in-law. Does he have a name, by the way?'

'It's Elliott – Elliott Wilmington the Third! Not quite as famous as the Rockfellers, but in much the same league.'

Fran spared a silent thought for her mother's Cornish neighbours, who were doomed never to hear the last of the triumph she'd always known Felicity would achieve. Then she gave her sister a little hug. 'I don't care what league he's in, as long as he makes you happy.'

'What about you?' Felicity asked. 'You and Richard, I suppose I mean. I'm sure he's got over me; I was always much against his better judgement, poor love!'

'He hasn't quite forgiven you yet for changing our Christmas plans; apart from that I think he's happy.'

'I asked about you, as well.'

Fran smiled at the insistent question. 'While not in *your* ecstatic condition, I'm content, thank you very much, and now rather anxious to get you installed upstairs. Anita's gone away, so you're sharing her flat with Juanita, who should be arriving with Maud Entwhistle in time for dinner. I sent Richard off to Heathrow to collect them.' She smiled suddenly at her sister. 'You'd better tell your Elliott to be here by seven. It's become a rum sort of party, but by the pricking of my thumbs I think it might be going to work rather well. At least if we run out of food it's nice to think Elliott can afford to treat us to the Hyde Park Hotel! Now you'd better come and inspect your quarters upstairs; not what a millionaire's moll has probably grown accustomed to, but you'll have to make do!'

Felicity smiled, but her eyes were suddenly full of tears. 'I've missed you – I always miss you when you're not around. You'll have to keep hopping across the Atlantic in future.'

Fran promised that she would and, smiling at the idea, they climbed the stairs to Anita's attic floor.

Twenty-One

Timing was becoming critical to the success of a complicated evening, and Fran smiled on Richard for managing to deliver his passengers while Felicity was still upstairs. She could quickly explain that an unknown American called Elliott Wilmington would be there by the time he returned for dinner before he tactfully went away; then her sister came down to meet the new arrivals and install an excited Juanita upstairs. Everything about her visit seemed wonderful to her, but an attic bedroom apparently added the final touch.

Fran steered Maud to more ordinary quarters and smiled at her with great affection. 'Oh, it's lovely to see you again. Christmas seems pretty well perfect now, with Felicity here as well, and the American she's going to marry also turning up to join us presently! The love affair is serious this time, and at last she and Richard can stop feeling guilty about each other.' She examined Maud's face and then nodded as if satisfied. 'I shall have to hear about Cantanzos later, but you look fine, and Juanita is obviously blooming.'

'Am I allowed to ask about you?' Maud wanted to know. 'Pascal reminded me a boring number of times that I was to give you his love and say that charming Spanish ladies seem to have gone to ground – at least, *he* can't find any.'

'He's not trying hard enough then. Surely Seville will be able to produce one or two.' Fran put the problem aside to consider more pressing matters. 'Settle in, dear Maud, while I attend to my concoctions in the kitchen. A large drink will be waiting when you're ready.'

'I *knew* we were right to come,' said Miss Entwhistle in tones of great satisfaction, and saw Fran's thin face break into a smile.

Richard had come back and they were all gathered in the sitting room when Felicity's Elliott arrived – punctually at seven o'clock, Fran observed. He was clearly a competent sort of man if he could defeat London's traffic, but no doubt his sort of wealth demanded competence in its handling. She went with Felicity to the door, and her first impression was of a man of medium height and build with his arms full of chrysanthemums, pure white except for the lovely tinge of green at their hearts. He stared at Fran, thinking that on the grounds of looks alone there was nothing to identify her as the sister of golden Felicity.

'Elliott, this is my dear Francesca. Do you think she'll do?'

He didn't answer the laughing question at once. Not only competent, Fran decided, but a man who wouldn't be hurried, even by her impetuous sister. When he did speak, his voice was quiet – another surprise; she'd imagined that a powerful American would make a lot of noise. His smile was pleasant, too. 'Oh yes, I think she'll do very well! I hope she can say the same about me.'

Fran smilingly agreed, still coming to terms with what was Felicity's final choice. Only the perfection of his tailoring, and the air of having been very beautifully laundered spoke of Elliott Wilmington's circumstances; otherwise he seemed an ordinarily courteous and civilised man. However, at a second glance his face was more intelligent than most, and more sensitive. If she could find humour in him as well, she would be delighted with her prospective brother-in-law. She thanked him for the beautiful flowers, then left Felicity making the introductions while she hauled Juanita off to the kitchen.

'Think of yourself as Marilar,' she suggested, 'while I try to fill out the role of Señora Fernandez! There isn't a lot of running about to do, because we eat in here; but fortunately there's a sort of scullery place where we can hide most of the mess.'

With traditional fare to come the following day, she'd kept the evening menu simple: a Spanish dish of boned lamb cooked with pimentos, tomatoes and garlic. After that came cheese and fresh pineapple, supplemented by the delicious marrons glacés that Juanita had brought with her.

With six of them to be fitted in round the kitchen table there wasn't room for formality as well. Fran knew it must be something of a culture shock for those of her guests used to the dining room at Cantanzos; and she could only guess at the dimensions of Elliott's Connecticut mansion; but no one seemed to mind the lack of space: the food was very good, the wine liberally poured by Richard, and the happiness and affection in the air unmistakable. Mindful that four of them had done much travelling that day, Fran vetoed midnight Mass; better to attend the Christmas morning service instead. It was Felicity's idea that they should go to Westminster Abbey – the best London could offer, she said grandly; the Catholics among them could give the Cathedral a try instead.

In fact, they all went to the Abbey together, and afterwards – at Elliott's invitation – to a snack lunch at his hotel. Then they parted company, Fran and Maud to go back in a taxi to Earls Court Square, the others setting off for a brisk walk through as many parks as they could manage.

'Heaven's being very kind to us,' Fran said. 'Juanita will return to rainy Galicia imagining that frosted grass under brilliant winter sunlight is what we normally see on Christmas Day in London!'

Maud nodded, busy with a thought of her own. 'I'd forgotten how lovely it is, though, when the conditions *are* right. The singing in the Abbey this morning – there's nothing that comes anywhere near the Anglican choral tradition; it's heartbreaking, the sheer transcendent beauty of it.'

Back at the flat she refused the offer of a siesta, and sat with Fran in the kitchen instead, peeling sprouts and chestnuts, and talking at last about Cantanzos. It was settled, she said, that Juanita and she would stay there until the end of the coming summer. Then it would be time for them to go to Milan, where Juanita was already enrolled in a college of art and design.

'She's working hard now, though,' said Maud. 'We do some general reading together; then she goes to a language tutor in between driving lessons and life classes. She's recovered the immense energy and drive that her father had – it's something else Luis gives *you* the credit for.'

Fran merely asked a different question: 'What about you – apart from the general reading?'

A smile spread over Maud's plain face. 'I'm rather enjoying myself, as a matter of fact – writing my memoirs! I've lived in Spain for nearly forty years. Franco was still El Caudillo when I first went there, a pot-bellied little man with a high-pitched voice and an abiding hatred of the Republicans who fought him in the Civil War. Spain has changed almost out of recognition since then – mostly for the better, I think. There are problems, of course: more crime, drugs, political infighting; but it's a happier country to live in now.' Maud gave a little snort of laughter. 'Need I say that my memoirs will be like me: outspoken and only notable for their political incorrectness!'

'A twenty-first century Richard Ford, in other words,' Fran murmured with relish, '. . . and a new *Handbook for Travellers in Spain*! I should think any publisher here would snap it up. Keep writing, Maud.' She finished the potato she was peeling before asking her next question. 'Juanita mentioned that Pascal is often away now – in Oviedo, or points further east – but there wasn't time to ask about her uncle and the Marquesa. I assume they're at Cantanzos?'

'Mostly, yes, although Luis has to spend more time than he likes in Madrid. He seems to have become an adviser to the President of the Regional Council and the Government on Galician affairs, and he also knows the King's son, Felipe, very well.'

'The mourning period for Marganita must nearly be over,' Fran suggested, relying on Maud to answer the question that had carefully not been asked.

'A spring wedding is what is planned, I suppose,' Miss Entwhistle said obligingly. Then she frowned at the Brussels sprout in her hand. 'It seems odd coming from me, but Inez is the one I feel sorry for now.'

'To be getting the Count as a husband?'

'To have fallen in love with the wrong man,' Maud replied. She saw Fran's expression and shook her head. 'It's true. There's no doubt that she does love Luis, but there's nothing else at Cantanzos that she wants. It's true that he occasionally entertains in a royal sort of way, and then she's a superb hostess, but she needs more opportunities to shine – in Seville or, better still, Madrid. Her dream would be for Luis to turn the castle into a parador so that they could turn their backs on Galicia.'

'He would never do it,' Fran said quietly. 'That green corner of Spain is in his heart and soul.'

'I think it's what Inez realises too,' Maud agreed, 'and therein lies her problem; but she's a very intelligent woman, as well as a strong-willed one. She'll find a solution in the end.'

Fran nodded, and abandoned the painful subject of the Marquesa. 'I've just thought of something else *you* ought to be doing: learning Italian, unless you know it already. Giorgio's English left a little something to be desired, and I don't remember Graziella speaking any at all.'

'I've started already,' Maud admitted. 'It's a pretty language, but I miss the rasp and good vituperative bite of Spanish. Still, perhaps it'll be better suited to my mellower declining years!'

They were both still giggling at this ridiculous idea when Felicity and Juanita reappeared, pink-cheeked, tired and happy. Fran refused offers of further help and shooed them all to their beds for a rest until it was time to change. Her Christmas dinner had reached the stage, she said, when she needed to be able to think quietly about the next thing to be done; a flock of gossiping assistants was help the cook was better off without.

Two hours later everything was ready: the capon, crisp and golden, was 'resting' under its blanket of foil, the candles on the table waited to be lit, and Richard's contribution of wine sat cooling in its ice-filled bucket. A conscientious hostess could now relax and tell herself that it was up to her guests to do a little of the work by agreeing to enjoy themselves.

It *was* a happy, joy-filled evening, only marred for Fran by one private, unlooked-for memory. Entering into the festive spirit of the occasion, Richard had appeared wearing the crimson bow tie picked out for him by Juanita long ago in Santiago, to wear at her birthday party. Fran was transported back from her own familiar flat to the terrace at Cantanzos, listening to Luis Esteban's voice informing her that it was time she went home. Inez had delivered the subsequent coup de grâce with more personal relish, but the effect then had been no more painful than the first time.

She was dragged back from the past by Juanita voicing a question she hadn't yet found time to ask herself. How had the children's venture in New York got started? Elliott smiled at Felicity across the table.

'Shall I tell the story, or will you?'

'I should tell it more quickly; you'll tell it much better,' she replied. 'Anyway, it's your story!'

He nodded and began. 'I have to go back to a time before Felicity arrived. My wife had been killed in one of those senseless motor accidents that should never have happened.' He reached out to touch Juanita's hand in a little wordless gesture of sympathy – sufficient, Fran reflected, to have *her* in thrall to Elliott Wilmington as well. Then he went on with his story.

'I was bitter and lonely, altogether in a mess, until by chance one day I met a man who seemed to have more to complain about than I did. His way of dealing with it, though, had been to start a refuge for the sort of children other people tended not to bother about. They were all damaged in some way, with nothing to hope for. I got involved financially at first, but I soon saw that just giving money wasn't enough; the children needed more than that. They're a mixture of colours and races and cultures, so finding the right people to look after them wasn't easy. We even sent an SOS to London one day, and it brought us Felicity!'

He smiled at her across the table and, watching her sister's face, Fran knew for certain that she need never worry about impulsive, harum-scarum Felly again; she'd found her home at last.

Juanita still had a question to ask – of Felicity this time. 'Was the job what you expected – what you were looking for?'

'I wasn't looking for anything; I was just running away,' she answered honestly, 'and my first sight of the hostel made me want to head straight back to London; but I knew what would happen if I did: Fran would have to pick up the pieces again. So I stayed, and fell in love with the children. Then we took them to Elliott's home in Connecticut, and I fell in love with him as well.'

'It's a perfect story,' Juanita said. 'I hate ones that don't have a happy ending.'

Fran caught Maud's eye across the table and knew that they were both thinking of the same thing: a Cantanzos story where the happiness of the ending seemed more in doubt because the people involved in it couldn't help wanting different things.

With dinner over, toasts drunk and the candles guttering, the cook was forbidden to do any more work. She and Maud were sent out of the kitchen while Felicity directed the others in the task of clearing up.

Sitting by the fire in the sitting room, Fran let out a little sigh of relief.

'You're tired and no wonder,' said Maud gruffly.

'No . . . just glad it's been such a lovely day.' Fran smiled at the memory of the story they'd listened to. 'Elliott's a nice man, don't you think? I used to reckon that seriously rich people lived in a different world from the rest of us, but he doesn't. My mother will be almost disappointed when she meets him, because she'll expect him to be all the things I like him for *not* being!'

'A complicated sentence, but I get its drift.' Maud let her glance wander round the room, noting the delicate watercolours enhanced by plain, white walls, the soft green-and-rose chintz of curtains and chair-covers, and the shelves overflowing with books. 'This, to use your own word again, is a nice room, Fran; it speaks of you, in fact.'

'*Muchas gracias, señorita!* It wasn't how I lived when I first came to London, in the cheapest, dreariest, bedsit imaginable.'

'So what happened – the streets *were* paved with gold after all?'

'No – one of my earliest patients was a rather irascible, lonely old man who seemed to make it a rule never to like anybody he met; but we gradually got on terms, and I went on visiting him. He was determined to teach me to play chess well enough to beat him occasionally! He lived here on the ground floor, but I didn't know until after he died that he owned the whole house. His will gave me a choice of the flats before the rest were sold – a wonderful gift that I wasn't even able to thank him for.'

'Another of Juanita's happy stories,' Maud commented. 'Let's assume that, irascible no longer, he's as chirpy as a lark in Paradise, knowing just how grateful you are!' She hesitated about saying something else, and changed her mind as Elliott came into the room to report that the working group in the kitchen had decided they could manage better without him.

'A plan's being hatched to introduce Juanita and me to

a pantomime tomorrow, a Christmas tradition that we must apparently sample at least once in a lifetime.' He smiled at the expression on Maud's face. 'My contribution is supper at the Hyde Park Hotel afterwards for those who can sit all the way through *Cinderella*!'

'I expect I'll manage it,' she admitted, 'as long as the Ugly Sisters aren't camped up too outrageously; fifty years ago they weren't allowed to be.'

'They will be now,' Richard warned her from the doorway, bringing in the coffee tray. 'Dear Maud, living in Spain has made you finicky; sheer rumbustious vulgarity is exactly what pantomime's all about.'

'Not *all* it's about,' Fran objected. 'There has to be some fairy-tale magic as well for the small girls in the audience, as well as ancient, incurable romantics like me!' She smiled at Elliott. 'You see what a strange hybrid animal it's supposed to be; we can't all be satisfied.'

But they very nearly were, she had to admit the following evening, and if, in his heart of hearts, Elliott hoped that one pantomime in a lifetime would be enough, there wasn't any doubt of Juanita's entrancement. Watching her spellbound face as Cinderella made her ballroom entrance, Fran thought what a mixture Mercedes' daughter still was: far older than her years for some of her experiences, but eager as a child for everything she didn't know.

Rounded off by the supper Elliott had promised them, Christmas came to a memorable end. The following morning Felicity and he set off to drive to Cornwall, while Richard and Fran took Maud and Juanita back to Heathrow.

'You're very quiet,' he said on the journey home. 'Exhausted, I expect. I don't know about Juanita's purity of heart, but she's certainly got "the strength of ten", and no one could call Felly restful.'

'True, but it was the happiest Christmas I can remember, and now we have a wedding to look forward to. I must make sure that Juanita gets invited to be a bridesmaid; she's already designing her dress!'

Richard grinned, but concentrated on the traffic, leaving Fran free to travel in her imagination with Maud and Juanita back to Santiago, and a grey stone castle whose tower flew the Leopard's flag.

Twenty-Two

T here was another brief reunion with Felicity before she and Elliott flew back to New York. He tactfully remembered that there were people he needed to see, so that the two of them could talk by themselves.

'How did it go?' Fran asked, almost before her sister was inside the door.

'Sticky to begin with, but I think we finished up friends! My darling Elliott wasn't quite what Melissa expected, and when a wedding extravaganza was firmly ruled out, I could see her deciding not to bother to attend. I'm not sure whether we talked her round in the end.'

'She'd like you to live here, not in Connecticut,' Fran pointed out. 'Allow something for that disappointment.' She smiled at her sister. 'Really *not* a lavish wedding? Don't I get to wear a bridesmaid's dress? Juanita was counting on it.'

'You have to be there: I couldn't be married without you; but it will be the simplest ceremony you ever saw. It's what we both want, just before Easter, Fran. We've got to find someone to fill my place in New York; I don't suppose you fancy the idea?'

'Thank you kindly, but no – I think one of us had better stay here. Will you miss working with the children? I imagine that life as Mrs Elliott Wilmington is going to be rather different from the daily round of a working girl.'

Felicity nodded, looking unexpectedly serious. 'Being Elliott's wife is something I have to learn to live up to, and it will be difficult even with his help. We shall have the children with us during the summer, of course, but I want us to start our own family as soon as we can. Elliott didn't give you quite the whole story when we were here. His wife was pregnant when she was killed, so he lost his child as well. She was a lovely person, by all accounts, and he hasn't ever forgotten her.'

Fran was silent for a moment, reflecting that, even for her beautiful, charming sister, good fortune didn't come without its problems. She'd skimmed happily along the surface of life until now, but with damaged, complicated Elliott she was in much deeper waters.

'You'll manage,' Fran said gently. 'You'll make each other happy, Felly dear. Just tell me when I have to fly the Atlantic and I'll be there – *very* simply dressed, of course! Would grey flannel be overdoing it?'

Felicity's ripple of laughter answered the anxious question. 'You'll make Elliott a very good sister-in-law; he'd rather forgotten to laugh at life occasionally, but I defy him not to do it with you around.' She was tempted to ask whether her elder sister was as cheerful as she seemed, but new-found sensitivity advised against it; the question, asked at all, would mean that the effort involved had been detected. Instead, she kissed Fran, made her own effort not to weep at saying goodbye and promised to be waving at the airport when Fran's plane touched down.

It felt very quiet when she'd gone; in fact, the world seemed altogether 'stale, flat and unprofitable' now that all her visitors had left. The last day or two of a memorable year crawled too slowly into time past and done with, and she had to make a determined attempt not to seem miserable when Richard called round the following evening. A glance at her pale face was enough to remind him of the holiday plan they'd had to cancel.

'Darling, I'd insist on taking you away now, but there's scarcely time before term starts again.'

'There's no time and no need,' she said firmly. 'I expect I'm feeling grumpy after too much jollity, and I always reckon the new year should start immediately Christmas is over.' She smiled with all the conviction she could muster, but it propelled Richard along the road she least wanted him to take. He suddenly pulled her close and kissed her more lingeringly than usual. Unable to respond, she could only wait to be released, fearful that she knew what was coming next.

'Fran, we can't go on like this,' he said earnestly. 'I want so much to marry you – it's what we always planned, and you *need* looking after, dearest. We could marry now if you wouldn't mind waiting to go somewhere exciting until the Easter vac . . .'

His face was full of kindness and pleading and what she took to be hopeful excitement. She hesitated too long, reluctant to cast him down, and he rushed on. 'There's more to tell you, sweetheart, but our future's really the important thing. I know it's my fault that we got in such a muddle, but with Felly happy at last *we* can be now, as well.'

It was more than time to make him listen – the longer she shirked it, the harder it would become – so she put her fingers gently over his mouth, and tried to smile at him. 'What else is there to tell – are they going to make you Vice-Chancellor?'

'Good God, *no*! Fran, say you'll marry me, please.'

He could read the answer in her sad face, but she knew she must put it into words. 'I can't, my dear; I'm so very sorry, but I'm afraid it won't do. I've tried not to . . . to mislead you, but perhaps I haven't been careful enough.'

'It's still Felicity, isn't it? You say that mistake is over and done with, but I don't think it is.'

She shook her head, hearing a faint tinge of resentment as well as despair in his question. 'It's only Felly to *this* extent: she made me realise what I ought to feel if I was going to be your wife. You're the dearest and best of friends, but the sort of love she has for Elliott Wilmington I can't offer you. I wish I could, because I hate hurting you. Forgive me, please.'

Her grave voice denied the possibility that she could be

212

made to change her mind; he knew her well enough to understand that he must accept what she said, or lose her altogether.

'Tell me your other news,' she suggested quietly. 'I've a feeling that it is important.'

He realised that she was trying to haul them on to safer ground, where friendship and affection could still survive and matter; he must meet her halfway or seem to behave like a thwarted, unhappy adolescent.

'It's intriguing, at least,' he admitted slowly. 'A television film company is interested in the Spanish book – well, rather more than that. It's been in the wind for a little while, but I didn't want to talk about it in case the whole thing fizzled out; but they're committed to going ahead now. A series of programmes about the pilgrim route, culminating in arrival at Santiago in time for the Feast of St James on the twenty-fifth of July.'

Genuinely delighted, Fran was able to hug him as naturally as any friend would. 'Intriguing isn't the word – it's stupendous! What have *you* to do – write the script?'

He even smiled himself now. 'More than that: I'm to be the pilgrim – Professor Weston making his debut in the movie business! God knows how it will turn out, but they've looked at me in front of a camera and seem to think I can do it.'

'I'm sure they're right,' Fran said categorically. 'You'll be the perfect guide – totally in love with your subject. Most of today's dons who get televised seem to be chiefly in love with themselves!'

Richard's expression suddenly grew tragic again. 'It means spending the whole of the Easter vac out there – I thought we could have enjoyed doing it together, Fran. In fact, I'm not sure I can do it without you.'

She understood now what their deferred honeymoon was to have been: a working journey shared with a television film crew! Only Richard could have seen nothing odd in suggesting it, she thought.

'I've got a much better idea,' she said, smiling in spite of herself. 'The girl to go with you is Juanita and, being involved in the book, she has the right to be there. She's intelligent and forceful enough to put the fear of God into any stroppy film person, her Spanish is even better than yours, and she would happily work herself into the ground for you.'

Richard turned the idea over in his mind, initial dislike of it gradually melting away. 'I must think about it some more, Fran, but maybe you're right. I should have to clear it with Luis Esteban, of course; technically she's still a minor in his charge, but he'd know that I'd take care of her, I hope.'

'No doubt about it, and I can't imagine he'd refuse; but I shan't mention it to her until you say I may.'

Richard's face changed again as he stared at Fran. He wanted to remind her that he was a bitterly disappointed man, but that would only make her feel guilty; he wanted to insist that nothing could give him pleasure now, but it wouldn't be quite true. The next few months would have been wonderful shared with her; but having Juanita alongside him instead would at least be better than struggling on his own.

'I'd better go and get on with some work,' he said almost cheerfully. 'Heaven knows there's enough to do.'

She saw him to the door, kissed him goodnight, and realised only then that she couldn't have gone with him to Spain at Easter in any case. Apart from wanting to be as far from Cantanzos as possible when a marriage was going to take place there, she was committed to attending a different wedding in Connecticut, USA.

Richard's great project moved ahead swiftly after that, as it had to with a July deadline fixed by the immutable calendar of Mother Church. A rapturous letter from Juanita confirmed that, with her uncle's blessing and Maud's steadying presence there as well, she would be waiting for him when he got to Spain ahead of the film unit. The letter spoke of nothing else – not unnaturally, Fran supposed,

214

given Juanita's state of high excitement; but it seemed strange all the same that her uncle's approaching marriage shouldn't get at least a mention.

Then something arrived that explained the omission. Inez had another wedding to arrange unexpectedly and even she could only manage one at a time. The heavily engraved card announced the forthcoming marriage of Señor Pascal Vargas to Teresa, only daughter of the Marques Jimenez y Cabreiro. Overleaf was a message scrawled in Inez de Castro's flamboyant hand. She felt sure Francesca would like to know that her brother's happiness was now assured. The wedding had had to be hastily arranged because the bride's father was due to return to his embassy in South America. They well understood, of course, that it was too short notice for any of Pascal's English friends to attend.

Fran found herself sitting at the kitchen table with no recollection of getting there. She stared at the piece of thick, embossed card in her hand, seeing not its message but the Marquesa's triumphant face as she scribbled it. Maud had suggested feeling sorry for the woman, but Fran knew she couldn't manage it; Juanita's assessment had been nearer the mark. She could be sincerely glad that Pascal had taken her advice; her hurt lay in the fact that he hadn't bothered to give her the news himself.

His letter arrived two days later and, carefully as it was phrased, its underlying anger was unmistakable. Inez had sent the card without his knowledge, and told him afterwards. He relied on Francesca to understand that it wasn't how he'd intended her to be told. He was more fortunate than he deserved: Teresa Jimenez was a beautiful, gentle girl to whom he'd been introduced by mutual friends in Seville. It was his task now to make her happy; that being so, this was the last time he would allow himself to repeat what Francesca knew already: he would pray for her and remember her always. She had difficulty in reading the last few words, but the hurt that Inez had wanted her to feel was washed away by her tears. She could write to Pascal now as a friend who truly wished for his happiness. It was another loose end tidied away; with Juanita and Maud in Milan by the end of the summer, there would soon be nothing whatever to connect her to Cantanzos.

In the moments of depression that crept up on her unexpectedly when she wasn't prepared for them, she wondered whether she was connected to anyone at all. Over an impromptu supper in Anita's flat one evening and an ill-advised third glass of wine, she confessed – with what she thought was the right note of wry humour – to feeling jaded – past her sell-by date, in fact, at thirty-one!

'It's your own fault,' Anita pointed out bluntly. 'What do you expect with two perfectly good prospects shown the door? Richard might not be every girl's dream lover, but Pascal certainly was. I can remember his smile even now, and I only saw the man for half an hour!'

Fran perversely chose to regret Richard more – solid worth, she insisted, enunciating her words with care in case she was nearly tipsy, being longer-lasting than a charming smile; in any case she was prepared to bet that the Professor's shy appeal was about to make him a celebrity.

'The kiss of death,' Anita insisted. 'Those whom the gods would destroy they first make into TV personalities!'

'You're allowed to quote from poets but *not* tamper with their verse,' Fran said; but her smile faded, leaving haunting sadness in its place. 'Thanks to Maud Entwhistle, whom you didn't have the pleasure of meeting at Christmas-time, Count Esteban can probably outquote you! English governesses must be one of our abiding export treasures.'

Anita grinned and changed the subject to Felicity's approaching wedding. 'Is your mother going with you or not?'

'I think she might in the end, but she's seriously put out by the lack of fuss. If Felly were marrying a poor man, she wouldn't say a word; but it's the wasted opportunities that she can't forgive them for. She has no hope of *me* giving her a chance to shine as the mother of the bride – and she *could* shine: when she's happy she's still beautiful.'

'You might surprise her yet. Don't forget that people are vulnerable when they get to meet you – just the angel of mercy they need!'

Fran thought of her first encounter with Juanita – someone certainly vulnerable, but in no frame of mind for recognising angels. 'I impinge briefly on people's lives, get a little involved in them sometimes, and then a week or a month later I'm looking at a different collection of bones and muscles that need attending to. Does that sound hopefully romantic?'

Anita looked unconvinced. 'Did you "impinge briefly" at that Spanish place? I don't think so.'

'That was different: I was living on the job; but it's not an ideal arrangement, being roughly halfway between servant and guest!' She smiled to show how little it now mattered. Anita couldn't be blamed for mentioning Cantanzos; she'd called it to mind herself by talking about Luis, in order to ease some aching inner need of her own. One day it wouldn't be necessary any more: he'd have become a faint memory she could scarcely put a face to; but the memory was taking too long a time to fade.

'I think you need a change,' Anita said, staring at her. 'You spend too many evenings listening to Richard Weston talking about himself. Let him become a household name without any more help from you.'

Fran smiled more easily this time. 'I'm afraid solid worth still doesn't appeal to you very much! Anyway, I'm *getting* a change. Another month and I'll be off to the States for Felicity's wedding. She half-jokingly suggested that I should take over her job. Safe in my London rut, I turned it down, but maybe I shouldn't have. Perhaps I'll decide this is the year to start living dangerously!' She *wasn't* tipsy after all – no one could be who managed a speech like that so coherently. With a cheerful 'Goodnight' she went back to her own flat; but, left alone, Anita still looked thoughtful.

There'd been something in their conversation that she'd failed to spot – some clue that had been significant simply because it hadn't needed to be there. Like a terrier at a rabbit hole she prodded her memory and finally unearthed the tiny nugget of information that mattered. Count Esteban was a man who could quote from Shakespeare. Well, it might be unexpected in a Spanish aristocrat living in the wilds of Galicia, but it wasn't worth mentioning unless the man himself was important enough still to inhabit Fran's mind. Anita assembled the pieces of the Cantanzos jigsaw puzzle that she knew and fitted them into a picture. It wasn't hard now to understand why the worthy Professor and the Count's charismatic cousin had bitten the dust with her friend. Fran was staring at a future that couldn't contain Luis Esteban because the beautiful Marquesa stood in the way, and *she* was completely certain of where she belonged: on the right side of the green-baize door.

Twenty-Three

With Teresa Jimenez motherless, Inez was deeply involved in the arrangements for her marriage to Pascal. It was to take place in Seville, rather to his regret. He was beginning to regard himself as a Gallegan now, and he would have preferred Cantanzos as the setting for his marriage; but Inez had no patience with this point of view.

'You're being quite unreasonable,' she told him, softening it with a smile because they were only just recovering after their falling-out over the invitation card she'd sent to Fran. 'Are your and Teresa's friends to trek three-parts of the way across Spain to see you married? My dear, there couldn't be a more wonderful setting than the cathedral, and I promise I'll arrange a wedding for you that Seville will never forget!'

He had no doubt that she would. What she couldn't do was understand how little it mattered to him to provide a spectacle for the city's benefit; but there was some truth in her first objection: Galicia seemed like the end of the world to everyone they knew in the south.

Inez went down to Seville some weeks ahead of the rest of them to deal with the hundred and one details that couldn't, she said, be left to a nervous bride and a diplomat father accustomed to having his entire life arranged for him. Then, two days before the wedding, Pascal drove down with Juanita, Maud and Luis. In mid-March it was still cold and wet in the north, but once over the Sierra Morena they were in a different, spring-like world already veiled in greenery and blossom. Even Juanita, not enthusiastic about

Andalucía as a rule, admitted that it looked beautiful, and Luis had smilingly to agree with her.

It *was* a very splendid wedding. Marganita would have enjoyed it, Maud thought sadly. The Condesa had put a high value on beauty and style, and Inez shared the belief that perfection mattered in a world of crumbling standards. Second best could be accepted only by the faint-hearted. Her philosophy seemed also to appeal to the Marques Jimenez, and Maud looked on with interest as he appropriated his beautiful collaborator; she was just the hostess he needed, having no wife at his side. Maud could make out nothing of Luis's reaction to this; whatever he felt about it, his expression remained pleasant and totally unrevealing, while the bridegroom gave a convincing impersonation of a man blessed with more good fortune than he deserved. Maud doubted if Pascal quite believed it yet, but she reckoned that he would in the end. Teresa had two considerable advantages over Fran: she was deeply in love with her new husband, and she was *very* well connected. Pascal would learn to be happy with his pretty, agreeable wife.

In Maud's experience the departure of the bride and groom usually signalled a sharp return to earth after the wedding euphoria, and she observed it again now. No sooner had Pascal and Teresa been driven away to catch their afternoon flight to Venice than more normal behaviour quickly reasserted itself. Juanita began to remind them that she needed to be back in the north to meet Richard Weston, and Inez duly pointed out that their lives couldn't be expected to revolve from now on round the activities of the Professor and his friends.

'I've promised to be there, waiting for him. Don't you understand?'

'I understand that it's something you want to do,' Inez agreed coolly. 'You mustn't expect the rest of us to be quite so enraptured by the prospect.'

'Nor are *we* as enraptured as you seem to be by this place

and the Marques Jimenez!' Juanita flashed. 'He's a boring, vain man, and Luis thinks so too.'

Maud watched the older woman's face go taut with anger, but she managed a steely smile. 'Don't try to guess your uncle's views about Rodrigo Jimenez; they probably aren't those of an inexperienced seventeen-year-old who is a little piqued because he hasn't had time to pay her much attention! Your turn for admiration will come, *cara*; you mustn't expect all life's pleasures at once.'

Maud caught Juanita's eye and gave a tiny shake of the head. Then she deflected the Marquesa's fire towards herself. '*Is* there anything to stay for now, with Seville filling up, and the Semana Santa only a week away? I thought you shared Luis's dislike of the foreign hordes who crowd out the city.'

'I do, my dear Maud, but unlike both of you, apparently, I can wait to be back in uncrowded, boring Galicia again, where the main excitement of the day is whether it's going to rain or not!' She smiled briefly at them again and walked out, leaving silence behind. Then, before Juanita could open her mouth to speak, Maud forestalled her, sounding dispirited and tired.

'Don't tell me what I already know: You don't like your uncle's fiancée; but please remember that he does. You don't like Seville, but she does. Being impertinent about Teresa's father – a vain and boring man, I freely grant you – won't shorten the amount of time you have to spend here. Try to learn a little patience for pity's sake; you aren't in the least danger of missing your assignation with the Professor.'

Expecting another tirade, she was rewarded instead by one of Juanita's mercurial changes of mood. With Mercedes' smile suddenly transforming her face, the girl wound her arms round Maud's neck and kissed her cheek. 'There are times, *querida*, when you sound just like Fran – that's exactly how she'd have ticked me off! We both miss her, don't we?'

Maud nodded, smiling in spite of herself – *querida* indeed, from a child fifty years her junior! 'She's in America by now, I suppose, attending her sister's wedding.'

Juanita nodded in her turn. 'I liked Felicity, but she smiles too much, I think. I prefer Fran's jokes that she makes with a straight face. I shall insist on being *her* bridesmaid when she marries Richard, whether she asks me to or not!'

'That's the spirit,' Maud agreed cordially, 'though I dare say she will remember to invite us; we make an odd couple – not all that easily forgotten!'

'There you are, you see: you do it too, just like Fran. Is it an English thing?'

'I've no idea,' Maud answered after considering the question. 'I'm not even sure I can think of myself as English any more after forty years of living among *los españoles*! I've become Spanish to this extent, at any rate: it's time for my siesta. I may feel strong enough to face you again at dinner, provided you promise not to nag your uncle about going home, or start another fight with Inez.'

Juanita nodded, aware, after an inspection of her elderly friend's face, that she was serious about needing a rest. 'Don't worry, dear Maud. I'll "smile and smile" and *not* be a villain!'

'And I'm the ghost of Hamlet's father,' said Maud, recognising the quotation. 'Still, a few dregs of our work together seem to have rubbed off on you; it's something to be grateful for.'

Juanita grinned and went away, leaving Maud to close her eyes; but sleep was out of the question: there was too much to think about. The truth was that she shared Juanita's view: it *was* time they went back to Cantanzos. The truce between the girl and Inez was breaking down and they were back in their usual roles: fencers inspecting each other for the weak points where damage could be done. Luis's patience with Rodrigo Jimenez was wearing dangerously thin; but hardest of all to deal with was the tension now sparking between him and Inez. He couldn't help being aware of all that needed his attention at home, with Pascal also away; but this was anxiety, not the jealous spur that Inez's behaviour continually prodded in his side. She was committed to *him,* and for a proud man like Luis Esteban it was unbearable to have to watch her encouraging Jimenez to treat her like a free and unattached woman. Maud understood the strategy well enough: a new and high-profile admirer was a useful weapon in her struggle to win easier terms of future imprisonment at Cantanzos. She wanted Luis very much, but not the life he offered her on a rainswept, ocean-washed promontory on the most godforsaken coast of Spain. She couldn't resist casting a sidelong glance at the alternative future the Marques seemed very eager to provide.

Maud was finally half-dozing over her book when Luis walked into their hotel sitting room, but she came properly awake when he gently fielded the book sliding off her lap.

'Well done, Maud,' he said as he glanced at the title. 'Your Italian is coming on by leaps and bounds if you can enjoy Alberto Moravia!'

'Enjoy isn't quite the word: he's much too modern for an old trout like me; but I reckoned that the vocabulary in my ancient grammar book wouldn't equip me for life in present-day Milan.'

She saw his strained face relax into a grin. 'Almost certainly not, I should think.' Then he spoke in a different tone of voice. 'Do we ask too much of you, Maud? Juanita isn't your responsibility.'

Her face was full of affection when she looked at him. 'I think I could steel myself to tell you if I really didn't want to go. Anyway, your niece would say that I shall be all the better for a new experience, and I think she'd be right!'

'So we let the arrangement stand; but only on the under-standing that when you've had enough of Milan, or Juanita can manage on her own, you'll come back to Cantanzos – it's your home, unless you ever prefer a different one.'

She nodded, after a moment's hesitation, unable to say

that she doubted whether it was also the Marquesa's under-standing. 'Thank you, my dear.' Then she smiled at him. 'Juanita's getting anxious to leave; there doesn't seem to be a moment to waste when you're not quite eighteen!'

'And our problem is that Inez seems more anxious to stay here?' He asked the question wondering whether his underlying challenge would be accepted or not. It was, of course, as he realised he should have known it would be. When had Maud *not* accepted a challenge?

'It isn't Rodrigo Jimenez who keeps her here. I don't know why I even bother to say so; you must be aware of it better than I am.'

'I'm not as sure of anything as I was,' Luis answered ruefully. 'Inez thinks that some insane pride of ownership keeps me at Cantanzos. I can't make her understand the truth. The people there are still relatively poor: they have to farm and fish in the old ways that suit their land and their climate. I stay because they're my responsibility; they need looking after and representing. I accept that Inez can't spend her whole life at the castle: Galicia seems to have nothing she values; but she has to understand that I can't be somewhere else for half of every year, idling my time away.'

There was a little silence while Maud considered what could safely be said next. At last she abandoned the difficult subject of Inez altogether. 'You'll miss Pascal when he and Teresa find themselves a house in Oviedo.'

'I'll miss him very much,' Luis admitted, 'but they need a home of their own, and he spends too much time travelling in any case.' He smiled at Maud rather sadly. 'With you and Juanita gone by the end of the summer, Cantanzos will seem too empty!'

'Room for dozens of children, though,' said Maud, almost without thought.

'Dozens?'

It was her turn to smile at the startled question. 'I'm not expecting Inez to become the old woman who lived in a shoe and had so many children she didn't know what to do! At Francesca's flat last Christmas we met the wealthy American her sister is marrying. Elliott Wilmington has a mansion on the Connecticut coast, which he fills with poor children from New York during the summer months. It's how Felicity came to meet him: she went to work in the home he funds for them in the city.'

'He sounds a remarkable man,' Luis commented.

'That's what he is, but in a very nice, quiet way.'

Luis grinned more easily at this. 'A very English way of wanting a rich man to behave!' Then he reverted to the subject of leaving Seville. 'If we say our goodbyes tomorrow, we could go home the day after. Inez may decide that she can't bear to miss the Easter processions that she's seen dozens of times already, in which case she must come when she's ready.'

Maud could see that his decision had been taken. He wouldn't argue with Inez about a matter that she must settle for herself, but his own choice had been made: he was going home to Cantanzos.

The atmosphere at the dinner table that night couldn't have been described as cordial; but from the Marquesa's cool glance at her from time to time Maud thought *she* was suspected of having persuaded Luis to leave – perfidious Britannia in the shape of Maud Entwhistle, scheming and interfering as usual.

But nothing was said, and on the morning planned for their departure Inez, having been able to tear herself away from the Easter processions and the Marques, was ready with the rest of them.

The journey home, with one overnight stop on the way, seemed tediously long without the excitement of the wedding to look forward to. Juanita, under oath to Maud not to provoke the Marquesa, said very little. Inez said even less, and Luis concentrated on covering the distance as quickly as possible; but the tension was palpable, and Maud began to regard her removal to Milan as something that couldn't come soon enough. Spanish temperaments experienced at close range were becoming too much of a burden for a lady in her declining years: she needed a quiet, Italian life!

They were rewarded for getting home without a scene by the sight of Cantanzos looking its best. In the ten days they'd been away, the last remnants of winter had entirely disappeared. On a glorious spring afternoon the castle's grey tower heaved itself into a cloudless sky; nothing could have been greener than the surrounding hillsides, and nothing more deeply blue than the ocean that lapped against the wall.

Maud, sitting in front with Luis on the last stage of the journey, heard the little sigh of contentment that he gave as he braked the car.

'It's worth going away,' she suggested quietly, 'just for the pleasure of coming home.'

'Good reason, you mean, for doing it more often!' He waited while Pepé came bustling round to open the car door for the Marquesa, and Señora Fernandez also appeared to welcome the travellers home. With Inez and Juanita already in the hall there was no one left to overhear them.

'You think that if I agree to go away a little more, and Inez agrees to stay a little more, our problem will cease to exist. It's a solution dear to your sensible English heart!'

'It's the best I can devise,' she agreed calmly, 'but I can see that it doesn't quite match a Spaniard's death-or-glory approach to life.'

His smile was full of sweetness as he leaned over to open the car door. 'I hope you also see that we could never do without you. Welcome home, dear Maud.'

Twenty-Four

For Juanita and Maud it was time to set off again almost at once on another long journey – this one by train to Pamplona, where they were to meet Richard. Here, the several roads that had been bringing pilgrims into Spain from France for centuries finally combined into the true '*camino*' that would lead them to the shrine of St James. It was where Richard's series of programmes was planned to start; from there their route to Santiago would be covered in stages: Logrono, Burgos, and Leon.

Luis saw them off at the station and couldn't help smiling at the contrast they presented. Maud, survivor of many Spanish train-rides, was in her sensible travelling clothes, with the usual minimum of luggage. It was exactly how she'd have set out, he thought, to explore the Amazon or climb Everest. Juanita was excited, but determined to appear businesslike and grown-up; she had a position to uphold, she said, as the Professor's Spanish adviser.

'Quite right, *chiquita*,' Luis solemnly agreed. 'Be polite but firm – it's the only way to deal with the troublesome English!'

He kissed them both goodbye, thinking how much he would miss them while they were away. Inez made no secret of disliking Juanita: the girl was still troublesome and much too much given to airing her adolescent views; but Luis liked her frankness and intelligence. With Francesca Brown's considerable help, she'd recovered bravely from disaster. He doubted that she would ever achieve her mother's beauty, but in other ways she now often reminded him of Mercedes.

227

The train whistle warned them that it was getting ready to leave but, as he bundled them up the steps, he thought of something else he wanted to say.

'When the filming finishes you must bring Richard Weston back to Cantanzos; I shan't get a reliable report of the trip out of you!'

Juanita grinned down at him – not a position she would usually adopt, being six inches shorter than he was. 'I expect the Professor will want to rush back to London: he'll be missing Fran terribly by then. Oh, we're off now – *adiós, caro Tio!*'

He waved until he could no longer see her hand moving at the window, and then drove home, trying not to think of Juanita's final remark. Of course Richard Weston would be missing Francesca; any man who wasn't a blind, insensitive fool would. It was unfair, though, that a girl who made so little effort to attract should be so insidiously appealing. It required a constant struggle not to think about her, but even so a treacherous memory still offered him too many pictures of her in his mind's eye.

Over dinner that evening, for some reason that he couldn't explain to himself, he felt obliged to tell Inez about his parting conversation with Juanita. Her reaction was immediate and foreseeable, but he found it deeply irritating as well.

'Let Richard Weston hurry back to London by all means; if he comes here, he'll talk of nothing but his book and his stupid programmes – a man with an *idée fixe* can't help being a bore about it, it seems.'

'You're being a little harsh,' Luis pointed out. 'He's enthusiastic about his subject, but that probably makes him a good teacher; and whatever they are, his programmes won't be stupid.'

Inez smilingly held up her hands in a little gesture of submission. 'Very well, *querida*; we'll agree that he's a prince of historians! But I really don't need to be lectured by an Englishman about our Civil War, and I don't much care what a polyglot herd of pilgrims have been doing for the past five hundred years along every cart-track across Spain! Remember that we shall hear nothing else but that from Juanita when she gets back with Maud.'

'True, but I also remember that this time last year we could scarcely get her to talk at all. Don't you prefer her as she is now?'

'Yes, of course I do,' Inez agreed with a hint of impatience. 'Any reasonable person would. But I refuse to be dishonest about her: I shall be glad when the time comes for her to go to Milan. It will be good for her, and a relief for us; nor shall I be deeply upset to see the last of Maud Entwhistle.'

'Not a relief for me,' he said gently. 'I shall miss them both, and since I regard this as Maud's home, you may not have seen the last of her.'

There was a silence in the room, but it wasn't the quietness of two people who had no need to speak because they were in harmony with each other. Luis knew it, and recognised something else as well: a moment of decision had unexpectedly presented itself. They could avoid it by refusing to admit that it was there, but suddenly evasion seemed unbearable; the moment had to be accepted now.

He reached out his hands across the table and she was compelled to put her own into them. 'My dear, it's time we did something about *us*. An engagement is meant to lead to a wedding, not stand in the way of it. If you can do without the fuss and bother that we've just been through with Pascal and Teresa, let's get married, as simply and quickly as we can.'

His words fell into the room's silence without improving its quality in any way, and he admitted to himself that there was no reason why they should. As the speech of a man to his beloved, it had lacked just about everything she had a right to expect. Ashamed of his performance, he leaned forward to lift her hands to his mouth and kiss them. Then he offered her a sweet, rueful smile.

'Forgive me; that *wasn't* the way to suggest our marriage!'

'Well, no,' she agreed rather coolly, 'but perhaps a mis-tress mustn't expect pretty speeches; she's supposed to have heard them all already.'

Luis watched her across the table, aware of the spark of anger in her huge dark eyes. It made her still more beautiful, and he could have told her so easily enough in the past; but what had once been easy was difficult now.

'My dearest, let me start again, please,' he said quietly. 'You've been the most generous of lovers, but I don't want that situation to go on. It's time you were recognised as my wife – not *my* mistress, but the mistress of Cantanzos. I know that it doesn't mean to you what it means to me: I know that you'll want to escape from time to time, and I shan't always be able to go with you; but I want you to be known for what you are – my *mujer*, my wife.'

'So that it's made publicly very clear that I'm no longer available!' she suggested with a glinting smile. 'Dear Luis, you got upset quite unnecessarily in Seville. I hate hotel maids whispering about who I share my bed with; that's the reason I slept alone. Poor Rodrigo knew all along about our engagement.'

It was tempting to say that the Marques hadn't behaved as if he knew, but Luis refused to be sidetracked. Their future needed to be settled at last and he couldn't allow a trivial quarrel to be used as an excuse for not doing so. She recognised the intention in his drawn face; Luis Esteban with mind and heart set on a fixed purpose wasn't going to be deflected from it.

'Inez, listen to me, please. Forgive me if I angered you a moment ago; it was stupid of me to speak of the fuss and bother of Pascal's wedding. You did it all perfectly, and if that is what you want for us, then of course it's what we must have; but however we do it, we must now take the plunge into married life. We need to be sure of each other – sure enough to create a family of our own. I should like to hand Cantanzos on to our son when the time comes.'

'That makes the position clear,' she said after another

long pause. 'It's not convention, or passion, or even good old-fashioned lust, urging you to marry: you're afraid I shall soon be too old to give you children! Well, I'm afraid of something else: being trapped here until I can't bear it any longer and have to run away, as your own mother did.'

She saw his face whiten at the reference to Marganita, but he spoke with the calmness of a man determined not to lose sight of his objective. 'What happened between my parents doesn't have to happen to us. For the last time, I'm asking you to marry me so that I can claim you openly as my wife, and have the right to take care of you; but I can only do that here. If life with me at Cantanzos isn't enough, you must say so and be free to find someone else who *can* make you happy.'

'That *is* what I must do,' she answered very slowly. 'Set myself free, I mean, even though I don't expect to find love again – I've loved you. And I think I can say that you won't be happy either, because you have loved me. That's true isn't it?'

'Yes, it's true,' he agreed quietly, hearing the insistence in her voice, and knowing that no other answer could be given to her.

She covered her face with her hands, then, in a purely automatic gesture, smoothed her still-unruffled black hair. 'You'll be lonely here – without Pascal and even without your tiresome niece as well. What a terrible pity it is that you refused to see the beauty of my scheme; making this white elephant into a parador would have preserved it better than you can, and the state would have been responsible for the people working here. If that had happened, you and I could still have had a life together.'

Aware that she would never understand, he answered in a tired but level voice: 'The answer to your scheme is still no, I'm afraid. Cantanzos, which I don't consider a white elephant, remains itself at least as long as I'm alive.' Her disdainful shrug spurred him into making a suggestion that she would certainly despise still more. 'I don't need to be lonely. I'm advised to fill the castle with the sort of underprivileged children who don't know what it is to play on grass or watch the tide come in.'

'Don't tell me who your "adviser" is. I can detect Maud Entwhistle's interference easily enough,' Inez said contemptuously. 'On second thoughts, perhaps it came from that even more irritating nurse-person. What was her name . . . something Brown?'

'Francesca Brown,' he said, self-control still holding firm. 'I'm surprised you don't remember; she's the girl Pascal fell in love with before he married Teresa Jimenez.'

Inez smiled brilliantly. 'Of course – Francesca! You could always invite *her* to come back; she seemed eager enough to use any excuse to be here. What a thrill for humble Señorita Brown to transform herself into the Condesa!' Mock-regret took the place of sparkling malice. 'No, that won't do, of course; she's going to marry the worthy Professor.'

'She isn't going to do anything of the kind, it seems,' Luis pointed out. 'Juanita telephoned from Pamplona to say that they'd met up with Weston safely. As you know, she never hesitates to ask questions that other people might shirk, and the Professor admitted that he and Francesca are *not* to marry after all. She's in America instead, attending her sister's wedding, and the likelihood is that she will stay there . . . so unfortunately your kind suggestion is still no good.'

It was a long speech about Francesca – too long for him not to give himself away in the course of it. Inez heard the ache of sadness in his voice, the desolate longing of a man whose love had gone far out of reach. The truth was there in front of her at last, devastating but unmistakably clear. He'd accepted all that Inez de Castro had to offer, but would have chosen instead the insignificant nobody called Francesca Brown! She was tempted to scream the truth at him, but it was too humiliating to be admitted to. All she could do was salvage her own wounded pride by damaging his.

'I should like Pepé to drive me to the airport tomorrow.

If I fly back to Seville, I shall be able to see Rodrigo before he leaves for Buenos Aires. My impression is that *he* might be rather an exciting lover. Forgive me if I point out that your own performance, my dear Luis, has been very disappointing.'

She lay back in her chair, supremely confident of her beauty and her power to rouse any normal red-blooded man; the calculated insult was that Luis Esteban was not such a man. He watched her for a moment, sickened by the vindictive malice in her face, but aware that it was something he was responsible for.

'Let's not end up trying to hurt each other – it's altogether too demeaning,' he said quietly.

'You'll be asking next if we can stay friends,' she suggested with a derisive smile. 'I don't think so. Our connection ends now.' She stood up and stretched her arms above her head in a slow, provocative gesture. 'Forgive me for leaving you alone, but that's something you must start getting used to. I've got a lot of packing to do.'

He got up to open the door for her and she swept out, not bothering to look at him. Luis Esteban had already been relegated to a past she had no interest in. For the last time he smelled the exotic perfume she wore and watched her walk away with the self-conscious grace of a woman certain that she must always be looked at. Then he drew a shuddering sigh, went back to the table, and sat down. He poured more wine into his glass and frowned because his hand was shaking. It seemed necessary to keep telling himself that what had just happened *had* happened; it wasn't merely in his imagination that a future he'd thought himself shackled to had been obliterated in one brief conversation.

It had seemed mapped out for Inez as well, and he could only guess at her present state of heart and mind. Below the surface spitefulness there were surely some regret and sadness to match his own? They'd shared a relationship that had seemed important once upon a time; but he hoped she might also be sharing the emotion he was most aware of: simple, thankful relief. No more pretence was needed now that love hadn't quietly leached away like water lost in desert sand; no more effort to simulate the desire he didn't feel. He couldn't blame her for the lovemaking taunt, and she'd been right to claim that the failure was his, not hers.

That thought brought him finally to the nub of the matter. There was no comfort left, except that of knowing that Inez couldn't have guessed the truth; he wouldn't have wanted her hurt to that extent. The jibe at Francesca had been born of spite, but it had been incorrect. His English love wouldn't come back to Cantanzos; she would make sure of that. Inez had been quite wrong to think that a title and a privileged life might make the slightest appeal. Francesca would be happier in New York, looking after her brother-in-law's waifs and strays. Somehow, sometime, he would have to try to find another woman to share his life at Cantanzos, but for now the truth of one thing Inez had said must be accepted: his future looked bleak and lonely. The thought catapulted him back into the past, and suddenly he was a child of ten again, watching his mother and Maud drive away from the castle. Nothing, he told himself now, could be worse than that remembered anguish. He still had his friends, his work, his ever-increasing responsibilities; he would slowly grow used to being with a companion who only existed in his heart.

Twenty-Five

T he wedding in Connecticut was as simple and beautiful as Felicity had promised: a ceremony in a small, white-painted, clapboard church, attended by family members and a handful of close friends. Fran said goodbye to bride and groom as they left for a brief honeymoon in the Caribbean, and then was shepherded back to New York by Elliott's friend, the warden of the children's hostel. He was a large, bearded Jew, an immediately likeable man, who saw nothing remarkable in salvaging the ruined lives of the children in his care.

She wanted, of course, to visit the hostel, and asked to spend a day working there; other than that, she insisted on being a tourist on her own, doing the things that all visitors did: the Lincoln Centre, the Museum of Modern Art, the ride to the top of the Empire State. But her new friend, Andrei Ronnenburg, took her unforgettably one evening to hear opera at the Met, and insisted on their dining together on her last night in New York.

'Felicity hoped you were going to stay for good,' he said, when the business of ordering was out of the way. 'You could have Manhattan *without* the hostel, you know. I'd find you a different job tomorrow if you wanted one.'

Fran smiled at him, shaking her head. 'Thank you for the kind offer, but if I stayed it would be *for* the hostel. I should be very happy to work there.'

'So what's the problem that I can sense in you? If you're worrying about your sister, there's no need. Elliott will take good care of her. He's a man who accepts responsibility very easily for people who might stumble on their own.'

'I realise that, although she's much less likely to stumble than she was. Felly has changed since coming here.'

Andrei's kind eyes inspected Fran across the table – eyes experienced, she thought, in seeing the muddles and small despairs that could be kept hidden from most people. 'If you're happy about Felicity, what else bothers you here?'

She cast around for an answer that would satisfy him and came up with one that had the merit of being partially true. 'I think it's New York itself, splendid and exciting though it is. We have plenty of tall buildings now in London, but I don't feel dwarfed by them in the same way – like a caterpillar crawling through endless rows of hollyhocks!' She smiled her slow, sweet smile. 'Translation needed?'

'No, thank you; I know what a hollyhock is!'

To avoid another difficult question, she asked one of him: 'Do you ever leave the hostel and come to Europe?'

'Once every two or three years I take a trip.' Andrei tasted the wine that had been poured and nodded to the waiter. 'My ancestors were Lithuanian Jews, shown very little mercy by either Nazis or Russians. A few of them survived, including my father, who was then a small child. He came here as a young man, and I was born in New York, but we don't shed our past as quickly as all that; I still feel at home in Europe. It's easier for you to travel there, of course!'

Fran nodded, suddenly unable to speak. She knew what the trouble was that she hadn't admitted to. Ever since leaving Cantanzos she'd been aware of the cord that seemed to connect her heart to Luis Esteban. The real trouble with New York was that it was too far away, and the cord was stretched too tight; if it was wrenched out, her heart's blood would simply trickle away. She could see her host staring at her, perhaps fearing that she was about to faint, and she made a huge effort to smile at him. 'Someone must have walked over my grave! Do you have that odd expression over here?'

He nodded, suspecting that some memory of her own had upset her and not any wandering over graves.

'I think you've worked too hard at sightseeing, Francesca, and you have a long flight home in front of you, so I shall soon return you to your hotel; but you must come back often to see us. I guarantee that you'll do what we all do in time: fall in love with Manhattan!'

She smilingly agreed but, charming company though he was, it was a relief to be saying goodbye to him in the hotel lobby when the meal ended. The panic attack – that was what she called it – halfway through dinner had unnerved her, and she wanted more than anything else that seemed remotely attainable to be back at home where she belonged.

The time difference between New York and London allowed her to let herself into the flat by late afternoon the following day. She'd been away for a fortnight and it felt like months. Anita had been in, and had left mail stacked on the kitchen table: circulars and junk post in one pile, envelopes that looked interesting or urgent in another. Fran skimmed through these first, pulling out the postcards sent by Juanita on her way across Spain with Richard; but there was also an envelope with a Spanish stamp, and she recognised handwriting that she'd seen once before; it seemed that the Marquesa had decided to get in touch with her. The single sheet of notepaper inside was headed simply: 'El Castillo, Cantanzos, Galicia', and dated three or four days before.

Dear Miss Brown,

I'm sure you will want to know that my brother's wedding was a moving and beautiful ceremony. Pascal's joy in his bride was obvious, and I can be sure that he is happy at last.

My own news is very different; I am returning to Seville to live. Count Esteban is heartbroken, of course, but although I can scarcely bear to be the cause of so much grief, I cannot endure Cantanzos for the rest of my life. With Juanita and Maud soon to be in Milan, your own connection with the castle will also cease, I suppose. Did you know, by the way, that Juanita finds a distinct resemblance between you and Miss Entwhistle? It's an amusing thought, but I do see what she means.

Now may I offer you a friendly word of advice? Observing you here, I think I detected a little penchant for the Count – reasonable, of course, but so hopeless, I fear. Do, please, save yourself more pain by ignoring any further invitations to come here; one should always, don't you think, stay where one belongs? It's something the Count himself feels very strongly about, though he may have been too kind to mention it to you while you were here.

That was the extent of the message; beneath it was simply the Marquesa's signature. Fran read the letter a second time, then very carefully shredded it into small pieces. She threw the pieces into the kitchen bin, but hadn't sufficiently got rid of them; a moment later she emptied the bin into the dustbin outside. It was pointless, of course: the Marquesa's acid phrases were fixed in her mind like letters etched on glass. She couldn't flay herself by thinking about Luis Esteban – did *he* also know about her 'little penchant'? Had he and Inez laughed about it together? . . . Better to concentrate on Juanita's remark instead. It might have been meant as an affectionate comparison with Maud, but the Marquesa's malice had managed to sour it with the suggestion that Juanita had been poking unkind fun at her English friends. Inez's advice hadn't been needed: there would probably be no more invitations to visit Cantanzos; but if any came, Fran knew that she would refuse them. The Count and his friends would have to find someone else to laugh at.

She told herself that from that moment on she would think no more about Cantanzos; the time had come to put it all behind her and move on. The cord had broken now, thank

God, and, far from tearing her apart, it would probably mean release and healing in the end.

Yet in the sleepless night watches something in the Marquesa's letter that she'd scarcely registered came back to haunt her. Inez was leaving Cantanzos for good; had probably gone by now. There might have been relief in making her decision at last, but it would have meant leaving Luis Esteban too, and the knife-pricks in the letter were a measure of what it had cost Inez de Castro to do without him. Maud had been right to say that the woman needed pitying, but of Luis Esteban himself Fran decided that she couldn't allow herself to think at all.

Richard returned to London for the start of the new university term, but he was too busy to call more than briefly at Earls Court Square. With becoming modesty, he thought he'd done quite well, but Fran would have to judge for herself when the programme was shown at the end of the summer.

'Did Juanita enjoy herself?' she asked, knowing that it was the question he'd expect.

'She had a high old time, bossing everyone in sight – very efficiently, I have to say – but today's pilgrims came as something of a shock to her! She found most of them downright odd, and too few of them spiritually inclined; but we agreed in the end that *something* rubbed off. The moment of reaching the cathedral was truly magical, even for the staunchest cynics among the film crew.' Richard grinned at the memory, but hastened to finish his tale.

'I delivered Maud and Juanita back to Cantanzos, of course, and stayed one night. Inez was in Seville, but we had a very pleasant dinner nevertheless. Pascal Vargas was there as well, with his very pretty wife. Oh, and Juanita told me to say that she expects us *both* back for her eighteenth birthday.'

Fran registered the fact that there'd been a conspiracy of silence about the Marquesa: the others had surely been told that she wasn't coming back; but she didn't comment on it, nor on the birthday invitation. Instead, she made a little bet with herself: would Richard remember that she'd been away herself or not? He got almost to the door but then he thought of it.

'Good Lord, I nearly forgot. Fran, love, how did the wedding go?'

He waited only to hear that it had gone very well, pronounced it splendid news, and hurried away. She closed the door behind him, marvelling at the resilience of men – or was it what Jane Austen would have called their inconstancy? This time a year ago he'd been enthralled himself by the girl whose marriage to someone else he'd just remembered to ask about. Perhaps it was the reminder she needed herself even now – that nothing lasted for ever and most things not at all. She would let her old friend be an object lesson: no ache of longing for the past, eyes forward from now on.

As a rainy, changeable springtime settled into summer, she achieved her object very well, accepting too much work, and engaging in a social life that she deliberately allowed to become too hectic. At least it meant that she went to bed at night too tired to do anything but sleep until the morning's alarm set her in motion again. If she felt sometimes like a performing doll in danger of being overwound, it was better by far than having time to acknowledge the loneliness at her heart's core. She ignored the messages that Juanita left on her answerphone; but one evening Anita, whom she'd also managed to avoid, appeared in the doorway to reproach her for casting off old friends.

'It's not just me,' she said severely. 'Richard's worried about you – thinks something is wrong. *I* might be less charitable and reckon that you're having too good a time to bother with us, but you don't *look* as if you are; in fact, you look thoroughly worn out to me.'

'Thanks very much,' Fran said faintly. Then the ghost

240

of her smile appeared. 'Worn out is rather how I feel, as a matter of fact! I thought I'd give perpetual motion a try, but hectic parties aren't really my scene at all.'

'I could have told you that.' Anita hesitated a moment, then soldiered on. 'Richard said something about you both being expected back in Spain – Juanita's birthday party, I think.'

'I know, but I decided not to go. I *have* written to tell Juanita, but later than I should have done. I didn't want her to go on arguing about it, and she's a girl who likes to argue!'

Anita stared at her friend's face: thin almost to gauntness and too shadowed about the eyes.

'Something *is* wrong, isn't it?' she asked with more gentleness than usual. 'Anything a friend can help with?'

'No, 'fraid not, Ani dear; but thanks for asking. It's a pitifully ordinary story: I wanted something I couldn't have, and it's taken me too long to get used to the idea; but now there's some good news: Felly's expecting a baby. She telephoned last night, and happiness levels are pretty high in the Wilmington household, I gather!'

Anita nodded, but rather absent-mindedly, still following a thought-train of her own. 'If you've made up your mind not to go to Spain, why not come with me to Greece? My grandparents' island hasn't *yet* been ruined by the tour operators, thank God. I can promise you miraculous Greek light, a sea bluer than you've ever seen, and the sweet life of doing absolutely nothing! Think about it, Fran?'

She promised cheerfully that she would, and Anita went away to report to Richard that he could stop worrying: Francesca still refused to go to Cantanzos, but otherwise she was herself again.

Twenty-Six

As midsummer approached, she didn't go away with Anita either, but only because a ballerina she'd treated once before fell and injured herself. Begged to stay and give urgently needed help, she had to abandon the Greek trip and let her friend go alone. She remembered the Christmas holiday in Austria that Richard had suggested, and decided that she might do better just to make plans on her own in future; but as if to make up for what she was missing on Mykonos, the temperature in London soared to Mediterranean levels.

She came home one evening tired and uncomfortably hot, thinking of a cold shower as the only necessity in life; supper could wait until she was cool again. She was towelling her wet hair when the doorbell rang. It couldn't be Anita, probably sipping her evening ouzo by now; and Richard always telephoned before he called round. That left, most probably, the new owner of the flat downstairs: a smart-as-paint TV presenter of whom her half-Greek friend would undoubtedly disapprove when she returned. But such celebrities presumably washed their hair like normal women, Fran assumed, and she opened the door as she was, in cotton robe and turbanned hair, about to smile and ask what item needed to be borrowed. She found that it was Luis Esteban who stood there.

Was she hallucinating – going mad? Had unbearable inner need called up a vision of him that would disappear if she put out her hand? But clinging to the doorpost to support herself, she heard what he finally managed to say, and had to accept that he was there.

'I didn't telephone – I thought you might refuse to see me if I did.'

'I expect I would have done,' she agreed hoarsely. 'As you can see, this isn't my evening for being at home to unexpected callers.'

In the face of such a welcome, if only she could hold out a little longer, he'd surely go away; any normal man would. But not *el gran Condé*, apparently. He still stood there, staring at her.

'I came to talk to you, Francesca – preferably not at your front door. May I come in?'

She wanted to whip herself into anger – believe that she could hear in his voice the arrogant certainty that what the Leopard wanted he must always have – but the truth was that his brown face looked tired and fine-drawn, and she couldn't see arrogance in it, however hard she tried.

She held the door open and pointed to the sitting room. 'I'll be with you in five minutes.'

It took no more than that to pull on a skirt and shirt, and tie back her damp hair with a piece of ribbon. She left her face bare of make-up, determined not to be seen to have made the smallest effort for him; but basic hospitality insisted that she took with her into the sitting room glasses and ice-cold amontillado. Pouring the wine restored some kind of normality; she was any hostess dealing with an unexpected guest. She could even talk in a voice that sounded normal.

'I hope Juanita and Maud are well.'

'Well in health, thank you, but Juanita is puzzled and very hurt. She doesn't know what she's done to offend you.'

Fran thought she might have expected a frontal attack; he didn't deal in anything else. 'Juanita's upset because I've refused her birthday invitation?'

'Of course, but she thinks the rejection goes further than that. Don't you realise what your friendship means to her, or don't you care?'

The question was maddeningly unfair: how could she

defend herself without giving away all the pain locked up in her own heart?

'I didn't mean to hurt Juanita,' she answered slowly. 'I thought I could withdraw without her even noticing. Her life was back on the rails again, and her future mapped out. I reckoned that my usefulness was over.'

The flash of anger in his face was unmistakable; she'd provoked it too often before not to recognise it now. 'Is that what you think – that your connection with us depends on how useful you can be?'

'It's what I was *made* to think,' she said with a sudden fierceness of her own – 'too often not to have got the message loud and clear. I dare say Maud has heard it, too, from time to time.'

'Not from me – *never* from me.' But his anger was giving way to a faint, rueful smile. 'You're about to remind me, of course, of an evening when it was suggested that you and Maud might like to dine alone! And if I offered you the idea that kindness prompted the suggestion, you'd refuse to accept it.'

'Yes, I would,' Fran instantly agreed. 'I'll freely admit that the Marquesa de Castro has many virtues, but I doubt if kindness is among them.'

She supposed that even a woman who was no longer his would need defending, but he abandoned the subject of Inez and returned to his niece.

'Will you change your mind about coming to the birthday party?'

'I'm sorry, but I can't: I've an urgent case on hand here at the moment; it's the reason I haven't gone away on holiday with a friend.' She spoke now with simple regret, hostility suddenly seeming absurd between them, because his question had been asked with almost humble pleading. Yet without the spur of anger she couldn't endure the interview much longer; she needed him to say that, having done what he'd come for – to deliver Juanita's reproaches – he would now go away.

Instead of that he poured more wine and then sat down again, looking at her, noting the pallor and thinness of her face, deciding that, as he'd suspected all along, her eyes *were* more green than hazel. He hadn't seen her smile yet, nor had he felt welcome. A sane man, such as he reckoned himself to be, would have admitted that what he ought to do was bow politely and go away. He even thought he had opened his mouth to say goodbye, but what he said instead was something different.

'I'm sorry you're so involved here; I was hoping that, even if Juanita's party wasn't enough to bring you back to Cantanzos, the offer of another job might be.'

'Francesca Brown still able to be useful after all?' she suggested with what she hoped was a mocking note in her voice. 'I really don't think so, though. Apart from more work than I can manage here, I've a job waiting for me in New York if I want it.'

She might not have spoken for all the notice he took of it. 'I think it's the sort of thing you'd like. Maud told me about your brother-in-law's scheme in New York. You don't suppose he'd mind, do you, if we copied it?'

Only astonishment pure and simple was in her face now as she stared at him. 'You mean taking in handicapped children . . . at Cantanzos?'

His smile reappeared, rueful and suddenly sweet. 'That *is* what I mean, though your amazement isn't altogether flattering! It would have to be only during the summer months: our winters are too wet and windy; but it would give the children some sort of treat. I hoped you'd agree to help take care of them.'

She was suddenly tired of half-truths and evasions, but if he was to accept refusal she must offer him one more partial truth. 'You'll have gathered by now that the Marquesa and I didn't like each other; but she suggested more than once something that I had to accept: people should stay where they belong. I don't belong in your splendid, impressive castle; I'm not even sure that I'd belong anywhere in Spain.'

She spoke quietly but with the ring of finality in her voice; what she'd just said was true, not open to argument. Looking at her pale, set face, and knowing the strength of purpose when her mind was made up, he felt despair settling round him like a Galician *orbayu*. Pascal had meant well, and had been a more than generous friend, but his advice had been the wrong advice. There was only one thing left to say, and even that would be useless.

'There was a piece of information that I left out,' Luis added, almost by way of an unimportant afterthought. 'If you came back to Cantanzos, you wouldn't find Inez there. She decided that it and I couldn't offer the life she wanted.' He watched Fran's face as he spoke, waiting for some change of expression. There was none, not even a hint of surprise. 'You knew,' he said roughly. 'How can that be? Juanita insisted that she hadn't told you.'

'She didn't . . . the Marquesa wrote,' Fran mumbled, '. . . just to tell me – kindly, of course – how happy Pascal was with his new bride!' It was as much as she could confess to; the rest of Inez's message must remain buried in some unvisited corner of her mind.

Her face was too revealing, however, and Luis read the truth in it at last. His final conversation with Inez was imprinted on his memory, and now he could pinpoint the exact moment when he must have given himself away. In true Spanish style she had revenged herself for what had been seen as humiliation.

'Will you tell me what else was in the letter she wrote?' he asked.

'No,' Fran said steadily, 'I won't. It was a private letter.' She was becoming exhausted by the strain of having him there, and wanted only to be left alone so that she could recover from the pain of seeing him again; but one more effort had to be made – for him this time, not for herself.

'Your life must look empty now, so I can understand that inviting children to the castle looks an attractive scheme; but I doubt if you have any idea what it entails. Elliott and his friend in New York could tell you just how difficult and demanding handicapped children are likely to be. It's a drastic cure for loneliness.' She saw his faint smile, and rushed on, intent on making him understand. 'It's tempting to use work as a drug when you're unhappy; I know: I've tried it. All it does is leave you exhausted but still unhappy; and in any case, you probably work too hard as it is.'

'I'm not planning to neglect everything else so that I can look after the children myself, but they will be my guests. If you'd agree to come, I wouldn't expect *you* to do nothing but tend them. I haven't mentioned it yet, but you'd have other responsibilities – your chief role would be as mistress of Cantanzos!

There was a moment of silence in the room in which Fran feared that her heart might have stopped beating; or was she only paralysed by the fear of having misunderstood what he'd said?

'It's not something to make a joke about,' she finally managed to suggest.

'I agree; but I wasn't joking,' he said gently. 'I'm asking you to marry me, Francesca.'

It was clear now; either, in the Marquesa's charming phrase, her 'little penchant' had been observed by him as well, or Inez had been kind enough to explain it to him. The strange thing was to discover that she didn't mind him knowing at all. Loving someone was the highest compliment one human being could pay another; she trusted him to understand that. All she must do was make it plain that he need do nothing in return.

'It was a stupid lie to say that I felt out of place at Cantanzos,' she said gravely. 'Perhaps you guessed how much I loved being there. But you don't have to make it easy for me to go back – there are limits to what even *el gran Condé* feels obliged to do for kindness' sake.'

He wanted more than anything in life to wrap his arms about her and kiss away the aching sadness in her eyes and voice; but his dear stubborn love wouldn't be convinced by

247

Spanish *macho bravura*. Inez was still there between them; he could see the triumphant smile she'd give if she knew.

'Francesca, listen to me, please,' he began quietly, 'and believe what I say. I loved Inez a long time ago, but she chose de Castro instead. He was much older, but didn't have a castle in Galicia round his neck! When he died, she came back into my life, wanting to make up her mind to give *love* a try the second time around. It seemed to me that we could make a marriage work, and I was tired of living alone. Then came my sister's accident and the arrival of her shattered child. Nothing helped her, and in despair I came to London.'

A smile of the utmost sweetness suddenly transformed his face. 'You know what happened next: I found a quiet, gentle girl and saddled *her* with the job – impossible I thought – of coping with Juanita.'

'"Britannia on the warpath" was how you once described me,' Fran reminded him, sounding aggrieved.

'So I did, but you're not supposed to interrupt – *I'm* telling this story.' His face grew serious again, because the hardest part of it was now in front of him.

'While you were working your miracle on my niece, Inez was affected by you in a different way. She decided that she *would* marry me, and so the embargo I'd insisted on seemed pointless self-denial. We became lovers, rather unsuccessfully and, as she was careful to point out, it was my fault, not hers. I'm ashamed that it happened at all, but I believed that I was committed to her by then, with no possibility of withdrawing.' He walked to where Fran was sitting and took hold of her hands. 'Can you understand how inevitable it seemed?'

She nodded, faintly aware that she would agree to whatever he asked her to understand if his hands continued to enfold hers and she could see happiness ahead of her, gleaming like a pot of gold at the end of the rainbow.

'What changed things?' she finally asked, clinging on to something approaching rationality.

'I asked Inez to make up her mind: either marry me at once or cancel our engagement, because in Seville it had been obvious that Rodrigo Jimenez, Teresa's father, saw her as very suitable ambassadress material!'

'Which she is, of course,' Fran said fairly. 'I have to admit that she would have done Cantanzos proud, in a way I could never do. You must be aware that even the servants despised me when I arrived.'

'But not when you left,' he said gently. 'They all want to see you back . . . where they think you belong.'

She smiled at the idea of Señora Fernandez unbending enough to make her feel welcome, then grew serious again. 'I assume that Inez decided in favour of the Ambassador. Maud always said that I should pity her for loving the wrong man; I found it hard then, but no longer. The poor woman must have been torn in two – because I'm quite sure she did love you.'

Luis didn't comment on that. 'Our final interview went fairly well,' he said instead, 'until she became very spiteful about you. Then I gave myself away, I'm afraid, and her revenge was to send the letter you received.'

Fran looked at him with a candid but slightly apologetic glance. 'I suppose it was *she* who told you that the tiresome English creature was enamoured of Cantanzos and . . . and all it contained!'

Luis shook his head. 'It was Pascal who finally gave me a hint – with more generosity than I deserved, when he wanted you so badly for himself; but for that I shouldn't have come to London, would never have imagined that I had anything to hope for: we never had a single conversation that didn't end in you getting very cross with me! But dear Pascal guessed what George and Henry knew, because I told *them* often enough – that I was far gone in love for the tiresome English creature! Will you marry me, Francesca, and stay with me for ever and be my heart's true love?'

He saw the answer in her face, and held out his arms, and she went into them as a homing bird finds its nest.

With his mouth on hers she could only be swept up in the unimaginable delight of being loved but, released at last, she began to smile, and he asked to be told the joke.

'Not a joke,' she explained breathlessly. 'I couldn't help thinking of the coat of arms above the archway, that I always tried not to look at: the leopard about to pounce on the poor, defenceless unicorn.'

'But you now realise,' said Luis smiling in his turn, 'that the poor, besotted Leopard has been tamed by the gentle Unicorn and is her prisoner for life.'

'Something like, I hope,' agreed Fran.